BLOOD
ENEMIES

BLOOD
ENEMIES

Glover Wright

Arbor House / New York

Manufactured in the United States of America

10 9 8 7 6 5 4 3 2 1

Library of Congress Cataloging-in-Publication Data

Wright, Glover.
Blood enemies.
I. Title.
PR6073.R488B56 1987 823'.914 86-32127
ISBN 0-87795-899-8

To John Enoch Powell, with gratitude

A man cannot be too careful in
the choice of his enemies.

— *Oscar Wilde*

Acknowledgments

I offer my warm thanks to the following people for their invaluable assistance in the research for this novel.

In Reading, former Chief Superintendent John Webb of the Thames Valley Police Force. In Gloucestershire, my sister Rena Sparks, her husband Cyril and their son Roger, for their hospitality while I roamed the area and subsequently for doing the legwork while I sat at my typewriter in Jersey. In Cheltenham, the Public Relations Officer at GCHQ, the security staff who did not have me arrested as a spy while I filmed the sensitive complex, and for others who fielded my persistent questioning. To Derek Hitchin who aided me with the inner-workings of the 22nd Special Air Service Regiment. To those people on both sides of the Atlantic who prefer anonymity.

Finally, to the Rt Hon John Enoch Powell, M.B.E., M.P. for graciously granting me more of his time than I'm sure he could spare, for pointing me in the right direction when, at the outset, I was certainly heading the wrong way, and for allowing me the benefit of his considerable experience, vision and insight. With gratitude, I dedicate this book to him.

Geoffrey Glover Wright
JERSEY

Fact

On 26 October 1982, the Prime Minister of Great Britain was questioned in the House of Commons regarding an apparent leak of secrets from the Government Communications Head-quarters (GCHQ) at Cheltenham, Gloucestershire, over a period of fourteen years.

Former United States President Jimmy Carter referred to this possible spy scandal the day before, during a visit to London. He defended his own record at the White House by saying: 'I had no evidence of a leak of this magnitude.' But he added: 'It seems to be serious.'

The British Attorney-General had already faced a series of questions over allegations that Russian Intelligence had penetrated the top-secret Cheltenham electronic intelligence-gathering base which shares information and works in close liaison with the United States National Security Agency (NSA).

One Labour Member of Parliament asked the Prime Minister to give more information on a statement she made about a security breach in July 1982.

He said: 'The reason for asking is the considerable disquiet felt by the United States Government and the suspicion that the Prime Minister was not frank with the House of Commons. This goes far deeper than the Prime Minister wished to disclose in July and suggests, therefore, that there has been a cover-up.'

At the same time that the security breach at GCHQ had taken place, July 1982, a gunman was hunted down by armed police

1

aided by an expert tracker. He died after being hit by police bullets. The gunman had previously killed two police officers and a civilian.

During the manhunt facts emerged which, pieced together, formed an intriguing set of circumstances.

The killer – a so-called Special Air Service reject – who had evaded the best efforts of the police to corner him for a considerable length of time was discovered to have unexplainable links with sensitive communications centres in Britain and the United States.

Although these links were reported by the British press at the time as coincidences, no action was taken officially – or was reported to have been taken – to establish if the links were any more than a somewhat eerie chapter of chance.

When collected together, the links reveal a disturbing synchronicity which appears to deny any possibility of blind chance.

Coincidence number 1: The killer murdered a police constable less than two hundred yards from one of the masts belonging to Menwith Hill US Air Force base.

Coincidence number 2: He was observed near sensitive RAF installations in Lincolnshire – the murder of the civilian took place not far from these.

Coincidence number 3: The killer was known to have made his way to Dalby Forest on the edge of the North Yorkshire Moors near the Fylingdales Early Warning Station – a vital part of the Western World's radar system and linked to NORAD, the North American Air Defence Centre in Colorado Springs. Investigating police also found that he had travelled through America, camping in the mountains near the NORAD base.

Coincidence number 4: During the long hunt for the killer police staked out a site at West Drayton, another sensitive communications area in Britain. They were keeping observation on the man's VW caravanette which was known to have been parked there for several weeks and had been at the same location on other occasions.

Coincidence number 5: The registration number of the VW caravanette was logged by security officers after being seen on more than one occasion outside the perimeter fence of GCHQ Cheltenham.

A further intriguing fact concerning GCHQ Cheltenham and the month of July 1982 came to light when it was reported in the British press of 28 October 1982 (the same month and year that the Prime Minister was being accused of a cover-up over a security breach at GCHQ) that Security chiefs were investigating the mysterious death of a former employee of the Cheltenham intelligence centre, who, in that fateful month of July 1982 had taken off in his light Fournier aeroplane to practise aerobatics. After an hour in the air he was seen to fly slowly into a valley near Cheltenham and crash. Accident investigators found no evidence of mechanical failure and no medical problems with the intelligence officer.

In the wake of this mysterious death (an inquest jury returned an accident verdict) British counter-espionage officers were reported to be probing into the victim's background, together with those of several other GCHQ employees.

Later, in November 1982, Geoffrey Prime, a long-term intelligence officer employed at GCHQ, was sentenced to thirty-eight years' imprisonment, thirty-five for spying and three for sexual offences against small girls.

Since then no other Soviet agents have been uncovered at GCHQ Cheltenham or its subsidiary locations.

All the above is reported fact. What follows is fiction, which might – by coincidence – be only a part of something else entirely.

Chapter One

The man worked swiftly, with the deft sureness of an expert. When he had completed his task the liquid-gas cylinder, filled and delivered to the house that previous afternoon, was a lethal bomb.

Throughout he had worn surgical rubber gloves, their elasticated material stretched to its limits over his broad, flat hands. In the slim, focused beam of the pencil-torch he had affixed with Plasticine to a metal shelf-bracket above his crouched body, the cylinder shone bright yellow. He blew over its surface lightly, dislodging the fine silver dust – the result of his drilling – dissipating the tiny amount of powdered metal into the chill air. Carefully, he inspected the area of the cylinder that housed the release valve. The fine hole he had drilled and the minute blob of a certain chemical he had injected before closing the aperture with a quick-drying sealant were virtually invisible unless you knew precisely what you were looking for. This particular form of booby-trap could be overlooked even by the most cautious bomb-disposal expert. It had also the added benefit of being totally undetectable in the aftermath. – the detonation itself ensured that.

The man arose, unstuck the pencil-torch, pulled away the Plasticine, rolled it over the place it had been to pick up any residue clinging to the metal bracket, then pocketed the pliable ball. Edging past the front bumper of the Vauxhall compact which filled two-thirds of the darkened garage – but not touching it – he reached a side door leading onto a small paved patio.

Before extinguishing the torch, he played the beam over the

floor and the soles of his jogging shoes. The car was only three months old and its owner fastidious; the concreted floor of the garage bore no traces of oil or grease from that or any other vehicle he had previously owned. The man had expected this – the information he had been given on his target had been comprehensive and meticulously detailed – but still he made a habit of checking everything at least twice in all he did. Satisfied that he had left no evidence of his presence he flicked off the beam.

He stood perfectly still for a few moments, his breathing shallow, while his eyes adjusted to the darkness. Feeling for the pocket of his anorak he pulled out a pair of lightweight leather driving gloves and drew them on after peeling off the rubber gloves, placing these one at a time in a zipped pocket cut into the sleeve of the anorak. He worked the zip and felt the slight bulge for confirmation. Satisfied with his precautions his hand went unerringly to the handle of the side door despite the complete absence of light; pushing the lever down he opened a crack which let the chill breeze play across his face. He hesitated a moment then was out and away, flitting silently past a greenhouse crammed with dark shapes reaching high against the streaming glass panes. Orchids, he remembered. You won't be short of flowers. Bastard! A bloody expensive way to die.

The garden fence was no problem. One arm along the top for leverage followed by a rolling leap which lifted him clear of the obstacle, landing feet first and crouched, fingers splayed lightly on the grass, like an athlete poised for the gun. Remaining crouched he traversed the neighbour's lawn backwards, his gloved fingers working on the grass where his feet had crushed the blades.

He dealt with the wide flowerbed before the next fence by spanning it with one outstretched leg placed high against the stout stanchion, then stretched both arms forward along his leg in the manner of a ballet dancer practising at the bar. His fingers gripped the stanchion as his body leaned inward, locked, then pulled against the lever of his leg. He swung over, his weight transferred to his arms, then dropped lightly into the alley connecting the two streets at the eastern end of the housing estate, moving instantly into an even-paced jog.

He encountered only two other people before he reached his vehicle parked a little more than a mile away: an elderly man in an overcoat over pyjama bottoms and slippers standing impatiently by a grossly overweight black Labrador, back hunched and trembling as it struggled to defecate in the gutter – and a late-night jogger going in the opposite direction; like the dog, overweight and straining with effort. Thursday, a few minutes before midnight, was not a time to find many of the inhabitants of the respectable and gracious town of Cheltenham on the streets. The man had chosen his time with care, for Cheltenham – which housed Britain's Government Communications Headquarters, the nerve centre for electronic intelligence and surveillance – had more than its fair share of police patrols.

He reached his vehicle, a second-hand Volkswagen caravanette, seconds after midnight slipped by, reversed out of the side turning and pulled out onto the main road under tall amber street lights – recalling, as he did so, the stark yellow of the gas cylinder.

Harold Thurstone arrived home at ten minutes past seven the next morning. He bade goodbye to one of his neighbours who, like himself and many others, was handling coded night traffic at GCHQ Cheltenham. Thurstone himself had suggested the forming of a car-sharing scheme some years before and the idea had been welcomed enthusiastically by those of his colleagues at the top-secret complex who also lived on the housing estate. This daily contact with co-workers who performed their exacting duties in departments other than Thurstone's own, was to the decoding officer's advantage, as it widened his area of knowledge regarding the comprehensive activities of GCHQ.

Thurstone entered the neat detached house, hung his raincoat in the hall, walked straight through the kitchen and out onto the paved patio. From where he stood he could see through the door of the greenhouse. He uttered a grunt of annoyance, striding immediately to the glass structure. A large gas heater inside was spluttering as the last of its fuel gave out. It was this intermittent flickering of flame which had caught Thurstone's eye. The sickly odour of gas hung in the humid air.

Thurstone fastened the door open by its clip.

The fresh gas cylinder was in the garage and it took only a few minutes' effort to remove the old container and heave out the new. Out of breath from the weight of the full cylinder, he pressed the connector down onto the valve.

Thurstone's rear neighbour was just entering his breakfast room – a plate glass windowed extension to his house – when the blast occurred. He regained consciousness on his back to the high piercing screams of his wife and two children as they crunched around on the carpet of glass around him. It was only when he put his hand to his face that he understood the horror on their faces.

Ambulances, fire-tenders, and the police arrived quickly – the latter discreetly armed as the possibility of terrorist attacks are never far from official minds in nationally sensitive areas. Then, quiet men in overalls settled down to the grim task of sorting and piecing together the dreadful jigsaw puzzle of glass, human tissue and bone, metal, soil and vegetation. By eight o'clock that evening – in time for the mid-evening news on television – they declared themselves satisfied that the explosion was caused by nothing more sinister than domestic gas. A faulty cylinder, not mains. There was no reason for the evacuation of more families over a wider area. By midnight, Thurstone's neighbours were back in their homes, shocked and subdued. 'They'll sleep badly for a few nights,' one of the explosives experts was heard to remark, a thirty-year-old veteran who had seen far worse. 'It's one thing to have a neighbour die suddenly, quite another to find bits of him around your house.'

The incident was carried in the national press the next day with emphasis on the GCHQ connection and supporting articles on the dangers of liquid gas cylinders if carelessly used but did not carry through to the Sunday newspapers.

The man responsible for Harold Thurstone's fragmented departure from this world awoke on Saturday morning to the sounds of the English countryside. He felt fresh, ready to face the day, satisfied, no guilt, no twinge of conscience. He had no need to turn on the caravanette's radio to confirm the result of his work. When he did a job he did it well.

7

He was not an evil man or a mindless thug – nor were his actions the prerequisite to monetary gain for his material needs were spartan and his long-term desires non-existent. If flaws in his character were to be sought, they might be found in his reactionary views and a tendency to favour simplistic solutions – however, identical attitudes could easily be found in any pub across Britain. The difference was that he had certain dark skills which enabled him to move that one deadly step beyond mere words.

He swung off the hard bunk, sat for a moment collecting his thoughts, then, ducking his head, stepped down onto the damp grass which carpeted the small copse in which the caravanette was parked. Still in the jeans and sweatshirt he had slept in he performed a series of rigorous physical exercises, all of which came straight out of the British Army Physical Instruction manual, before switching to a routine which owed more to the Orient.

Finally he stopped and sank to his haunches, breathing deeply, his close-cropped, dark-brown hair matted to his scalp, his hands bleeding lightly from splits in the calloused skin. He twisted his head, his eyes sharp.

The farmer shifted his shotgun, broken and crooked over his forearm, the bright brass of its two shells gleaming in the breech. 'You planning on staying another night?' he demanded.

'Your land?' asked the man, still crouched.

'Best you get along,' stated the farmer frowning at broken lower branches on two trees.

The man stood up. 'Sorry about those.'

'Less said, soonest mended. You get along now.'

The man climbed behind the wheel of the caravanette and started it, the engine spluttering on full choke. The farmer walked alongside. 'Foreign, is it?' he asked, indicating the left-hand driving position.

'German.'

'You're not from there though.'

'Comes cheaper. Hard to sell, I suppose.'

They had reached the narrow hard-topped lane, the turn tight after mounting the rise from the copse. The man applied the brake when the manoeuvre was completed.

8

'You allow one, they'll all be doing it. Next you get gypsies. Then it's stealing and all kinds of rubbish scattered on the land. Can't move 'em on if they decide to squat. Law doesn't protect you any more. It's the layabouts that's got the rights these days. Owning a bit of land makes you a villain.' The farmer patted the shotgun. 'Don't involve the police myself. Never had to use it though. Just having it does the trick.' He stepped back. 'Get along then.'

The man engaged the long gear-lever and pulled away, his eyes steady in the rear-view mirror until he was around the curve in the lane. He was hungry, but decided to wait until he reached the motorway services outside Oxford before breakfasting. He enjoyed pushing himself to the limits of his endurance; it gave him a sense of achievement – and with hunger, the sensation of being cleansed. From experience he knew the clarity of thought which came from an extended period without food.

From his past, which remained dangerously close in his mind to the present – he could open a mental door on it and escape too easily from reality – he recalled the voice of their Arab informer. 'Fasting,' he would pronounce, in his classical Gulf Arabic, 'shrinks the body but expands the soul.' They had killed him later – for dealing both ways – not quickly, because they needed to know the extent of his treachery. The Arab had understood this; had accepted his treatment and his ultimate fate stoically – even with courage. He'd tried to shoot himself, naturally, which was the accepted thing on both sides – no one surrendered himself alive, that was lunacy – but they had stopped him. After that he resigned himself to the hard journey to death. The entire patrol had admired the way he had handled himself, so, in the end, they gave it to him clean: one bullet precisely placed. Of course afterwards they had messed him up a bit – to deter – but he was only meat by then, his spirit had already flown.

The country lanes now were past and he was driving on the fast dual-lane highway toward London; hunger was gnawing at him and he let the thought of food give him pleasure, momentarily, before closing the trap on it.

His scheduled contact that evening was many hours away – he had started off earlier than expected because of the farmer –

9

so he would have to kill time. He decided he would visit the little grave; buy some flowers somewhere, tend the grass if it needed it. He took comfort in being close to her but the anguish which knifed through him with memory was unbearable. It was the only pain he suffered any more – nothing else could hurt him now.

He was crouched over the wheel, as though the pain had winded him, and the sprawling roundabout caught him unawares causing him to brake fiercely as he swung the wheel hard into the bend. A white Rover police-car, stationary against the outer rim of the roundabout, emitted a cloud from its exhausts and drew out into the traffic. The man cursed silently, angry at himself for allowing his control to slip, watching in his mirror as the patrol-car followed him down onto the motorway. They pulled him in after three hundred yards.

He knew the form and stepped down from the Volkswagen before they exited from the Rover, his licence and insurance ready.

'Took that a bit late, didn't you?' queried one, the second walking past him and around the caravanette.

'Any reason for driving a left-hooker?' the second officer shouted over the blast of a big sixteen-wheeler truck.

'Cheaper,' the man replied, handing the documents to the one in front of him.

'Where you off to?' the officer asked, eyes down as he read.

'Services. Breakfast and a clean-up. Then London.'

'You live in that thing?' he asked dipping his head at the van.

'For now.'

'So where's home?'

'It's on the licence.'

'That permanent?'

'It's in my name.'

The officer looked up from the insurance certificate.

'Split from the wife,' said the man, purposely avoiding his eyes.

'Ah!' uttered the officer who was no stranger to domestic problems, both personally and professionally.

'Mind if I take a look?' called the other.

The man shook his head.

'What're you doing down here?' asked the first officer,

passing back the documents.

'Looking round the old Roman sites – Cheltenham way. Driving, bit of camping. Thinking.'

'Interested are you? The old ruins?'

The man shrugged. 'History, isn't it.'

The second officer slammed the van's side door and walked over. He shook his head. 'Seems all right,' he said, seemingly disappointed. The Rover's radio grated harshly.

'Watch how you drive then,' warned the first as they both turned back to their vehicle. He shouted again before shutting the door: 'Keep your mind on the road, not your problems.'

The man gave a thin smile and climbed back into the Volkswagen as they drove past him at speed. He pulled back into the traffic, staying in the inside lane, then took the slip-road into the service area as it came up.

After parking, he made straight for the washrooms, taking with him a change of shirt. Inside, he stripped to the waist and gave himself a thorough wash then worked on his stubbled chin with a battery razor before putting on the fresh shirt and making for the cafeteria. He bought himself a cooked breakfast and sat alone at a table. A family came in, colourfully dressed as if going on holiday; the three children rushing headlong for the self-service counter laughing excitedly. One tripped, out of his view, falling hard. He heard the high scream of pain and the hair rose on his neck but his eyes remained fixed on his food while people around him turned to the sound.

He took the plastic cup they had given him for his tea out to the caravanette and sat sipping the hot drink, his arms resting on the steering-wheel, his eyes sharp like a fox. He crushed the cup, lit a cigarette, then drove off, accelerating hard on the slip-road and into the inside lane, taking the first turn-off he came to, then back-tracked to his original route.

His progress was slow once he hit the suburbs of the capital – it being Saturday and the weather fine – but he held his impatience in check, driving steadily and carefully. One brush with the police was enough. At a road-side flower stall he bought some blooms then pushed on again.

The cemetery was protected by railings which had rusted and had then been repainted repeatedly, giving them a crusted

11

surface and a misshapen look; black but sprayed at intervals with brighter colours, the work of vandals. Inside were graves, too many to count, poorly tended and spreading out unevenly into the distance like debris left in a field. The wide path from the gates was hard, it edges trimmed; a neat thoroughfare for the living, while the dead were lined on either side stretching backward to mossy walls – not entirely forgotten, for here and there were fresh flowers and solemn people. But mostly there was evidence of indifference, as though the pace of life was too fast and had passed the dead by.

He reached the small grave some way in, near the wall, its white marble polished, the grass cut back with long-nosed scissors – he could see the uneven measured cuts along the edging. The headstone read AMY CADE and the dates gave her an age of six years; under these was the message: ALWAYS LOVED. He never quite knew what to do when he faced it. Inside he wanted to weep but he knew that once he broke he'd be destroyed. So, as ever, he stood looking down blankly, disbelieving; half-reality, half-nightmare. He dropped to his haunches, gently, as if not to waken, flowers clutched hard against his chest, the knuckles of his hard hands like ivory. It took some while before he could reach forward to lay the blooms on the stone.

The woman had arrived some time before him, had seen him approach the grave, watching cautiously as she tended another – her mother's. Now she walked towards him.

Her clothes were too young for her and her hair, though full and shining, too blonde by far to be natural. Her face was small and sharp under the tangled explosion of curls, and finely lined in the way in which thin faces age. She wore high-heeled boots, tan-coloured, to the knee; the leather soft and in folds at her ankles. Her straight skirt was tight and short, leaving too much of her thighs exposed. In contrast the raincoat she wore – despite the warm sun – was long; an expensive Burberry, beige, to match the fluffy angora wool roll-neck which held her throat in its soft grip. She exuded a coarse but potent sexuality.

She came up beside him, standing – almost defiantly – above him as he crouched before the small grave. Finally she said: 'Jack?'

Perhaps he knew she had been there all the while for when he stood and turned his head toward her he registered no surprise.

'You look rough,' she said, then moved her head, dislodging a few curls; a practised gesture. 'Nice flowers. You've broken some.' Her London accent was strong.

He had turned back to the grave.

'You knew I'd be here,' she accused. 'It's Saturday. I always come Saturdays.'

'I'm not here for you,' he answered brutally.

'I don't want trouble, Jack. It's not on any more. There's someone else anyway.'

Now, he turned. 'Why do you keep telling me that?'

'So's you know. You've got to know, haven't you?'

'I *know*. You told me – *last time*, then again on the 'phone. I know! All right?'

Her face had hardened, though a smile twisted her lips. 'Just so's you understand.'

He began walking away from the little grave. *She shouldn't hear this*, he found himself thinking. I'm bloody mad! *She's dead.*

The woman followed him. 'I'll need a lift,' she told him, as though it were his responsibility.

'Where's your feller?'

'He's got the betting shop to run. It's Saturday, they're flat-out. Doing well, bought me a fur, Christmas.'

Outside the gates she saw the ageing caravanette. 'You sleeping in it? That why you look rough?'

'Shut up.'

She stood beside him as he unlocked the door: small, even against his average height. 'Other side,' he said.

Ignoring him she climbed in, sliding under the wheel and across the bench seat, her short skirt riding high. She made no attempt to pull it down.

He glanced at her thighs and she caught him. She grinned. 'Where?' he said.

'The house.'

'You haven't moved in with him then?'

'None of your sodding business.'

'Is he in with you?'

She swore at him.

They drove in silence, heading toward Central London. She broke it, her voice tight, anger caught beneath it. 'Anyway, he brings me all the way here. Doesn't have to – she was your kid, not his.'

'And yours,' he retorted, the edge of his own temper sharpened by her – just as it had always been. She wants me to belt her, he thought. That's what does it for her. He could predict what would come next.

'You eaten?' she asked after some fiddling with the radio.

'Breakfast.'

'I'll feed you. At the house.'

'It's all right.'

'Don't be so bloody-minded.'

'I'm not hungry.'

'Not for anything?'

And there it was, the same as always, the itch she had to have scratched, the challenge she would not let pass by her. Not just him. Others. Sometimes he felt it could be anyone. He wanted her but he knew what it would be like afterwards. The unclean feeling, the need to purge himself.

They were nearing their destination. '*Come on!*' she urged.

He knew from the way she held herself and the sound of her voice when she needed a man badly. He stopped, leaving the engine running.

She made no attempt to get out. Her hand had shifted to her breast, the fingers moving lightly. He switched off the ignition and got out of the van, walking straight to the front door. He forgot he no longer had a key.

She came up beside him and used hers. 'Quickly,' she said.

He knew exactly what she wanted and stripped off his clothes, revealing a hard, solid torso ridged in muscle, then lay on the bed.

She stood before him and pulled the soft angora sweater up over her naked breasts, teasing her nipples with the wool. He dragged her down, hard, the way she wanted it.

It had begun to rain by the time he left. Their parting was normal: she bitter and half-accusing him of rape; he, flat and empty. With her he was weak; he admitted it to himself for the

14

first time, but the admission changed nothing. He used to be able to pretend that he was using her as much as she him, but that convenient piece of self-deception no longer held true. Afterwards, the truth lay as naked as she had on the tangled bedclothes. He wanted love from her – she wanted . . . just wanted. It had worked between them, once, with a child – his daughter – as proof, but since . . . He closed his mind, fast, before her screams – as he had imagined them a million times – escaped and shredded his sanity.

He drove away, taking the long route up to central London because he had time to kill before the contact, stopping at a small grocer's to restock the camper's cupboard and at a garage to refuel and make routine checks. Traffic started to build as he carried out his tasks and he made the West End with a half-hour to spare. Seven twenty, he had been told with a fall-back one hour later at an alternative location.

Parking was difficult because he was in the theatre district and crowds were heading full-tilt for their Saturday evening out. In the end he swung into a space that the owner of an overlong Mercedes finally gave up on, conceding defeat with a petulant squeal from fat tyres. Locking up he hurried through the drizzle toward Covent Garden, making the wine-bar with three minutes to spare.

His contact was early, the older one of the two men who had recruited him and, supposedly, named Harlow. He stood at the side of the wine-bar, foregoing the high stool beside him, umbrella dripping, his glass raised to his lips as he leaned on the narrow shelf running the length of the wall. A gentleman. Well-bred, well-fed, with smooth skin undoubtedly pampered for it belied his retreating middle age, and soft down on his plump cheeks where a razor was forbidden. Today he was dressed informally but equally well: a tweed jacket, twill slacks and a cravat at his throat bearing the same stripe as the tie he had worn at the first meeting. Beside him on the shelf was a national newspaper and a second glass of white wine. He lowered his glass, nodded, then shook his umbrella. 'Damned rain,' he said. 'All well?'

Cade nodded and took the stool. Folded inside the newspaper he could see a large envelope; he reached across and took the waiting wine. The wine-bar filled so quickly that

Cade wondered irrationally if Harlow had arranged it.

Harlow ducked down, his face close to Cade's. 'Whichever way you choose, make it convincing.'

'My problem,' said Cade.

Harlow turned his face away, then moved in close again. Someone pushed against him and apologized but he ignored the interruption. 'You've no doubts as to the necessity of . . .'

Cade stopped him, contempt touching his eyes. 'I'm doing what's been asked. You can't use your own people, so use me. Just don't question me. I'm doing what's *right*. Aren't I?'

'Of course it's right.'

'Then don't spill your conscience over me.'

Harlow coloured. 'It's nothing to do with conscience, I'm as convinced as you are.'

'*You* convinced me,' Cade said, coldly.

'Everything's there.' Harlow touched the paper. 'There's money too. Take the paper as well.'

'I don't want paying,' Cade snapped.

'We know that. It isn't a fortune. Expenses, you'll need money.'

Cade nodded.

'Brock might meet you next time, usual method.' Harlow hooked his umbrella over his arm.

Cade finished his drink as Harlow pushed his way through the crowd, then vanished. He looked round. Complacent bastards, he thought, surveying the crowd. You're all in a fucking sinking ship and too thick to know that there's holes in it. Don't care, either, who's making them. He stood up, transferring the newspaper and the packet it contained under his arm, then forced his way out none too gently.

Back inside the camper he opened the plain sealed envelope, placed the wad of notes beneath the rubber matting under his seat, then shook out the photograph he knew would be inside. There were three shots on the one oblong print: full-face, and both profiles, left and right. Male, forties, thin lips primly together, heavy eyebrows, arched as if surprised – probably the flash, he thought – and light brown eyes beneath them. The hair was thinning and tinged with a shade of copper, though not a true redhead. The face had probably been thin but had fleshed out with age. Cade guessed the body would still be trim; the vain eyes gave away the discipline of a man who would watch his waistline. And, Cade guessed – instinctively, for he had yet to read the detailed notes still inside the envelope – *bent*. In fact the notes termed the man as 'possible homosexual' with an appendix declaring: 'Investigated in depth over extended period. No homosexual friends, acquaintances, or encounters of a casual nature. Bachelor, lives alone, dedicated to duty, little or no private life outside GCHQ organized leisure activities. Nothing recorded against. Positively vetted and cleared.' 'Bent,' Cade murmured aloud. He would not countenance the modern term 'gay'.

He pushed the envelope, with the photographs back inside, under the seat – beneath the matting, with the money. He would study the notes later, when he settled down for the night in the camper, somewhere secluded, on the journey back to the Cotswold Hills.

He was hungry. Okay, a good hot meal and maybe a drink afterwards. He deserved it. He locked the camper after checking the latches of the sleeping compartment windows then made his way through the busy streets toward Leicester Square. There was a restaurant he had used occasionally – before and after his marriage; he remembered taking Carol there, presenting her, showing her off, until her constant flirtations soured the atmosphere for him. He chose to eat there not out of any masochistic yearning but because everywhere else seemed to have changed around him: he felt like a stranger in a familiar land. When he arrived, the restaurant had vanished. There was a red-brick wall up to and around the corner where once the plate glass windows had been: where faded but genuine velvet curtains enclosed candle-lit tables and music played on 78s crackled through a horn shaped like a foxglove. Now there was only the wall. And messages in dayglow paint informing him that London was now a nuclear-free zone; that punks ruled; gays were people too; and that the people would soon be free. Also, that the government was fascist.

He walked away.

There was anger in him, deep, like betrayal, and the betrayal was all around him. Street corners peopled by creatures with

17

bizarre clothes and hairstyles, who, to him, might easily have arrived from outer space. I've been away too long, he thought in a brief moment of rationalization: too rigid, too much training, too much uniformity. I'm out of touch. The thought died because his longing – his need – for the old, organized order, would not let it live.

Somewhere, hidden from ordinary people, devious minds were deciding the shape of the future. His future. His fists were balled tight, his mind also. Then he relaxed as he pushed hard through a group blocking the pavement who thrust into reluctant hands the sum total of their radical solutions to all ills. He relaxed because he knew he at least was doing something while the rest sailed along, accepting any wind which propelled them. He took the literature, screwed it up, and pitched it over his shoulder without-even a glance at the content.

Someone called 'Fascist!' so he turned and raised his foot, dragging it down the nearest shin before walking on. A figure fell, screeching, into the mêlée – it might have been male or female, he could not tell and did not care – then a number of them chased after him, giving up the moment he swung around and fixed them with his eyes.

He found a pub which appeared unchanged, purchased a pint of dark bitter and two pies heated in a microwave oven. The clientele were mainly theatricals, stoking the fire between performances. Here and there were well-known faces, each with a small, fawning audience who measured their responses when addressed personally by the great ones, all vying ruthlessly to up their places in the pecking order.

Cade studied them, munching his pies and sipping his beer. Creeps, said his pale eyes. One or two caught the look but none disputed its message.

His own fire was stoked now so he sank the beer and ordered a large scotch as a chaser. The young barman serving him poured the drink precisely because his fine profile yielded a greater return – in that vicinity – than the proceeds of his nightly sleight-of-hand with the measures.

Cade ordered another scotch, swallowed it immediately and left. Already he was over the limit for driving but his head was hard enough for him to push aside that consideration. Part of

18

him recognized that he was crashing head-first through the barriers of self-discipline he had erected, the rest said: Bugger it.

He walked back to Leicester Square and entered a dance hall where a big band was featured who made the kind of sound he enjoyed. Inside, the bouncers skirted the packed dance-floor like sharks patrolling a crowded beach, poised for any flurry which would be their signal to strike. He strolled upstairs to a bar overlooking the bandstand, ordered a beer and let the bright brass echo up to him. A group of girls came toward him in a jumble, shrieking over the sound of the band as they exchanged notes on their male targets for that night. One of them, dark with streaks of blonde and glitter in her high heavily lacquered hair broke from the group and made for the bar, settling beside him, both elbows on the wet surface. Her breasts were full and showed through the gaping arm-holes of her tee-shirt.

'Vodka-tonic,' she told the barman who broke off halfway through serving a knot of young men with close-cropped heads and short-sleeved shirts, the sleeves rolled tight to display bulging biceps.

'Oi!' one yelled.

The barman bent over toward the girl, giving her what he imagined was a look guaranteed to seduce, then swung away and flashily fixed the drink.

The skin-head who had protested came over, brows furrowed, picked up the drink and thrust it back at the barman. 'You finish us first, mate,' he demanded.

The girl said: 'Piss off,' and reached out for the drink.

The skin-head slapped her hand, hard. 'Yer out of order,' he said. The barman had backed away, his eyes flicking into the dim lighting for the reassuring sight of a white shirt beneath a black tuxedo.

The crack of the slap had turned Cade's head.

'You gonna do something about it?' the skin-head demanded leaning right across the girl, his face close to Cade's. The girl kneed him in the crotch. He howled and dropped both hands to his groin. His friends reacted instantly, assuming Cade was responsible, rushing straight at him.

He took the first swinging blow high on the head, rolling

19

with the punch off his stool, making space for himself. The one who had landed the punch jumped forward for more and Cade broke his arm at the elbow before slashing high with his foot at another face. The girl screamed as she was splattered with blood and tooth-fragments. Cade regained his balance but was struck by a number of kicks to the body. Standing his ground and accepting the blows he chopped down with both hands connecting each time. The odds lessened quickly as numbed and bruised thigh muscles gave out. Two dropped to their knees directly below him. He punched each hard, in the face; short rapid blows which travelled only inches before impact. There was only one left standing, hands raised and open, away from his body, backing off. Cade's hand struck low, too fast for his victim to pull back his groin. He shrieked as the fingers locked and applied pressure.

The bouncers had arrived, four of them, but they remained at a distance, shoulders dropped and hands curled. Cade stuck his free hand over the skin-head's mouth, shutting off his cries, then shouted over the blaring music at the bouncers: 'It wasn't my problem. They made it mine.'

'Okay, mate. Let him go. It's okay. Everything's okay,' one replied.

The skin-head gurgled under the hard hand.

Cade's eyes flicked over each of them then pushed the quivering body away from him in disgust. 'He's yours,' he told them. 'Leave me out of it.' He walked away, his drink unfinished on the bar.

The girl was slumped on a bar-stool, still shocked, picking at her bloodied tee-shirt, her friends gathering around for the details.

Cade was already out in the square, mentally shrugging off the incident and glad to be getting away from the spoiled metropolis once more.

When he reached the camper, the level of traffic had swelled and it took him a while before he could cut into the stream.

Two hours later he filtered onto the motorway feeling wretched. A growing depression weighed him down – loneliness as well, though he would never admit this. The image he had built for himself was an extension of his professionalism: self-sufficient, decisive, controlled, emotions battened down.

20

Since the death of his child he had encased himself in the hard shell of supreme self-confidence. Yet there were times when that shell turned to pulp.

He had been driving automatically, his black mood and the effects of alcohol numbing him. As if awakening he became aware of wire fencing and prefabricated huts, and beyond the lighted windows of the massive block which housed part of the eleven thousand people employed by Britain's Government Communications Headquarters outside Cheltenham.

He cursed himself violently.

Up ahead was the large roundabout which sprawled before the guarded gates of the top-secret complex. There was no way he could avoid it. Somewhere, he could not remember where, he had taken the wrong turning and in so doing had made himself visible and perhaps placed himself and his mission in jeopardy.

The roundabout was upon him and indecision forced him to make a second sweep before deciding to head directly through the spa town of Cheltenham. He fumed at his stupidity, knowing that one of the discreet observation points or an unmarked security vehicle would – just for the record – have noted his number. In their position he would have done so. It was late and traffic was sparse. The caravanette was fairly anonymous but the sound of the Volkswagen air-cooled rear engine would be distinctive and clear in the night air. He knew from his own experience that men on surveillance or observation duties were plagued by boredom and would treat any incident, even marginally out of the ordinary, with an inordinate degree of suspicion. He had no doubt whatsoever that the camper's number had been logged.

The mistake had been made so now it was a case of assessing the potential damage.

The registration number and description of the camper would be put on the police computer. So what? He owned it. It gave him mobility and temporary shelter and backed up his cover of travelling around to view the ancient Roman sites which abounded in the area.

He started, almost stabbing his foot on the brake pedal. The two policemen on the motorway – they would also have taken his number. Two computer checks in one day. Not good at all.

21

He lit a cigarette and drew the smoke in deeply. Stupid! It's her. She's buggered me up again. He drove on, furious with himself. He knew he might pay heavily for his temporary loss of discipline.

So get rid of the camper?

Not yet. Sleeping in an ordinary car would soon reduce his physical appearance, which would arouse suspicion. Also, the police had a negative attitude about people sleeping in their cars, usually assuming the occupant was sleeping off a drunk. And using hotels or lodging houses meant signing registers which could provide neat signposts if things went badly wrong. He had little faith in false names – the police rarely began investigations with a name; if they had anything at all it was usually a description; and hotel staff remembered faces.

No. He'd stick with the camper for a little while longer. Brazen it out if he was pulled. He relaxed, beginning to think more clearly – like his usual calculating self. So he'd made a balls-up. OK, he'd cover it. Think!

There were two more jobs to be done after the queer – Brock and Harlow had told him right at the beginning there would only be four – so he'd bring the queer forward. Close him off by Monday, latest. Assuming the bastard hadn't done a runner after reading the papers! Cade gave a tight smile. No way. He was too bloody good. The gas explosion could never be thought of as anything but a genuine accident. He knew what they looked for after an explosion; knew it all backwards: he'd worked both ends in his time, the blowing up and the piecing together.

Where now then? Pushing it a bit to park the camper on public land with its number on the 'suspicious vehicle' list of every police patrol-car in the area. The farmer that morning – what was it he said? 'Don't involve the police myself.' Then he'd patted the shotgun. He'd do.

Cade began watching for signs, spotted the right one then had to make a twenty-minute detour before coming out on the road he wanted. Half an hour later he was back in the narrow lane – but this time he drove past the copse, braking to a stop as a five-bar gate was caught in the beam of his headlights. He backed up, unlocked the gate, drove through, then stopped and locked it again. Farmers did not appreciate their farm-gates being left unlatched.

With the aid of his pencil-torch he fiddled in the Volkswagen's rear engine compartment until the motor developed an unsteady beat, then drove on up the long poorly cared-for rutted driveway.

The farmhouse and various outbuildings were set around a muddy yard strewn with hay-spillings. The camper sloshed to a halt outside what seemed to be the main door. Cade left the engine running, its sound now appalling. There were no lights inside the house but he cracked down the knocker anyway. A bulb came on above him – on an extended, angled bracket – so that he was held in a circle of light. When the door finally opened it was on a heavy business-like chain, black and oiled against rust – it confirmed a lot of Cade's earlier opinions about the owner.

'You again?' snapped the farmer from behind the door, his face hidden. Cade guessed there was a crack in the thick wooden door. He also guessed that the shotgun – with its bright shells locked in the closed breach – was not too far away.

'I'm asking permission this time. My motor's bad – I can't work on it in the dark. It won't last much longer if I keep going.'

'Why didn't you find a garage?'

'Out here? The ones I passed are all shut anyway. All I need is somewhere to park and sleep till morning – I can see then.'

'You can fix it yourself?'

'I'm a trained mechanic, 'course I can.'

'How much'll a garage charge you to fix it?'

Cade shrugged. 'Can't tell, can I? Not till I have it apart.'

The farmer's face came into view but the chain stayed on. He stuck his chin out. 'Over there, behind you – the big shed. Machinery inside.' He moved out of sight then thrust a heavy brass key through the gap. 'Bring the key straight back,' he warned. 'There's heavy-duty jacks and stuff. You pay me half what a garage would charge. I'll trust you.'

'Deal,' Cade said.

'Get on with you, then. Don't forget the key.'

Cade drove the chugging camper across the yard until the big double doors of the 'shed' – in reality a large barn-like

23

structure – were in his headlights. The lock, like the key, was brass and as serious as the chain on the front door – as were the hasp and screws. Fortress mentality, thought Cade. He had met it before in men who lived – usually alone – in remote areas. Better still.

He drove the camper in, then trudged back. The farmer had the door wide open – the chain made redundant by the shotgun laying, unbroken, on the tall heavy oak chest close by the man's hand. 'It stays by the bed when I sleep,' he informed Cade.

Cade nodded. 'I appreciate it.' He twisted his head at the barn. 'You got any machinery needs fixing? I'll do it if I can.'

'Maybe.'

'I'll get some sleep, then.'

'The key?' said the farmer.

'Oh yeah!' Cade passed it over

The farmer had put on gumboots. 'I'm going to lock you in,' he said.

Something flickered across Cade's eyes, then was gone. 'If you feel better,' he answered, reasonably.

They walked to the barn together, the farmer picking up the shotgun first – casually, like his raincoat, but Cade heard the double click of the hammers, cold and metallic in the night air.

'Thanks again,' he said, inside the barn.

'I'll unlock you early,' the farmer told him as the big doors closed and the lock clicked.

'Good night!' Cade called.

There was no answer, only the sucking sound of rubber in mud, then the hard slam of a door. Cade did not hear the chain but he knew it would be on. He extracted the envelope Harlow had given him from under the seat then stretched out in the back of the camper with the interior lights on and began his reading.

Number Two lived with his mother – no age given for her but he was fifty-one so she was no chicken. But mobile: she apparently still ran a Morris Minor. He drove to work and owned a Rover – the old 3500 V8. Name, Blaikley: Maurice Bertram, actual position at GCHQ not given. Cade had not been given that information with Number One either. It did not bother him – he knew what they were up to so it was

24

certain they did not clear garbage. He recalled Brock's words – the young tough one with the hatchet mind and confident eyes – at that first irreversible meeting: 'GCHQ's a sieve with the Soviets underneath, except they're getting a whole lot more than just the drainage. There's four holes we know about – definite, no question – and we want them plugged. Permanently. We want you to close them up, fast, before the Yanks get wind of it and they flush us down the pot for good and all!'

'Why not use your own?' Cade had queried.

'*Verboten*,' Brock retorted, instantly, with a sliding look at Harlow who nodded.

Harlow had taken it up: 'Look at the wretched papers. Leaks, recriminations between departments, official enquiries brought on by media pressure. That's only what you read – what you don't see, what is never revealed, is the near-panic behind the scenes, the fear that there's always someone whose conscience – or political leanings – will cause him, or her, to drop a neat billet-doux, anonymously of course, into the eager hands of some TV producer or investigative journalist.'

'Even in your lot?' Cade had asked, shocked. Meaning the Security Service or MI5, which was who they had said they were – with ID to prove it.

'Especially our lot,' muttered Brock with venom.

'The trouble is', Harlow rejoined, leaning forward in his chair, his smooth face pained by disillusionment, 'it's got to the stage where the sort of methods we're discussing here – at the best of times on the shaky side of being legal because no one ever wants to have his name as the final signatory – well, they're like flapping a red rag in the face of a bull.'

'*Red* is right!' Brock had snapped.

'So why me?' Cade asked after a whole lot of thinking – and a lot of anger building.

'Because we checked you thoroughly,' answered Harlow. 'Because you would do it for the right reasons. You're a patriot – that shines right through your army record. You're a patriot still, even after they treated you so appallingly.'

'Because,' cut in Brock, 'because you took some action. You bloody well *did* something.'

'I bloody well got shoved in the nick,' Cade snapped back. 'Four years hard.'

'Shocking,' said Harlow.

'Typical,' said Brock.

'I was a hero,' Cade fumed. 'Before it happened, I was a hero. Not for the whole fucking world to see, I didn't want that – you don't join The Regiment if you want the glory.'

'You were and still are,' Harlow put in sympathetically. 'Undercover work always produces unsung heroes. In Northern Ireland especially.'

'They introduced you to the PM,' Brock reminded. 'Unprecedented, that.'

'She wanted to meet someone who worked undercover. I was available. Didn't count for much later, did it?'

'Political expediency,' said Brock.

'You shot dead four young Irishmen – it caused riots at a time when they wanted calm. There were delicate negotiations in progress.'

'I shot four IRA hoods who rammed my motor because they'd sussed me out. They weren't interested in negotiating. They wanted me dead.'

'You fired four shots,' Brock murmured. 'And killed with each.'

'They underestimated you,' offered Harlow.

'They overestimated themselves,' Brock put in, shrewdly.

Cade had not commented: it was not his way.

'So you'll do it?' Harlow asked, pressing for commitment.

'We'd understand if you have other considerations,' Brock said, deserting his hawkish stance momentarily.

'There aren't any,' Cade commented. He was ready to do what they wanted, willing even, but like anyone being given the hard sell he hesitated before final commitment.

'If it's a question of money . . .' Harlow began but Brock was already chopping him down.

'Cade didn't come here to extort!' he almost shouted. 'His record tells us he's not buyable.'

'Of course, I apologize,' Harlow agreed, quite shaken.

Harlow is the senior, Cade had thought, but Brock is the one who's made the decisions. Brock and whoever is behind and above both of them. Cade was no fool, the two of them had clout but in the nature of the game they were no more than heavyweight errand-boys. How high up did it go? he wondered, who had the real power to say: Kill? He did not want to know. Not then, and certainly not now when the operation was running and he was at his most vulnerable.

He read through the information on Maurice Blaikley then began again. The first time he wanted facts, the second he wanted the *feel* of the man. The problem was that once Number Two was hit there was a very real danger that it might frighten the game. In other words: if all four were members of the same cell – a fact not proven by Brock and Harlow – or even if they all worked separately, each to a different control yet aware of their comrades' activities (highly unlikely, but possible, had said Harlow, who owned to an expert knowledge of Soviet Intelligence operations), then the sudden demise of both Thurstone and Blaikley would trigger shrill alarms in undoubtedly already nervous minds. Cade knew he needed a set of circumstances which would make Blaikley's demise totally convincing. Convincing enough to fool his mother, the investigating police, and, in their wake, the Security Service – because Harlow had warned they could not hinder MI5 investigations. Also, Moscow Centre.

He gave the problem over an hour of concentrated thought – until his mind blanked out and it was morning. As usual it was the first idea he had thought of which slammed into the forefront of his mind. The one he had shelved, yet dragged out time and time again, each time with rejection as his conclusion – but now, with the uncluttered singleness of thought that morning brings, he knew it to be the logical answer. The entire project was fraught with risks – which, as a straight executioner, should have caused him to say: forget it. And mean it. He actually grinned widely as he sat up from the bunk, his old army blanket around his shoulders against the dank chill of the windowless barn. He was pleased – and not a little surprised – by his deviousness. If he pulled it off, he would cloud the issue so much that even the sodding Russians would be thrown. The answer lay – so simply – not in covering the link between the two deaths but actually establishing one.

'You in there!' the farmer bawled, followed by the sound of something wooden cracking repeatedly on the barn doors.

'Hear you!' Cade shouted back.

Daylight, grey and lifeless, drifted into the gloom – bringing the rain with it. The farmer stood between the gap in the big doors dressed in an old-fashioned oil-cloth bicycle-cape – bright yellow like the cylinder which had obliterated Thurstone – and his gumboots. He carried a heavy knurled stick in both hands, low across his belly.

Cade stepped down from the camper. ' 'Morning. I'll get to work. Thanks.'

'You have anything to eat in that thing?'

'I'm all right,' said Cade.

'Not if you're going to do any work for me, you're not. I need work done properly. A worker with an empty belly is only half a worker.'

'You sound like my old RSM,' Cade countered with a twisted smile.

'You army then?'

'Was.'

The farmer looked at him suspiciously. 'Not on the run are you? Not deserted.'

'Leave it out! I loved the army.'

'Oh-aye? Why'd you leave? You're still young.'

'Thirty-five. You stay in too long and there's nothing when you come out.'

'I suppose,' nodded the farmer, back to his tough but reasonable self. 'Hard enough for anyone to find work these days.'

'That's right.'

The farmer pointed his stick at the farmhouse beyond the wall of the barn. 'She'll fix you something – my sister – sleep through a war she would. Didn't hear the racket that thing of yours made last night, didn't hear anything. Going deaf I reckon as well. Get on in, she knows you're coming.'

'Thanks,' Cade said gratefully.

'Thank me when you've fixed some of that lot!' The stick swung up at a diesel tractor and what looked like a petrol-engined generator. 'Think you can handle that?'

Cade shrugged. 'Depends what's wrong, doesn't it?'

'Oh-aye . . . well get on with you then. Don't dawdle over your food or she'll be gossiping to you all morning.'

'Give me fifteen minutes.'

The farmer moved out into the rain as Cade began tugging

on a pullover. 'That stuff you were doing in the wood, yesterday,' he called, his gumboots working patterns into the mud as he moved around scanning the outbuildings.

'What stuff?' Cade shouted back, his head inside the camper as he collected his anorak.

'That Japanese fighting – seen it on the telly – where'd you learn that – army?'

'Chinese,' Cade corrected, joining him in the rain, the hood of his anorak over his head. 'Well, Tibetan really. Originally. Yeah, army.'

'They teach that now do they – never heard of in my day.'

They were walking to the house now, but slowly, as if the rain did not exist. They might have been father and son. 'You were in then? Which bunch?' Cade enquired.

'Oh! long time since. The war. Foot-slogging. Nothing special.'

'I thought farmers didn't get their papers – dispensation – you know, because of the food shortage.'

'My old dad was the farmer – I was just help. Still, could have stayed out if I'd wanted.' His manner had become defensive.

'Volunteered?'

'Did my duty.'

'Did you catch anything?'

The farmer glanced at him. Cade sensed embarrassment, even shame, and knew he was lying.

'Wounds?'

'Lucky,' growled the farmer in a way that closed the subject.

His sister was standing at an open side-door, a polythene strip over her head. 'Bring him in,' she squealed in a high voice. 'He's dripping, can't you see? Will! You're the limit.'

The farmer waggled his stick at her. 'Worse than a wife – not that I've ever succumbed.' He carried on talking about her even when they were inside. She might not have been there. 'Never been anywhere. Spent her life between here and the village. If it weren't for the TV set she'd think the war was still on.'

'Lettie,' she said, wiping her hands on her apron but not offering one for shaking. 'We're Sullivans. He's probably not told you that either. He exaggerates everything. I once went to London –'

29

'Fifty-two,' put in her brother. 'God knows what for.'

'The Ideal Home I think it was. Exhibition anyway.'

'Came back pickled, they all did. Went on a coach, whole village. Women anyway.'

Lettie Sullivan allowed a smile to drift over her lips, lighting her eyes as it spread.

'Daft,' her brother explained.

'Sullivan?' Cade queried. 'Must have been Irish.'

'Once,' Sullivan growled. 'Poverty-struck bog-farmers, I should think.'

'It was – oh – quite a big farm,' she disagreed. 'Long time back, mind you.'

'You'd have been there?' asked Sullivan. 'Army and that.'

'Did my duty,' Cade smiled.

'Oh-aye.'

'Let the boy eat, Will.'

'Boy? He'd better do a man's work!'

'Take no notice,' Lettie Sullivan insisted. 'It's only his bark.'

'He can bite, too,' Cade said, joking, but remembering the steady eyes over the shotgun the morning and the night before.

Sullivan opened the door and peered up at the grey clouds. 'I'm out to the fields then,' he announced. 'You see what's wrong with that foreign van of yours then look over the tractor and the other.'

'The tractor's never worked,' said Lettie. 'Not since he first bought it.'

Sullivan was outside, the rain patting on his oil-cloth cape. 'It worked well enough for the first ten years!' he shouted. 'She still thinks we're back in the fifties.'

'I'll have a go!' Cade called as Sullivan padded away.

Lettie produced his cooked breakfast then stood over him as he ate, replenishing the plate even as he filled his mouth.

'Got to get a good start to the day,' she muttered – more times than Cade could count.

He felt good. At home. Welcome. But disturbed. This was everything he had never had. Responsible, caring people who fussed over him. Parents. Quite suddenly the loneliness washed over him, engulfing him, his filled stomach empty and cold. He pushed himself up. 'Thanks, Ma,' he told her. 'Terrific, best I've had. Better get a move on.'

'I'll fetch a nice mug of hot tea to you,' she said with a firm nod. 'That old shed's damp.'

Cade stepped outside, running for the barn as soon as the door clicked into place. His black mood had destroyed his earlier feeling of self-satisfaction, bringing to the fore the dangerous route he was planning on taking.

'Fuck it!' he snapped aloud, with a rare obscenity, then began work on the old tractor, interrupted only by Lettie Sullivan's promised mug of tea.

By lunch-time he had the old tractor chugging unevenly — after discovering that there was nothing seriously wrong, simply a jammed solenoid. Sullivan obviously had no mechanical knowledge whatsoever. Cade stopped the engine and unscrewed the plugs, then cleaned them and set the gaps. With the plugs back in it ran as smoothly as it ever would. He turned his attention to the small petrol-driven generator but soon realized that this would need replacement parts. Good, he said to himself, if he wants the job finished he'll have to let me stay a bit longer.

Lettie Sullivan interrupted him as he lay under the rear of the camper, tugging at his boots with an accompanying high, 'Yoo-hoo, come and get it.'

Cade followed her into the farmhouse, the rain now no more than a haze evaporated by a warm afternoon sun. Sullivan was already at the table tucking into a roast.

'Never waits,' she complained, almost pushing Cade into a chair.

'So you got that old lump of iron going,' Sullivan said.

'Jammed starter,' Cade explained, staring aghast at the enormous portion placed before him.

'Let the lad eat,' snapped Lettie. 'There's more when you want it.'

'That all?' Sullivan raised his thick, greying eyebrows.

'Plugs needed work — that's done — you'll need to change the oil, I couldn't find any fresh.'

'Wouldn't know where to begin. You could do it if I got some, eh?'

Cade chewed on the delicious beef, nodding. 'The generator needs parts. I can fix it but not without them.'

'What about your foreign van? Got that going?'

31

'Same problem – parts. I'll have to look up a Volkswagen dealer in the yellow pages.'

'Under the telephone in the hall,' Sullivan muttered, mouth full.

'You want me to fix the generator, then?'

'May as well finish what you started. We're giving you food and board.'

Cade grinned at Lettie: 'Better than any restaurant, Ma!' She beamed. 'I'll work out the cost of the job on the VW,' this to Sullivan. 'Half you said – for the facilities.'

Lettie exploded, slamming down both knife and fork onto the scrubbed wood of the kitchen table. 'You'll not take money from the boy!'

Sullivan's head ducked a little into his worn checked jacket. 'That was last night. Different now, isn't it? The old tractor's got going.'

'He got it going,' she snapped, face flushed; quite shocked by her own outburst but not displeased with herself.

'Problem is,' Cade put in breaking the silence, 'it's Sunday.'

'He'll have to stay over,' she said.

'And I'll have to take you away from your work to drive me all the way to Cheltenham,' Cade pointed out.

'He can take the cycle,' she said, decisively, getting an astonished look from her brother.

'A bike?' Cade laughed. 'I'll be gone for a week.'

'Motorcycle,' Sullivan corrected. 'It's almost new. Well, years old really, but hardly used.'

Silence, and exchanged looks between brother and sister halted their eating.

'You get it started and you can use it,' Sullivan said at last. 'It's got bags on the back if you've got stuff to carry.'

'Yours?' Cade asked but no answer came.

'You married, son?' queried Sullivan. 'Suppose not – army and that.'

'Separated. A few years now.'

'Not divorced then?'

Cade sighed. 'Should be. She starts, then stops. Never got around to doing anything about it myself. Should do really.'

'Sad,' said Lettie. 'Especially if there's children. Poor little souls, they're always the ones to suffer.'

32

Cade's face had become a mask.

Sullivan put his knife and fork together on the emptied plate. 'She's got yours then – your wife?'

'Mine's dead.' The words seemed to be dragged from Cade.

Lettie's thin red hand flew to her mouth.

Sullivan stood up. 'I'll show you the motorcycle.'

The two men strolled back across the yard, leaving Lettie still seated, her lined face woeful.

'She had one of her own,' Sullivan explained, half-glancing back at the house as if afraid she was watching. 'Got in the family way. Left it too late to do anything about it.' He shrugged. 'Our old dad half-killed her – not with his hands you understand, he'd never have done that. With words. Catholic y'see. Both of them. Not me – not now. She daren't go near a church to this day. Old Dad really finished her off. The boy too, in the end.'

'The kid died then.'

Sullivan picked up a stone and pitched it at three fat crows perched on the barn's roof. He actually struck one. It tumbled, scrabbling on the slates, then got its wings beating enough to lift it up and away.

'Did it himself,' he said. 'Oh, years ago now. Went fishing – never came back. The bike's his. Police found it on the bank – with his tackle. He'd eaten his picnic lunch and his tea – all at once – then must have jumped in. Brought the bike back, they did, that day. Took them a week before they found him. Had to go myself to look at him. Dad refused – she couldn't. I think seeing him – like that – would have made her believe, I mean really, that God had punished her for good and all.'

'How old?'

They had stopped, briefly, Sullivan scanning the roofs of his property – whether for more crows of for signs of disrepair was uncertain. 'Old? You mean how young. Eighteen if I recall. Long time gone now.'

Cade moved off. 'Show me the bike – it'll need to be checked over if I've got to use it.'

Sullivan followed. 'Oh it works all right. Makes me start it up regular she does – not that I can ride. I can kick the starter, that's all. Never went for motorcycles – got my Land-Rover for transport. I'd let you use that but now that she's said use the bike . . . well, you've got to really. No one's ever ridden it since him – you understand that, don't you?'

'I guessed.'

They had entered a stable, without horses. The motorcycle was under a tarpaulin in one of the two stalls. An old Triumph, maroon, the chrome gleaming as if it had just been rolled out of the showroom.

'She polishes it every week,' Sullivan explained.

'It'll be worth a bit these days.'

'She'll be dead before it's sold. Me before her I shouldn't wonder. Can you ride it?'

'Sure.'

'Have a go then. I'll keep an eye on her while you run it round the yard. Don't know how she'll take it really.'

Cade unscrewed the petrol cap on-the tank and peered inside, sniffing.

'There's half a tank,' called Sullivan, already out in the yard. 'I have to keep some in for when I turn the engine over.'

The Triumph started at the first kick, roaring wildly in the confined space of the stall. Loose straw flew like a whirlwind around Cade as the exhausts lifted it from the cobbled floor. Momentarily Cade was back in his own teens – a young tearaway who had stolen a BSA for an illegal Sunday run down to the south coast. His stomach had been like jelly from fear, making him ride even faster just to push himself beyond the limits of fear itself – into that strange purgatory between stark fright and death where you float, uncaring, because you've made yourself believe that if it's going to happen then it's going to happen anyway. He'd lived half his life in that place.

Yeah! he shouted in his mind, then aloud, as strongly as he could, though his voice was no match for the blast of engine.

Lettie had come out into the yard to watch him as he wheeled in circles, spraying mud and straw, a lot of it over Sullivan's gumboots. The old man frowned at first but when he saw his sister's face and the open mouth wide with laughter the lines on his forehead faded and he threw back his own head, joining her.

Cade lifted the front forks, performing a 'wheelie' and Lettie's fists crushed her cheeks but the smile stayed fixed right until he skidded to a halt beside her, grinning from ear to ear.

'Thank's, Ma!' he shouted. 'You've taken years off me.'

She let the tears spill over her clenched fists, then turned back inside.

'Enough for one day;' Sullivan said, beside him again.

'I'll put it back,' Cade nodded and, more sedately rode the bike back into the stable, replacing the canvas. He rejoined the farmer in the yard.

'Enjoyed that, didn't you?' said Sullivan.

'Terrific!'

'I've got a small problem with the Land-Rover,' Sullivan said, pointing vaguely beyond the yard.

'Sure. Let's take a look.'

They walked away, toward one of the surrounding fields, Lettie watching from her kitchen, her eyes reddened but her smile returning. She flew to the door. 'Don't be late for your tea!' she shouted after them.

Sullivan said: 'If you're staying over you'd best sleep in the house. It'd please her.'

'Great,' Cade said. He felt better inside than he had done for longer than he could remember. What had to be done was for people like these: good solid, honest people who spent their lives working the land he loved. He would happily kill anyone – man or woman – who would sell that land to an enemy.

Cade was proud that his country had chosen him to execute its traitors.

Chapter Two

It was Monday with evening taking an eternity to close down the long summer day. Jack Cade sat in one corner of the pub waiting it out, sticking to beer and limiting his consumption even with this. Earlier he had made two telephone calls from the pay-phone in the pub. The first to the Sullivan farm with the excuse that he had some mechanical trouble with the motorcycle, not serious but he was going to be back late, and – this directly to Lettie who insisted on taking the telephone from her brother – that he was really disappointed he would miss the supper she had prepared. Otherwise all was well, he would eat something out and see them both later. The entire conversation seemed, absurdly, to be a communication between a family with close ties and predictable habits. A son, concerned that no one at home should worry unduly; and parents gratified that they had bred a caring and responsible person. Cade half-believed the fiction himself, allowing himself to sink into the warmth of Lettie's – albeit transferred – mothering and Will Sullivan's gruff paternalism. Their trust in him was terrifying, scaring him more than the risks he would have to take that evening. There was no longer any place in his life for love or friendship, yet here he was accepting – if only in part – the responsibility for their affection.

The second telephone call had been to the home of the late Harold Thurstone, his first victim. He had let the telephone ring for a long while but no one lifted the receiver. Gratified he returned to his corner with his second beer. At closing time he left and walked to the street in which he had parked the Triumph – following the firm instructions of the special-ops officer given during briefing sessions for undercover work during his time with the 22nd SAS Regiment: 'Your presence is noted not only by your physical being but by your accoutrements – and that includes your form of transport. Never give people anything to remember you by. If you must use a vehicle, make it grey and ordinary. If it isn't – park it elsewhere. Be grey yourself – the average person doesn't want to remember grey indistinguishable things: they are reminded too much of themselves.'

On the basis of this excellent advice, Cade's use of the left-hand drive Volkswagen caravanette was a mistake, but at the time of purchase he had not yet been approached by Brock and Harlow so could not have foreseen his present situation. The vehicle had been cheap but sound and suited Cade's needs at that rather shaky period in his life: no home, no job – and, with a dishonourable discharge from the army plus a prison record, very little chance of one – and limited savings. Brock and Harlow's 'expenses' did not stretch to the purchase of another vehicle and he certainly was not going to ask them for more money. Money was not why he had accepted their proposal; it was neither inducement nor reason. He believed, simply, that traitors deserved death.

The gleaming maroon paintwork and polished chrome of the Triumph had worried him – plus the fact that it was a classic motorcycle and therefore easily distinguishable from the modern Japanese imports that now ruled the market – but he had solved this problem simply by riding the bike hard, letting rain, mud and traffic-spray do the rest. As insurance he had stowed the old canvas cover in the panniers and had thrown this over the Triumph when he had parked it earlier at the end of the dull suburban street.

On reaching the motorcycle he stripped off the cover, thankful that the crash-helmet Lettie Sullivan had dug out from some secret corner for him had not been stolen from underneath, then rode toward Thurstone's house but stopping short of the housing estate itself.

Before, when he had booby-trapped the liquid-gas cylinder, he had had the concealment of the caravanette for any quick changes he needed to make, but now he had to make use of natural cover. His stopping place was perfect: a deep, darkened hedgerow backing onto a field which lay un-ploughed so he had no problem with mud. He might have been drier and had more light in the public lavatories he had spotted on the ride from the pub, but to have changed there would have been insecure and Jack Cade always put security above all else. In his past this had saved his life more times than he dared recall.

After changing, he emerged from behind the hedgerow in his guise as the late-evening jogger once more, leaving the Triumph well-concealed, on its side and covered by the canvas cover.

He started off at a fast pace to build up some sweat, needing the physical effort to stifle the fear he always experienced when he was going in underprepared.

He had no reason to believe that Thurstone's house might be under surveillance by the police Special Branch or the Security Service itself but he was not prepared to take any chances. He decided to make a double circuit once he entered the estate: the first time for signs of 'watchers', the second for the break-in. If MI5 men were actually inside the house – perhaps having discovered Thurstone's espionage equipment and hopeful that his KGB controllers might try a break-in to recover deeply stashed equipment that members of MI5's A1(D) section might have missed – then he would have to take some very quick and possibly drastic decisions.

The paradox of having to worry about MI5's own people when he was employed – however clandestinely – by Five himself did not confuse him at all. Brock and Harlow had been very clear on this issue: 'Decisions have been made at the top which – due to the current, regrettable, situation regarding leaks – are known only to a select few. So you might find yourself up against our own people. If that happens you will have to handle things as the situation dictates. Rank and file members of the Service have no knowledge of this operation – even the most senior officers know nothing. If you are caught or compromised don't under any circumstances admit to involvement with the Service, nor that you have been in contact with people employed in an official capacity. Unofficially we will do what we can to help but officially we'll deny all knowledge of you. We don't exist, our names are not entered on any computer, our positions are subject to such deep cover that even the most penetrating search could not uncover us or our superiors. Our meetings, if revealed, will quickly be construed as part of some fantasy you have built up inside your embittered mind, brought on by the trauma of your past. So for your own sake don't get caught!'

Well, thought Cade as he pounded the hard pavement, it boiled down to one factor: How far was he prepared to go to avoid being caught?

He jogged on, leaving his decision open – for the moment itself.

The house came up on his left but he ignored it, scanning instead the cars parked nearby under the street-lights, his eyes checking for the usual giveaways. The immediate area seemed to be clean as far as vehicles were concerned but MI5 could have taken over one of the houses opposite – which wasn't unheard of – with the rightful owners now enjoying a free holiday in the sunshine. But he doubted this for whilst preparing for Harold Thurstone's dispatch he had made notes of all vehicles parked regularly in the street, in driveways, and which were garaged overnight. None had changed or had been added to – no late-staying visitors on a foul Monday night who might be genuine or straight cover. He felt his confidence building as he jogged past. Everything was as normal – at least on the outside; whatever was inside the house was there anyway. There was nothing he could do about that.

He made his second circuit, switching his route at the last moment to take in the narrow interconnecting lane between the streets which ran parallel with Thurstone's garden – his original escape route. Once around the sweep of the curve and out of the line of sight of houses opposite, he leapt cautiously over the battered wooden fence – flattened by the blast and re-erected and shored up by the police for reasons of public safety – landing with a tinkling crunch on the lawn. He had forgotten about the glass. It lay everywhere, like the aftermath of a hailstorm, jagged splinters discarded by the police after they had sifted among them for what was left of Thurstone's body.

The house loomed up before him, its smart white stucco walls blackened by the blast and every rear-facing window blinded by roughly nailed boards. Cade chose not to disturb the boards but entered through the connecting door to the house in the garage. He had been prepared to pick the simple lock but somebody had forgotten to turn the key. Oddly it was the one entrance Thurstone had overlooked in his search for security, for inside Cade discovered some very serious hardware on every other door and window.

He stood quite still and silent in the small antechamber, hung with coats, which led onto the hallway, then moved forward, breath held, listening for the breathing of others. Breathing, in the silence of night while in an enclosed space, could carry directly to attuned ears and Cade's senses were on red alert. Nothing, the house was as dead as Harold Thurstone, Cade was certain. Nevertheless, he progressed as though there was violence awaiting him behind every door, using his hands and his senses in place of his pencil-torch. He searched both floors this way, waiting for the blow and ready to roll away from it. In the end he flicked on the thin beam and, throwing caution to the wind, he pulled down the fixed attic ladder and searched that too.

Relieved, he took a stick of chewing gum – the wrapper discarded earlier – from his track-suit pocket and sat at the top of the stairs, coming down a little as he chewed. After a few moments he got himself going again, searching for what he wanted. There were numerous photograph albums and Cade sorted through each with a critical eye, laying aside those which suited his purpose best. Good, he thought. Bloody good. Just the right hint in each shot to make the idea feasible. There were loose prints too; Thurstone had obviously been a keen amateur photographer of above average talent – well, he had bloody good teachers, didn't he! Cade thought furiously – so these helped fill the blanks left by the missing prints. Finally, from a table stacked with large, framed, colour prints in the drawing room, he removed a very posed studio portrait of Harold Thurstone smiling in a slightly supercilious manner at the camera.

Cade was pleased with this find and stowed the silver-framed portrait inside his track-suit jacket. Next he checked his own route through the house, covering his tracks. He gave a brief nod of satisfaction as he made his way down the stairs back to the connecting door to the garage, then moved swiftly out into the garden again, passing the brick rectangle which was all that was left of the greenhouse on his way. With one bound he was over the fence and was jogging away from the scene.

Done, he thought. Now for the next traitorous bastard.

Maurice Blaikley lived in a house owned by his widowed mother near the summit of Chosen Hill outside Gloucester, overlooking the A40 highway which ran directly through to Cheltenham and the heavily guarded perimeter and gates of GCHQ itself. The arrangement suited Blaikley perfectly, for his relationship with his mother was idyllic. He was by nature a fussing man and his mother enjoyed the constant and minute attentions he showed her.

Rarely was the late Ralph Blaikley mentioned and when he was it came from others – usually dinner-party guests, for the Blaikleys entertained often and well at home. Blaikley senior had been Indian Army, a full-blown brigadier, and identifiable as being just that at a thousand yards in civilian clothes, or, as he would have had it, in *mufti*.

The house, large and beamed, was filled inside with memories of the Raj which, upon Ralph Blaikley's death, both Edith Blaikley and her son would joyously have torn down and speedily discarded. This never happened for the simple but practical reason that there would have been too much empty space to fill upon their removal. Naturally, neither mother nor son had actually voiced this secret desire, for their pretence of adoration and respect for 'the Brigadier' held firm, even after his accidental departure from life under the wheels of a milk-truck some five years earlier. As did their fear. Blaikley's portrait, depicting him in full-dress uniform and moustachioed, over the drawing-room fireplace could still make them both quail under its hard-eyed glare – almost as if it were the man himself and not oil-paint on canvas.

In reality, Ralph Blaikley was no Victorian authoritarian; strict certainly, but no more so than was considered both correct and necessary for the times. The real problem which, beneath the surface, split the family was that Edith Blaikley was, and had always been, a liberal, viewing the plight of the

41

underprivileged as being the direct result of the callousness of the privileged classes of which she had been born, to her everlasting shame, a member. Ralph Blaikley had crushed her liberal spirit, or more accurately, had driven it beneath the surface of her well-bred exterior leaving no outlet for it in his presence. Inevitably, the single child of this mismatched union became the willing receptacle for the mother's besieged ideals – the one open gate to a semblance of freedom.

It was hardly surprising that Maurice Blaikley, upon being approached by a Soviet KGB talent-scout while at Cambridge, accepted the proposition of long-term penetration of the British Establishment and, some day, actual treachery toward it, with alacrity; indeed his eagerness to betray had caused his controller some sleepless nights from fear that, in reality, he had netted a particularly bright young prospect whom the British Secret Intelligence Service had already made their own. His fears, however, were negated by the young Blaikley's continuing zeal in the communist cause and, over the years, often spectacular returns during his deep passage as a mole. Money had not been involved – excepting carefully calculated sums, injected periodically, to aid the agent's 'surface' career – which made Blaikley infinitely more valuable to Moscow Centre; for an agent who believes he is 'paying' rather than one who is being paid is rightly considered to be more secure and obviously more deeply committed. There was only one price to be paid by the Russians and they paid it readily: young men, always attractive, always charming and always willing. Also, for reasons of security and the safety of the agent, always Russian. No rendezvous was ever set up within the British Isles, so out of necessity they had to be arranged each year during Blaikley's annual leave, spent on the continent with his mother. It took the Russians six weeks and a minimum of thirty men on the ground to *sweep* and prepare a location each year but with each ascending step in Blaikley's career the effort became more profitable. The fear that Blaikley might slip and succumb to his desires with some young man outside Soviet control never retreated, but his political commitment and his awareness of his precarious position seemed sufficient to control his desires. Moscow Centre often had reason to wish that more of their agents had the iron discipline of Maurice Blaikley.

42

His mother knew none of this and, for all her deeply held liberal beliefs, would have been appalled by such a revelation. Appalled not by her son's homosexuality – which she had always suspected and believed suppressed – but by his treachery; for Edith Blaikley was of that particular breed of liberal who preach, earnestly, that class-distinction is morally wrong, yet paradoxically believe that without the existence of a privileged class the underprivileged would have no champions at all. So she did her good works, aided selected causes – none of them remotely left-wing to her limited knowledge – and wallowed in the love of a son who sought out no other woman for a deep relationship. Life for her was perfect. She believed, sincerely, that it would never change.

The Blaikley residence was set back from the rising slope of road, nestling in its own modest grounds. It was easy for Cade to approach it from the rear, across adjoining fields. As a precaution, for the last one hundred yards, he removed his jogging shoes, moving forward in his thick woollen socks to avoid leaving a patterned impression on the soft ground. He kept firmly to grassed areas, treating soft soil as if it were a mined position, moving around it or, when necessary, leaping over.

Darkness was no problem to him; his night vision was excellent and a watery hint of moonlight gave him all the illumination he needed. He traversed the back of the house like a shadow, moving from one dark cleft in its defences to another. For some moments he stood quite rigid against the rough wall, listening with silent patience for the life he would soon terminate.

He moved onward, past drainpipes to the side of the building, catching, as he rounded the corner, a dull glow seeping through heavy curtains. With his face close to but not touching the leaded glass he heard the muted blur of a high-pitched voice, then another, deeper, as though in response. Then silence again. He might have heard the shutting of a door but with his senses raised so high he could easily have imagined this.

Tonight then, he thought. Not tomorrow. Not next week or next year. Tonight. No reprieve. He untied his shoes from around his neck and put them on over his wet socks.

The lock on the kitchen door had yet to be turned for the night and Cade slipped in without a sound, finding the wide main hall at the end of a narrow passage. The hall light was on and Cade paused momentarily before entering, getting his bearings right. He stepped quickly across and entered the room which had been behind the curtains.

Maurice Blaikley sat at a large roll-top desk, his back to the door, at his feet a fine black-hide briefcase. On the desk before him were sheets of typescript and beside this long folded loops of a computer print-out.

'I shan't be long, Mother,' he said, not turning. 'I'll pop in before bed.'

Cade eased the door closed until the lock clicked then stood waiting, a revolver in his right hand, low against his thigh. He pulled back the hammer.

As Blaikley turned Cade's arm rose, rigid, locked at the elbow. His free hand moved to his face, one finger against his lips.

Blaikley sat transfixed, the green desk light behind him revealing his shiny scalp through his thinning swept-back tinted hair. The sudden fear in his eyes changed to supplication, then, though not a word passed between the two men, to dull acceptance. He had always known that one day they would come for him, never believing that they would give him a public trial. They could not reveal the extent of the damage he had done. They did not dare.

'Not her,' he said, very quietly. 'Please, not her as well.'

'That's up to you,' answered Cade, his voice a flat whisper.

'Take me away from here. Don't make her a witness. Please!'

Cade was thrown by the man's courage; he had expected the opposite. 'You'll need a pen – the one you use for your best letters. And paper, good stuff, not a note-pad. Bring something to drink too. Whatever you like best.'

The study was oak-panelled with two of its walls lined with books, dark heavy tomes that made the already gloomy room even more oppressive. Cade felt hemmed in and wanted to be out of it. 'Quickly,' he ordered.

Blaikley stood up, leaning against the panelling, his face

44

grey, the skin seeming to have lost all moisture, a paper mask, dry and ready to crack. His mouth fell open, suddenly full of saliva, jaws working as he began gagging.

Cade forced him over, head down between his legs. Spittle dropped to the parquet floor but the vomit that had threatened to erupt from Blaikley's throat remained inside his stomach. Cade pulled him up, not roughly, then rested the sagging body against the wood. 'You're doing all right,' he said.

'Is this what happens?' Blaikley croaked. 'You've seen it – tell me!' His hand had reached for Cade's anorak, the gun between them, its barrel close to Blaikley's heart; they might have been in an embrace.

'You're better than most,' Cade answered. 'You're all right.'

'How did they uncover me? I have to know. I wasn't careless. I've spent my life not being careless. Tell me. I want to know!'

'Don't ask me.'

'You won't tell me?'

'I don't know.'

Blaikley nodded, wearily. 'You wouldn't. Of course you wouldn't.'

'It's time,' said Cade. 'Get the things. Bring your car keys as well.'

'Promise me you won't kill her.'

'I told you: that's up to you.'

From somewhere upstairs music began, played softly yet very clear. It could have been in the room with them. 'She loves music,' Blaikley said as he gathered the materials Cade had asked for. 'She goes to sleep with the player on sometimes.'

'Will she come down – before she goes to sleep? Say good night?'

'I go to her.' Blaikley was facing him now, ready.

'Tonight? Did you tonight?'

'Not yet.'

Cade stared at him, letting the seconds fall away.

'Let me?' Blaikley pleaded. 'I won't say a word. What can she do anyway?'

'She'll know. She'll see it in your face.'

Blaikley smiled hopelessly. 'I'm a spy. I've been one for as long as I can remember. She's never seen that in me. She never knew I was hiding so much from her. *Let me!* I'll do whatever you want of me.'

'You'll have to anyway.'

'I'll make it easier. Let me – please.'

'I'll follow you upstairs,' answered Cade. 'I'll be right outside the door. Say whatever you say clearly. If you whisper I'll kill both of you. Do everything you do normally.'

'Thank you,' Blaikley said.

Outside in the hallway again, Blaikley laid the bottle of brandy and a leather-bound writing case on a table then made his way up the staircase, gripping the polished wood rail of the bannisters tightly with each upward step. Cade followed behind, the revolver ready all the way. He stepped aside and out of sight as Blaikley knocked first then walked into his mother's bedroom, leaving the door partially open.

Cade rested his back against the wall, the gun up high beside his face, staring forward but seeing nothing, doubting his readiness to kill an aged woman because of her son's treachery. He heard the voice of one of his instructors in the black arts coming down at him through the years: 'We are all killers – every sodding creature on this planet. The difference is that the rest only think about it – maybe only once in their lives – but that once is enough to make them the same as us. We're the sharp end of that urge. We *do* it. Just don't ever think it will be easy. *Nobody*, no man, woman, child or dog gives up a whole lifetime in a couple of seconds willingly. They'll fight you till their very last breath and even then they'll try to kill you with their eyes.'

Oh, Jesus! thought Cade, who had already seen those words proved more times than he had years behind him.

Blaikley's voice was completely audible through the open door. He said: 'Good night Mother, sleep well. Try and remember to shut off the player before you fall asleep.'

Edith Blaikley answered: 'You'll do it, darling. You always do.' She paused. 'You look drawn, darling – you take on too much responsibility. I honestly don't know why you're quite so zealous. They're not worth it, you know.'

Blaikley had moved into the doorway. 'Who, Mother?' he asked.

'Don't be obtuse! This government – as you well know. Too

46

strict. Too much prying. For example, that snooper-factory you work in.'

Get out of there! Cade shouted inside his mind.

'Sleep tight,' Blaikley said.

The music was very soft and Cade wondered, bringing himself down, why it had been so clear downstairs. The speakers are on the floor, he told himself, the sound passes through the beams. Stay loose!

Blaikley stepped out into the passage and pulled the door closed. He saw the clear warning in Cade's eyes and gave a brief shake of his head. There were tears in his eyes.

Even traitors have someone they can cry over, thought Cade. But they don't shed any tears for the ones they sell down the river. Remember that he's a selfish bastard who's done what he wanted to do and sod the rest of us. He tilted his head at the stairs.

They left the house through the kitchen door, turning left through a gap in a knee-high brick wall which led onto the gravel driveway to the garage.

'Don't try anything,' said Cade, over the sound of their feet crunching on the chippings.

'Is there any point?'

'No.'

'Is there anything I can bargain with?'

'No.'

Blaikley's calmness was chilling; Cade wondered if it was courage or weariness at the end of the long clandestine path he had taken over the years.

They were at the gates of the garage. There was no lock, only a simple double-bolt.

Inside Blaikley reached for the light but Cade stopped him. They faced each other in the darkness, the doors closed behind them. There was one window, very high in the farthest wall; it cast an oblong of pale grey onto the shining waxed paint of the Rover's roof.

'I want to tell you *why*,' Blaikley stated. 'It's important that you understand.'

'Sod off!' snapped Cade. 'I'm not interested in your excuses.' He pushed Blaikley away from him. 'Give me the key.'

'I never lock it.'

47

Cade opened the driver's door and the interior lights came on, very bright, but he had already shielded his eyes against the sudden glare. He sat backwards in the car, one hand searching in the glove-box then under the dash and both front seats while the other kept the revolver sighted on Blaikley. He did the same in the back.

'I don't own a firearm,' said Blaikley. 'I have no idea how to use one.'

'You're a liar.'

'I mean it. They wanted me to learn in case things became desperate. I couldn't. I couldn't kill anything.'

'Liar.'

'You must try and understand that I'm sincere. I have ideals –'

'Get in the back.'

Blaikley had begun whimpering, a drop of mucus ran from his nose and settled on his upper lip. He'd taken longer to break than Cade had expected.

'Shut up,' Cade snapped.

'*I can't believe this!*' Blaikley sobbed, his eyes squeezed tight. His entire face was suddenly very wet, the muscles flaccid as if he were melting in his own fear.

It was all an act, thought Cade. He'd built up an image over the years of how he'd take it if it happened. Now it's here. He climbed into the front passenger seat after locking Blaikley in the rear. 'Pour yourself a drink,' he said.

'I'll be sick,' whispered Blaikley, rigid with terror.

'You won't. Do it.'

Blaikley had chosen to bring a cut-crystal goblet; he splashed cognac into it haphazardly, spilling a lot over his trousers and green velvet smoking jacket.

All part of the image, Cade thought, watching him. He wanted to show a bit of dignity. A touch of class at the end. 'Drink it,' he said.

Blaikley drank all of it, choking, but keeping it down.

'Stopper the bottle and put it on the seat with the glass. Now get out your pen and paper and write what I tell you.'

'You want my confession?' Blaikley asked. He seemed to be grateful.

'Just write.'

48

Blaikley unfolded the leather pad, managing to undo his gold Parker despite his near-useless fingers.

'If you have a lover, what would you call him?'

'*Oh no*,' Blaikley uttered, closing his eyes. 'Not *that* way.'

'What would you call him.'

'I won't do it.'

Cade said: 'This way it comes without pain.'

Blaikley just stared. He seemed not to be capable of thought. Finally he said: 'I'd call him by his name.'

'In a love-letter?'

Blaikley slumped hopelessly. 'If I loved him deeply, I'd write: My beloved.'

'Write that. I've seen your handwriting. I know what it looks like.'

Blaikley's Parker scratched in the silence. He straightened up, breathing deeply, regaining control.

'Write: "I can't go on without you." '

'I wouldn't say "go on". I'd say "live".' Blaikley's tone was unpleasant as if he had nothing to lose. Cade had witnessed the same see-sawing psychological pattern many times before. The Irish were the worst.

'Write "live". Now sign your name – just Maurice. Now give it to me.'

Cade took the single sheet of paper, glanced at it then said, 'Finish what's left in the bottle.'

'No.'

For the first time there was a hard glint of defiance in Blaikley's eyes. Cade reached forward and took a handful of thinning hair pulling him up and toward him. He pressed the barrel of the revolver into Blaikley's groin, low, with just enough pressure to avoid bruising. He said: 'This way comes with pain.'

'*Don't!*' Blaikley gasped.

'It's up to you.'

'*Please!*'

Cade released him. 'All of it,' he ordered. 'Forget the glass.'

Gagging intermittently, Blaikley tipped the bottle to his throat. He drank half of what was left and tried to push the bottle away but Cade put his hard palm on the base, forcing him. When Blaikley began to choke he released it, letting him slump over sideways on the seat, vomiting. But the damage was done; he was exhausted and a lot of the alcohol remained in him. The vomit would help; most suicides throw up at the end. Cade had allowed for that.

Leaving Blaikley prone on the seat Cade got out and, working quickly, unravelled a long length of the flat type of garden-hose with a sucker-cap fitted at one end. From his anorak pocket he took a prepared piece of canvas-backed adhesive, then, at the rear of the car, pushed the cup-fitting over the Rover's exhaust, affixing it firmly with the tape. The other end of the hose went through a gap he opened in one of the rear quarter-windows.

Blaikley was moaning and retching in the car, only partially aware of what was being prepared for him. Cade ignored him, satisfied that the garage was far enough away from the house for the sounds not to carry – and the old lady was either asleep by now or would have her music on. Either way he felt he was safe. He recalled an assassination he had performed in Northern Ireland, years before, with the SAS, using the same method. The target then had resisted wildly. Blaikley made a pretence of courage at first but he soon showed what he was: a weak snivelling traitor. This time there would be no resistance.

Cade reached into the car for Blaikley, pulled him upright and turned his vomit-streaked face toward his own. Blaikley's eyes were bulging with terror, his mouth and jaw jelly. 'Turn your head away,' Cade said, but Blaikley heard nothing, nothing that was intelligible to him. He could only see the flat, almost dead eyes before him. It penetrated his brain that the revolver was no longer in the man's hands yet somehow he seemed more deadly without it.

'Turn your head,' Cade repeated.

Blaikley's head moved but his eyes stayed fixed on Cade even as he slowly turned. He actually saw the hand move, saw even that the central knuckle was extended more than the others. He fouled himself at that moment, an instant before the blow connected – with minimum force – in the thickest part of his hair behind his right ear.

Cade eased him upright on the seat cushions then examined the area behind the ear. There would be very little bruising, if any, and no broken skin at all. He closed the door, then from the front pushed the unconscious figure against the closed rear-window, adjusting the head so that the place the blow had landed was in contact with the glass. A fall-back just in case some bright forensic boy decided to really make a case of it.

All that was left to do was position the 'suicide' note and the framed photograph of Harold Thurstone he had stolen, scatter the loose photos on the seat as though done in despair, and start the engine. Carbon monoxide fumes would do the rest.

Cade completed these tasks, then, with the deep throbbing of the Rover's big vee-eight muffled behind the locked doors of the garage, reversed his route down the hill to where he had left the motorcycle.

At the bike he drew off his rubber gloves and placed them in the sleeve pocket of his anorak, patting the place once – just to make sure. The luminous dial of his watch – regimental issue, never returned – informed him that it was four minutes to midnight. Almost exactly the same time he had reached the carvanette after arranging the demise of Harold Thurstone. He pulled on his shoes and helmet then kicked the Triumph into life and headed back toward the Cotswold Hills, looking forward to spending a few days with the Sullivans – if they'd have him. He really would enjoy kicking about the farm and tinkering with the machinery. It would keep his mind occupied. He didn't want to remember anything. Not *anything*. He just wanted today to be here if it had to, and tomorrow didn't matter at all. Mostly he didn't want to see any little children, because that was the hardest part of all.

Later, after a couple of days had passed and the papers had said all they had to say, if anything, about Maurice Blaikley, he'd call the number Harlow and Brock had given him – an answering service – and he would set up the meet to deal with Number Three.

It made him feel good that he was needed; that he was allowed once again to do his duty for his Queen and Country. You can strip a soldier of his uniform, even strip him of his honour, but you can never take away his sense of duty. That was Jack Cade's one last unshakable belief. They used to call him Sergeant Superior in The Regiment and perhaps he still believed that too.

51

Chapter Three

The British section of the Office of Communications Security (OCS), the counter-espionage arm of the United States National Security Agency (NSA), is situated in Grosvenor Square behind the American Library.

NSA is the most important source of intelligence in the United States, larger nowadays because of advanced electronic engineering than the Central Intelligence Agency in Langley, Virginia.

NSA headquarters are located at Fort Meade, between Washington and Baltimore, Maryland, with a total staffing of around seventy thousand personnel. Its sheer power and influence within US government departments is described by those who monitor intelligence matters as being awesome.

The British equivalent of NSA is the Government Communications Headquarters (GCHQ), Cheltenham, Gloucestershire. Both NSA and GCHQ are extremely closely linked in all aspects of their electronic intelligence gathering: from interception of simple telephone messages through to high level military and diplomatic decoding, onward to high-technology special sections dealing with spy-satellites (ELINT) and radar intelligence (RADINT).

The head of NSA's counter-intelligence section (OCS) in Britain was Max Weidenstein, a former German-Jew whose parents had fled the Nazi pogroms, barely surviving as stateless refugees, usually only one step ahead of the all-conquering armies of the Third Reich as yet another European country fell under their might. The Weidensteins finally ended up in a land they had never dreamed would exist in their lifetime – the newly created state of Israel. Here they quickly learned that their troubles were far from over and soon found that their only son, still very young, was mixing with grown men who were proving to be utterly ruthless in determining the future of their promised land. Much of that ruthlessness had already permeated the character of the academically gifted boy; and his parents, liberal and sickened to the heart by violence and intransigent nationalism, foresaw only the destruction of a bright, constructive future for their son. Swiftly, once their minds were made up, they arranged for relatives in the USA to accept their son into their peaceful east coast home from where he could rise to better things through diligent study and, hopefully, to a deeper understanding and acceptance of humanitarian ideals.

Max Weidenstein certainly studied diligently, for he soon understood that America feted success and scorned failure. Humanitarian ideals, however, never quite touched his soul. His limited but very real experience of life on the weaker side supported only one, very American, ideal: Do unto others before they do it to you.

America loved him. He was small, after his mother, but his largish head contained a breadth and height of intellect that could easily intimidate his heftier college fellows. Above all, America loved his covert ruthlessness. He was an achiever; a winner who abhorred failure – but one who recognized that winners were those who recognized the lessons of failure. None of life's experiences, however dismal, were to be discounted; they were to be invested – for the future.

Inevitably, post college and highly qualified, he succumbed to the overtures of the secret world for he knew that within its higher echelons the only stature that ultimately mattered was the size of one's thinking.

He joined the CIA and while still with them predicted, silently, to himself, that the then newly formed NSA would grow and eventually overtake his own organization in the power-stakes. Perfectly in character, but not without considerable objections raised by his employers at Langley, he resigned his post and drove directly to Fort Meade. NSA took him on the spot, as he knew they would.

Now, as head of NSA's London-based counter-intelligence

arm (British Section), OCS, his personal power-base was secure, and firm enough to be a launching pad toward much higher objectives.

These were his feelings until a signal flimsy arrived on his solid glass desk on that Tuesday morning, midway through the poor summer of that year. Quite suddenly he found himself atop political quicksand and in dire danger of being sucked under.

Immediately, he ordered his deputy into his presence and upon his arrival waved him to an empty chair.

Within the intelligence fraternity, Max Weidenstein had earned himself the epithet: the Silver Fox; his longish, prematurely silver-grey hair accounting for the first half of the tag, the rest needing no explanation whatsoever to those who had call to deal with him. At that moment, the fox in him felt decidedly hunted – but also frustrated for he could not identify who his hunters were. He did, however, have suspicions.

'Someone wrote,' he murmured, head down over the signal on his desk, 'that once is happenstance, twice coincidence, three times is enemy action.' He crushed the signal and tossed it across the desk.

His deputy made no comment, well-schooled in the correct reaction to crisis situations, knowing by heart the dictum that it is politic for those who are second in any chain of command to remain silent, offering mute support but no positive suggestion which might, when the dominoes began to fall, topple them also.

Simon Adeane was a slim elegant man with a background of serious money on both sides of his family and a sharp, often intuitive, intellect. Like his superior, he was ambitious and something of a politician, prepared to divide his loyalties if the need arose – and, if the rewards were sizeable enough, was ready to take a calculated risk. At that moment he wondered if his ambition had drawn him too close to the edge of the risk-margin and how far his loyalty could stretch before self-preservation became vital.

Weidenstein began again: 'It's the British.' He placed his sharp chin on the knuckles of his interlocked fingers – then shook his head impatiently. 'I'm not prepared to lose the most important disinformation operation since the cold war because they've discovered they've got some dirty laundry.'

Adeane scanned the signal once more. 'You said it yourself, Max. Twice is coincidence.'

Weidenstein leaned forward, rising slightly in his leather executive chair because of his lack of height. 'Except that this game has no coincidences. It has connecting factors. We have two factors here: Thurstone, Harold and Blaikley, Maurice. What connects?'

Adeane was familiar with the form of his superior's thinking – and the tortuous routes his mind could take to achieve an acceptable conclusion. He let his body relax in the chair but his attention remained keen: Weidenstein never wasted his mind on minor or irrelevant matters. 'Both are known to us as Soviet agents,' he said, quoting facts they both knew for the sake of the exercise. 'Our agent has blown both of them to us.' Then he added: 'To *you* Max. You hold control. I'm in on a need-to-know basis. Fall-back control when you go Stateside – or if you suffer an accident or fatality. The British don't know. They would never have given us permission to run ORACLE on their sovereign territory, within their most sensitive intelligence-gathering organization.' Adeane was acutely aware of the political explosiveness of the NSA operation and his added statement was for the benefit of the voice-activated recorder which monitored every conversation in Weidenstein's inner sanctum.

Weidenstein knew this of course, but, certain of his power – and his political backing – stated: 'But we went ahead and did it anyway.'

'Illegally. An illegal operation by a friendly power on allied territory. No rights, no permissions.' Adeane paused. 'Max, if the British did know, they'd be here, *now*, blowing the walls. This is GCHQ we're discussing. We'd be screaming if they were running an agent inside NSA without our knowledge.'

'Moscow, then? They've bought ORACLE back. We know *that's* possible. They're closing the others in case they were contaminated too. They're expendable.'

'On the basis of current intelligence, everything we feed ORACLE is going back to Moscow, verbatim,' Adeane pointed out.

'Disinformation,' Weidenstein said. 'And Moscow Centre could be discounting the entire fiction.'

Adeane frowned and gave a small shake of his head. 'They're acting on everything. Lenin could have written the reports himself. Our stuff is backed up by rock-solid collateral – genuine British secrets we've ordered Oracle to pass on. And not chicken-feed, you know that better than I, it's your responsibility.'

'I had no choice. Moscow Centre would spot low-grade intelligence immediately when its laid against what we are asking them to believe. The more expensive the wrapping – the more the receiver anticipates what lies beneath.'

' "Lies" in the other sense being the operative word in this case. I think Moscow believes us – just an opinion, Max – they *want* to believe and that's probably most important of all. We know the extent of their penetration of GCHQ and we've let all their other agents run clear and free. No interference, no burning. If the rest are straight why should the best of them be bent? That's how they'd sit down and evaluate it. CIA would, SIS too. Maybe even MOSSAD.'

Weidenstein grinned. 'The Israelis don't believe meat is kosher unless they have a rabbi there to verify it. Leave them out of it, they've got their own way of thinking and it doesn't resemble anyone else's. So what do you think, Simon? Is it kosher?'

'Maybe the truth is simple? Two deaths. All right, two dead *Soviet agents* – both penetrating the same British intelligence organization. Maybe they *were* lovers? Maybe Blaikley *couldn't* face the pressure without Thurstone?'

'We have evidence that Blaikley was homosexual. But Thurstone, no way. Vain, narcissistic even, but heterosexual. We even fed him a girl ourselves once – remember? Just to get a profile? She had a great time, came back exhausted. Some fag!'

'The British police believe it. They have evidence. A suicide note and photographs. Thurstone was a spy, Max. He was used to cover.'

'The police *say* they do.'

'Max! You're talking conspiracy on a grand scale here. The case does not warrant it. Not to the British, anyway. They're not conscious of the network. There isn't any connection for them to make. Nothing to conspire against.'

'Maybe.'

'If they were conscious, we'd know it as soon as it happened. The Company would have found out immediately under the intelligence-sharing arrangement and they'd have informed us immediately.'

'CIA is not conscious of our interest.'

'Of course not. But they'd have let us know the instant the British uncovered a couple of Moscow Centre moles inside GCHQ. There's one hell of a lot of our own material processed through Cheltenham. The Company would be hysterical!'

Weidenstein showed no sign of conceding. 'Maybe the Brits have only just found out? Maybe the *Russians* told them? Maybe Moscow Centre has got MI5 doing their wet-work for them?'

'That's *wild*, Max! Where's the logic?'

'Suspicion. Maybe our fiction is just too good to be true? Maybe any number of things? Something may have made them distrust their entire network? They've done it before. Just one hint of suspicion and they cut their losses. Chop their own people. This time, maybe they want to do it with clean hands? So how? An engineered leak? Meant only for the ears of those who could take decisions? That would take it right to the top, wouldn't it? This particular British government would do anything to avoid the disclosure of long-term Soviet penetration at high level inside GCHQ. They'd sanction a closure on the whole network to keep *that* story out of the press with an election imminent.'

Simon Adeane was a confirmed Anglophile – but one who believed he held an unblinkered view of the race he so admired. He had also the conceit of one who is convinced he knows his subject thoroughly – even intimately. Weidenstein's last declaration had to be challenged by his superior – and often proven – knowledge of the British Establishment.

He said: 'This is *Britain*, Max. Their administration is too leaky to hold *that* kind of secret. Even at Cabinet Office level.' Adeane showed his fine teeth. 'You don't get to take their Civil Service exam unless you lean a little to the left when you write the paper.'

'That the sort of witticism going around Whitehall these days?' Weidenstein responded.

'That's the truth, Max – give or take. You need proof? Read the Company's report on the British Civil Service. It's not that they're all hard left, God forbid – although they've got more than they need of those tucked away – they're simply too liberal for their own safety.'

Weidenstein matched Adeane's smile – less its condescension. 'There speaks a true conservative.'

Adeane touched his pin-striped waistcoat. 'Here speaks a realist.'

Weidenstein touched a small panel on his desk console. 'Coffee,' he ordered abruptly. 'All right, if it's not the Russians, nor the Brits, then who?'

'No one. Maybe just death? Accident and suicide.'

'Coincidence? That'll be the day.'

A young woman came in following a sharp double tone from somewhere near the solid sound-proofed door, her obvious good looks caged behind plain spectacle frames and severe, tailored, business clothes; standard livery under Weidenstein's rule. She smiled fixedly at her chief then allowed warmth to escape as she placed Adeane's coffee before him. Adeane lifted one side of his rakish face in response.

'I hope you're not,' said Weidenstein, after the girl had departed.

'I don't break house-rules,' his deputy replied, still smiling.

'Does she know that?'

'Not yet.'

'Tell her.'

'Yes, Max.'

'I mean it.'

'Max, perhaps you should loosen up a little.'

'I do. I just don't do it within the department.' Weidenstein reached for the signal flimsy again. 'This man Rattray . . .?'

'NSA's liaison officer at Cheltenham. There just to keep the cogs working smoothly between us and the British. Naturally not conscious of anything.'

'This all he knows? Suicide, early hours of the morning, carbon-monoxide poisoning . . . messy?'

'Probably. It's not his job to delve deep. Certainly not with the British police. All they need to tell him is that there is an aspect to the death which makes it our business. You're right, the homosexuality factor makes it messy. We wait now for the British Security Service to clean it up.'

'Oh, sure! With strong antiseptic. In five months' time we'll get a pristine, germ-free, hand-bound report.'

'*If* you are making the assumption that MI5 is behind the two deaths. That presupposes that the entire Soviet operation inside GCHQ is blown – and all evidence we have points to the contrary in fact. Our agent is alive and well – and operating – and the Russians are swallowing everything they're fed. I say again: If Five have blown the networks then we and the Company would have to be told. That's how the relationship works, and you know that only too well.'

'Tell me more,' Weidenstein put in, his twisted smile a mere hint. 'Convince me that the Brits are clean.'

Adeane bridled, realizing that he was being led. It had happened before and no matter how hard he resolved not to be manipulated by his superior he still found himself sucked in. This time was no exception. 'If you're talking conspiracy, ultra-high-level orders for terminations from someone, or some cabal, within or near Cabinet level – then you're really talking cover-up. Watergate with blood, Max. That's serious business.'

'It's possible. Lay the problem on the computer – you'll get that as one possible scenario.'

Vexation touched Adeane's eyes. 'The British have had their fair share of spy scandals – more than most – but they've always brought them out into the open. Okay, reasonably out into the open – within the bounds of security. British governments try their traitors, they face the censure of the Opposition and hope that the electorate will, when the furore dies down, be sympathetic and – hopefully – forget. That's the way they do it here – and generally so do we. Neither one of us thinks or acts like the Russians. If we did . . . well what the hell are we supposed to be protecting anyway!'

'Idealism even!' Weidenstein exclaimed, amusement in his grey eyes. Without warning he became deadly serious. 'Two British Intelligence officers, senior grade, both based at GCHQ Cheltenham, have died within one week. One accident, one suicide. Not astronomical odds, given the few thousand employed there. Both are known to us as being part of a long-term KGB penetration operation. That cuts down the odds – and I mean cuts them. Both men were linked together by a homosexual liaison supposedly proven by photographs and a damning suicide note. Now what, Simon, does that smell of to you?'

'Sure, if I were sniffing at the air hoping to get a scent of something, then yes – KGB smear-tactics. *Except* both men are – were – *KGB agents*. Why smear their own men? Why kill off an apparently successful, even vital, operation?'

Weidenstein leaned back in his chair. 'Why indeed? There *is* no logic. Which leaves only one other interested party. The British. Simon, the homosexual story is cover, dirty and complex, written up by MI5's creative team just for media consumption – and maybe for us too. They've uncovered our operation, know we've been shitting on them, so they're cutting it out from under us. But silently, letting us assume their ignorance, maybe believing – because in their eyes we're paranoid, half-civilized, and subliminally fascist – we're bound to look east for our enemies, to see Red in our anger. All this to save the "special relationship" which even the retarded masses know keeps them from being swept down the drain. You admire their culture and their gentility, Simon, but let me inform you – the British may like us all to view them as gentlemen but at no time has their history ever proven them to be gentle.'

Adeane studied the stitching of his hand-lasted shoes for a few moments. 'So what do we do about it?' he asked finally, meeting his superior's eyes.

'You go to them – you're a blood-cousin, I'm a Jew and deep down, when it's crunch time, the British do not trust my race. Show them the depth of American goodwill. Flatter them, make them believe you believe in them – that shouldn't be hard – and all the time watch their eyes. They're lying and I want to know the extent of their lie. Who gave the order? From what level in their establishment did it originate? If this is only a piece of private enterprise from within Five – someone trying to save their neck – then we can deal with it without too much pain. If it came from higher up – then I've got choices to make.'

'They won't tell me anything,' Adeane stated. 'Why should they? If it's clandestine it'll stay that way.'

'You don't ask them anything directly. You're going there to renew their faith in us. You love them dearly – but you're worried by this homosexual link between the two deaths – who wouldn't be in our business? – and you need to be reassured that the two departed lovers loved only each other and not some higher ideal also.'

Adeane studied the fine pin-stripe of his trouser leg and ran a fingernail along one tracing its path, then splayed his fingers and studied those. 'How high does it go on our side of the park, Max? If I'm going along to prod at a nerve I'd like to know who is strong enough to hold the patient down if he reacts violently?'

'Sorry, Simon. Maybe we're going to have to break some rules pretty soon but the one that stays rigid is that you know only what you need to know.'

Adeane looked up, sharply. 'I've briefed ORACLE, Max. I've played control when you've had to go Stateside. I know damn well that the fiction being passed to Moscow Centre is going to make certain we have an umbrella in the next century that will be one hell of a lot stronger than any foreseeable Russian rainstorm. We're feeding them failure and long-term problems and that is surely not the case. I would hazard a guess, Max, that even NATO doesn't know how far forward we've progressed – and that means the British. Now if I'm fronting on this, I need to make damn certain that if the entire operation aborts and the truth comes out, I'm not left out under the spotlights on centre stage while the director and the producer exit the theatre. You're ambitious, Max, that's why you agreed to go along with this – well, hell, so am I! I can guess how high this goes on our side – and if the British are eliminating the network because they know what we are doing, then forget the idea of someone in Five covering his back because it's certain to go higher than that. Much higher. And I do not want to be caught in the cross-fire of any power-play at those levels!'

'You've got no choice. Nor have I. So we just make certain that we protect the operation.'

'Protect by *any* means?'

'By whatever means prove to be necessary.'

'And that is the view from on high?'

'That is the only view,' Weidenstein replied heavily.

'The British are our allies – long-term allies. Friends.'

'The Russians were our allies, once. Times change, so do circumstances. I don't have to give you a history lesson. The British have changed; there's a very strong socialist undercurrent in this country which has to be taken seriously at decision-making level. If radical socialism wins control of power over here we'll all be on the next flight out – and there are some people in Washington who believe that just might happen and are not prepared to leave behind the details of our most advanced technology as a gift to the East – because that's where it will end up.'

'The British people would never allow Parliament to fall into the hands of the mob.'

'No doubt someone said the same thing of the Roman Senate.'

'*Mobile vulgus*. The fickle mob,' Adeane conceded, drily.

'You said it,' Weidenstein retorted and stood up. 'Go to Charles Street, make them acutely aware that we get very unhappy when British Intelligence officers in highly sensitive positions which could affect the security of the United States of America turn out to be homosexuals sharing a bed. Remind them of Burgess and Maclean – and throw in Blunt for good measure. Make them realize that we're watching their game very closely. But do it with style, woo them as you dissect them – then come back and tell me how they took it. Every word, all the nuances – and all the little looks in between.'

Weidenstein turned to face the venetian blinds of his large window – blinds that were proof against electronic eavesdropping of the most sophisticated sort, with the added benefit of being able to stop a high-powered bullet or bomb splinters. Adeane had never seen them opened, not at any time in the five years he had been deputy chief in NSA's OCS in Great Britain.

Adeane moved to the door, then stopped. 'Max, when you were a boy – in Israel – how did you feel about the British then?'

Weidenstein chuckled. 'Probably how some of them feel about the strength of US power now. But the answer to your unasked question is: no, I have no subconscious or concealed hatred for the British – it's simply that *we* have the power now and we have to start learning very fast to use it as effectively as they did. I admired them – once. No one really ever hates the British. They tolerate them or they fear them, because underneath they're the hardest, coldest race on this planet – that's why I believe that they're the ones behind all this. You love the British, Simon. I understand them. Just one last thing: If it comes down to choosing between your country or your friends – just make damn sure you choose your country.'

'I'm an American, Max.'

'That's all I want to hear. I'm flying to Washington today – should be back on the night-flight tomorrow. Whatever you manage to dig out of Five we can act on when I return.'

Max Weidenstein was a solitary man, a loner who had little time for socializing if it gained him nothing. His confirmed philosophy was that any meeting should increase the substantial information already stored in his brain and not just add an inch to his waistline which he would then have to work off, for, as a small man, he could not afford to put on weight. For this reason, it had become the pattern that Simon Adeane, with his English manners, attended the functions the servants of Whitehall regularly organized.

Inevitably, Adeane's circle of contacts had grown to quite astonishing proportions, beginning mid-way on the hierarchical scale and ending – as the protocol demanded with his number two position – just one step below the highest echelon. Therefore, when Weidenstein had said: Go to Charles Street – the Headquarters of MI5 – what he had really meant was go to the men who would have an interest in the Security Service – interests that were not always accompanied by goodwill, for manoeuvring, conspiracy and bitter jealousy are an integral part of the daily life of government departments the world over.

It is an accepted fact that those who co-ordinate intelligence are the most powerful, and resented, of men within the secret world. These are the officials who have direct access to the princes of government and, through them, the ear of the ultimate ruler. They do not themselves gather intelligence or set in motion operations which protect state security. They do not suffer the strains, nor the disappointments. They judge, evaluate, accept and hand down accolades, or pass on rebukes – or worse – for failures while managing to remove the stain of fallibility from their own career-dossiers. These are clever men, often charming, able to think on their feet and are adept at side-stepping or shelving potentially dangerous or controversial operations.

One such was William Salisbury, deputy to the Co-ordinator of Intelligence in the Cabinet Office.

'You realize that this week the place has hot and cold running KGB men?' Salisbury said as he allowed a waiter to seat him in the restaurant of the Mayfair Hotel in London, that Wednesday. 'Hungarian week,' he elucidated, indicating enthusiastic musicians in national costume who weaved their way through tables and Hungarian gypsy dances with equal dexterity.

'Then it's the safest place in London to have a serious talk,' Adeane replied with a bright smile. 'They'll be far too busy watching their charges for any sign of "Westernitis" to take any notice of us.'

'Too bloody witty, you Americans. I understand that the State Department is running courses in social repartee!'

'Sure, they import British civil servants to lecture.'

'Sign me up, will you, I could do with a nice fat fee right now.'

Adeane accepted a menu from the head-waiter, who recognized the American immediately, and ordered lavishly, giving Salisbury the lead to do the same.

'I hope I'm worth it,' the Englishman said after the head-waiter had departed with their orders. 'Though God knows nobody's tried to seduce me for centuries.'

'Marriage does that, puts you out of bounds. How is it by the way?'

'Don't know yet. How's that ravishing beauty that Weidenstein keeps wrapped in corsets? I wouldn't feel hesitant with her.'

'Forbidden.'

'Tough.'

'Max or his house-rules?'

'Both.'

Adeane tasted the wine placed before him and nodded approval.

'So?' Salisbury said when they were alone again.

'We received a report that Gloucestershire Constabulary have evidence of a homosexual connection between the two deaths at GCHQ this last week,' Adeane began, as an opener.

Salisbury took a mouthful of claret and savoured it before swallowing. 'Yes, so did we.'

'Comment?'

'They're everywhere now – what's so special about GCHQ?'

'The security aspect, naturally.'

'Oh, I don't think so.'

'You sound remarkably complacent?'

Salisbury sipped this time then wiped his lips with his napkin. 'We're not *worried*, if that's what you're after.'

'Then you have considered it?'

'Certainly, but if there's one intelligence arm we feel confident about as far as security is concerned, GCHQ is it. But don't worry, Five has its people up there at this moment taking the two deceased gentlemen's lives apart.'

'So they do take it seriously?'

'Five are policemen at heart, with a policeman's Victorian moral attitudes. A homosexual to them is not gay – or even queer. He's *bent* – just as a villain is bent. Crooked, not following the rule of law. So they'll worry at the case for a while, like a dog at a juicy bone, but when it begins to get dry and unappetizing they'll bury it. Am I the first you've approached on this?' Salisbury added, a little defensively.

Adeane knew that there was no point in lying. 'Actually, I called a mutual friend before I invited you to lunch.'

'Really. Who?'

The American named a well-known journalist, renowned for his contacts in the secret world.

'Oh dear,' Salisbury moaned. 'Now we'll read of nothing but scandalous rumours for the next two weeks. I do wish you Americans would trust government sources a little more.'

'Oddly enough he couldn't have been less interested. His point was that in this permissive age Five know exactly who the "queens" are – his term – but dare not get too heavy with them in case they infringe their civil rights.'

'He's right. We take the middle ground now and accept that if they do their work well and keep away from the more sordid practices which might leave them open to a good old-fashioned KGB *burn* then they are left alone. Mind you, they are given a pretty tough vetting – tougher than the norm, although that's not publicly admitted to, of course.'

'And occasionally you set the watchers on them.'

'Occasionally. In practice, actually, they turn out to be more patriotic than we heterosexuals.'

'Better the devil you know,' said Adeane, smiling.

'As good a way of putting it as any.'

The Hungarian troupe surrounded them through their first course making conversation impossible.

'Bravo!' Salisbury exclaimed and beamed enthusiastically at two business-suited men seated four tables away, their chairs adjusted so that both had a direct view of the entrance – and exit – of the restaurant. He leaned forward. 'They've had a hike in their allowances to go with the new "enlightened" Kremlin image – the first thing they did was rush down to bloody Simpsons. Five were buzzing around like hornets trying to find suitable men to work as temporaries in the menswear department. All they found out was that good KGB men dress on the left.'

Adeane laughed. 'What about the bad ones?'

'The bad ones were really professional, they clasped their hands over their balls and kept their secret intact.'

They began their main course in silence, then, halfway through, Adeane said: 'Max would like a sight of the Glouces-ter Police report. You know Max, senses conspiracy in all things.'

Salisbury looked up from his raised fork. 'You mean he doesn't trust us?'

'Trust doesn't enter into it. He simply wants to view the evidence himself. It's his way. It's the Jew in him.'

'More likely the German,' Salisbury retorted. 'What evidence?'

'The Blaikley letter – the photographs?'

'They're not dirty if that's what he thinks. Studio-posed

portrait and some outdoor stuff. Thurstone was a fitness fanatic it seems. Superb physique. Weightlifting. Lots of muscle definition – that sort of thing.'

'So he might well have been gay?'

'What makes you think he wasn't?'

Adeane ducked the question. 'So you saw the photographs? Did you see the letter also?'

'The content. Cheltenham police – or Five by now – have the original.'

'And it convinced you?'

'Of what? That Blaikley was Thurstone's grief-stricken lover or that Blaikley did asphyxiate himself?'

'Both.'

'The answer is yes in both instances. Max *is* distrustful, isn't he? Impatient too. Can't he wait for Five's report?'

'Their wheels grind slowly – Max's brain works at the speed of light.'

'Which makes it difficult to change course if his thinking is speeding in the wrong direction.'

'He's been uncomfortably correct on many things in the past.'

'This time, however, I'd say he was wrong.'

Adeane looked over at the musicians, now gathered around the table belonging to the two business-suited men, who were not pleased by this attention.

'One up for the Magyars,' quipped Salisbury, noting the KGB men's discomfort. 'They'll pay for it later, though.'

A small frown had settled between Adeane's eyes.

'So you don't like my appraisal of the Blaikley–Thurstone business. You still think I'm being too complacent? Does the whole of Grosvenor Square feel as you do? Or is it just Max playing the cunning fox once more?'

It was time for dessert but both declined, ordering coffee and cognac instead.

Adeane sipped his coffee, forming his thoughts with precision. Whatever he said now would be repeated at the highest level. He tipped his head at the two KGB men. 'I'll put forward an hypothesis. They – or others like them – are capable of unpleasant acts.'

'That's fact – not hypothesis,' interrupted Salisbury.

'Let me finish. If Moscow *were* running Thurstone and Blaikley then discovered that the two had developed a danger-ous affection for each other – let's say consummated by the physical act – would it be in Moscow's best interests to remove these emotionally unstable and potentially dangerous immor-al elements – KGB jargon, you know how they view homosex-uality – from the scene?'

Salisbury swirled his cognac in the oversized balloon.

'Your hypothesis works – only if you are assuming deep and possibly widespread penetration of GCHQ. A network, or networks. Also, if Blaikley and Thurstone were very low on Moscow's scale of importance, they could, without too much damage being done to the whole operation, be dumped. Permanently.' He savoured the brandy, then said: 'Now, if you're telling me that this is what you Americans believe – or suspect – to be the truth, then I'd have to say that I would consider your service to be criminally incompetent. It is ob-vious to any fool that you would be risking codes and your own secrets as well as ours if there were any basis in fact for your suspicions. You'd be insane if you had not reported your suspicions to the Security Service. That *isn't* what you really believe, is it, Simon? Because if it is, I'm going to be very unhappy and suffer terrible indigestion from what has, up to now, been a memorable gastronomic experience. And my discomfort would be nothing in comparison to that suffered by the government front benches in Parliament. Now you just tell me that this is nothing more than another example of American paranoia!'

Adeane grinned widely. 'Weidenstein paranoia – leave the rest of us Americans out of it.'

Salisbury seemed genuinely relieved and leaned back in his chair. 'I think the US Treasury owes me another measure of this marvellous cognac but it will have to be on some other day I'm sad to say. England expects every man to do his duty – even after a lunch such as this.'

Adeane hoisted a hand for the bill which came promptly. He put his signature to it as Salisbury mimed violin bow-strokes then applauded the Hungarian troupe. He even waved at the glowering KGB men.

'Show me a Russian with a sense of humour and I'll show

you an anti-Party reactionary,' murmured Salisbury as they made their way out to the front of the Mayfair.

'Except for Gorbachev,' Adeane retorted, as the doorman signalled for two taxis.

'That's not humour, that's guile,' the Englishman called, as he entered his cab. He saw Adeane's fleeting smile as the American climbed into his own taxi before being driven away.

'Where to, guvnor?' the cabbie bawled over the clatter of the diesel motor.

Salisbury checked his watch. 'Find me a public telephone quickly that hasn't been vandalized and I'll double the tip.'

'There's one in Berkeley Square that worked this mornin'. You can walk to that.'

'Drive me there. Then wait.'

The square was just around the corner. Salisbury alighted, change ready in his hand; in the stinking cubicle he dialled a London number. As he was about to give up a clipped, cultured voice came on the line.

' "Brock" here,' said Salisbury.

'Yes?' the voice enquired.

'Our cousins are worried. Not about us.'

'We assumed they might consider that their competitors were involved. On balance it seems logical. Let them follow that direction – it won't lead them anywhere. They'll soon accept the situation at face value.'

' "Blue" tried to be too clever.'

'Yes. Regrettable. It was best done without complications. Keep on top of the situation yourself. Lower the temperature. These things aren't as scandalous as they used to be, more's the pity. "Blue" is still secure?'

'There's no reason to think not.'

'Is there any hard reason to delay further action? For the moment that is?'

'Nothing hard, no . . .'

'But?'

'Perhaps our time-scale is too tight?'

The voice cracked down the line like a whip. 'Every day that passes is one day too many. They damage us, betray us and make fools of us for their own gain. They are draining our lifeblood and you want to give them more time?'

'No!'

'This *must* be done.'

'Next time the reaction might be hostile,' warned Salisbury.

'Not toward us.'

'They'll be at each other's throats.'

'But not at ours.'

'There'll be questions – next time. It might go to Cabinet level.'

'As long as Blue is convincing that should be no problem. Even if there is suspicion we are clear of it. We have nothing to gain. Until now all we have done is lose.'

Salisbury stood sweating in the airless rancid cubicle.

'Three,' the voice ordered.

Salisbury replaced the receiver and stepped thankfully out of the cubicle.

'It'll be smashed by tonight,' called the cabbie. 'Where to, guv?'

'Downing Street,' Salisbury ordered.

Chapter Four

Gerald Parminter lived each hour of his life under the shadow of two terrible secrets. The first was that he had, years before, sold his soul to the Soviet KGB and the second, perhaps more heinous, was that he was an active paedophile with an obsession for small girls.

The KGB believed they controlled his life totally, extracting from him every fragment of information he gleaned from his sensitive position inside GCHQ's Joint Technical Language School at Oakley and his frequent trips to Behall, the Centre's main complex. To them he was an easily manipulable British traitor who had sought them out for reasons of idealism but, in the classic manner, had continued in their service out of greed – and fear. Amazingly, they had not the slightest suspicion of his darker activities.

That Thursday morning, although he knew that many important signals would cross his desk at Oakley, the hunger in him was too fierce to be denied. He lay awake for over an hour, letting the minutes slip by, his fevered thoughts pushing aside his secret responsibilities, his hands clutched over his genitals as if denying them their perverted needs.

By nine thirty he knew that he was not going anywhere near Oakley.

Downstairs he made two telephone calls. First to his wife's place of work informing her that after she had left the house earlier he had suffered a severe attack of diarrhoea – no lie, for his bowels instantly became fluid at the thought of what he was about to do – so would probably stay away from work, perhaps making a trip to the doctor or a chemist. The second call was made to the personnel office at GCHQ explaining his absenteeism. Freed of these necessary chores he returned upstairs and lowered the ladder to the house's attic. There he uncovered a set of clothes he kept hidden from amongst the jumble and took them down the ladder into the bathroom. Here he washed his face and hands only, neither bathing nor shaving, then dressed himself in the brand-new clothes which nevertheless gave off a musty odour due to their airless confinement. Every item would end up, that very day, on the garden bonfire, to be replaced at a convenient time with a further set – purchased carefully at differing shops – once again hidden in the chaotic attic.

Dressed, he prepared a light breakfast, ate it quickly, and left the semi-detached house in a hurry as if late for work, his new clothes covered by his regular raincoat, briefcase in his hand and an umbrella over his head against the slight morning drizzle.

He drove his three-year-old Ford Cortina along the same route that Cade had taken in his Volkswagen caravanette that previous weekend but broke off the dual carriageway at a roundabout to head directly for the town of Gloucester.

Parminter knew exactly where to go and the time he should be there. He had two hours to kill and both were spent in agony of mind and body, dawdling meaninglessly in the town centre after parking the car, forcing an unwanted pastry and coffee into his churning stomach and finally, in a pub, swallowing two large brandies in quick succession.

At mid-day he drove up near the gates of the nursery school, watched the small children being collected by fussing mothers and targeted his victim. The gorge rose in his throat and he dropped his head down against the steering-wheel, fighting the need to expel the vomit. The moment passed – as it always did. He turned the ignition and let the car roll forward until it stood outside the school gates.

The child was agitated at being left until last. Her mother was invariably late for the pick-up because of her part-time job and her friends often teased her about this. She scuffed her shoes along the metal railings of the gate, attempting to swing but defied by the solid bolt. She was neither pretty nor plain, just an ordinary child with a defiant thrust to her

72

tiny jaw and a show of temper in her eyes.

'Mummy's not well,' said Parminter, leaning across the seat, the passenger door already open. 'I've been sent to collect you.'

The child turned from the gate but still clung tight to the railings.

'Mummy's at work,' she said. 'She went this morning. I know she did.'

Parminter smiled understandingly. 'I know, I've seen her. But she didn't feel well after she got there. She sent me to get you – she can't come.'

'Has she got her asthma?'

'That's right, a bad attack. She's not at all well – you must come quickly!'

'Are you her boss?' asked the child, stepping off the gate and moving closer.

'Yes,' Parminter replied fast, seeing a young red-headed woman approaching down the gravel path of the school entrance. Panic struck at him like a physical blow, his legs beginning to shake on the pedals.

'Susan!' the woman called, her voice high-pitched, the syllables split like the double peal of a fine bell.

Parminter made his voice harder. 'Susan! *Hurry* please! Mummy's ill – she'll be worse if you don't come right away. Hurry up!'

The child scrambled into the car, all suspicion dissolved by the sudden overwhelming terror of losing her mother and Parminter's commanding tone.

'*Susan!*' the teacher shouted, running now. At the gate she saw the speeding back of the dark blue car, its exhaust smoke dark and blowing up over the already besmirched number-plate. 'Oh God, no,' she cried and ran back up the gravel path, her legs half-buckling as if the bone had been sucked from them. Her shouts carried all the way to the school building, her weeping continuing unabated while the police were called and the child's mother arrived with a face as white as death. Only under the harsh questioning of a police inspector who had to raise his deep voice to get through to the teacher did she finally begin to spill out what facts she could recall.

The car meant nothing to her and the number was inde-cipherable – a fact the inspector showed no surprise over – but one possibly life-saving fact soon came out: the red-headed teacher had a better than average talent as a painter – indeed, one of her portraits in oils had actually been shown in her native city of Edinburgh – and the one thing she did remember, with all the clarity of a painter's eye, was the frightened face of Gerald Parminter as he had leaned out of the open doorway of the Cortina toward his young victim.

Cade was ready to ride the Triumph motorcycle to London for his next meeting with the man he knew as Harlow that Thursday night. Naturally, he had asked permission for the use of the bike from both Lettie and Will Sullivan, giving as his reason for going, his decision to see his estranged wife regarding their divorce and also to tend his daughter's grave while he was there. Cade hated lying to the couple who had taken him – a stranger – into their home, treating him as if he were some lost son returned, but he did not want to risk using the caravanette whilst the police might have a watch out for it.

'That foreign van of yours still not fixed then?' Will Sullivan asked in his gruff manner. 'Should've got yourself something British. British Made always meant something in my day – not any more. Serves you right. Well, you'll know next time, won't you?'

Cade nodded obediently, astride the bike, mid-morning, so as to avoid the worst of the traffic.

Lettie had cut flowers from somewhere on the farm and brought them to Cade in her arms, her eyes brushed with tears. 'Poor little mite,' she said very softly, placing them one by one in the Triumph's panniers with leaves of tissue for padding. 'Don't go on at the boy, Will. The cycle needs to be ridden. He *should* ride it!'

'*Motor*cycle,' Sullivan growled at his sister. 'He isn't going to pedal it all the way up there, is he?' They all laughed at that which at least stopped Lettie from a full flood of tears which Cade felt certain was due at any moment.

The ride along the motorway was exhilarating with the weather holding most of the way. He did in fact visit the small grave of Amy Cade although the act of doing so again after so few days had passed since the Saturday left him feeling drained and empty, destroying the well-being he had felt inside during the time he had spent with the Sullivans. But he had no option: there was no way in the world that he could throw away the flowers Lettie had picked for his daughter's grave.

Simon Adeane rented a flat overlooking the river Thames at Chelsea. He liked to think that at some time in the old building's past, some highly talented artist had struggled to create where he now lived, for his large drawing room boasted an enormous window a full twelve feet tall and twice that measure in width. He had decided, long before, that only a painter – or perhaps a sculptor – would need that much natural light.

On that Thursday evening, with Max Weidenstein still in Washington, he had allowed himself a night of relaxation away from his responsibilities at Grosvenor Square.

Adeane was a film-buff with a collection of rare vintage celluloid footing in sixteen-millimetre and was looking forward to stretching out on his leather Chesterfield sofa with a decent meal – he cooked well – on the low marble table before him while he watched, for the umpteenth time, Garson Kanin and Carol Reed's apocalyptic story of war in Western Europe: *The True Glory*.

He had already set up the projector and screen so poured himself a very dry sherry and, while his thick fillet was under the grill, took the drink and a lighted cigarette toward the massive window to watch for a few moments the passing water-traffic on the river Thames. On the way he lifted the remote control unit off the television set and pressed the button for the Channel Four News.

He was fascinated by the Thames and its collection of motley craft and would often spend a complete Sunday afternoon simply watching the slow progress of the water and the craft which plied their trade upon its surface.

Behind him, the television droned mutedly on with news of fresh disasters, great and small which plagued the latter end of the twentieth century. As an intelligence officer his mind was trained to listen from a distance, selecting only the information that would concern him while discounting the rest – in virtually the same way – albeit electronically – in which the advanced computers at NSA stations could 'listen' to whole

75

telephone conversations while reacting only to certain programmed key-words.

Perhaps because Simon Adeane was at his 'painter's window' the words: 'Scottish painter' made him turn around. He saw briefly the puffy face of a red-headed girl, obviously distressed, and then a drawing, well-executed in charcoal, of a man in his mid-forties.

Adeane stood transfixed, it took seconds before he raised the volume on the remote unit. The newscaster continued with the item:

'. . . Gloucestershire Police would be grateful for any assistance in tracing this man who may be able to help them in their enquiries into the abduction of four-and-a-half-year-old Susan Franks from outside the Marydeane Nursery School at just after mid-day today. Telephone numbers to call are . . .'

Adeane pressed the mute-button on the way to the telephone, lifted the instrument, then, the cool professional in him regaining control, replaced the receiver. If there were a conspiracy, as Weidenstein suspected, then almost certainly, MI5 had bugged his telephone, either officially, via a Home Office warrant, in which case his flat had recently been entered and his telephone had been rewired so that it acted as a microphone relaying all sounds in the room to a voice-activated tape-recorder – an operation they code-named Special Facility or Azure. Or, if MI5 were engaged in an unofficial, clandestine, operation to save their own necks: Operation Cinnamon, by-passing the Home Office warrant and bugging the junction-box. One way or another, if they really wanted to, they could have done it.

He had the equipment to perform a preliminary sweep of the flat but now was not the time – he would have that done in the morning by a team borrowed from the CIA's London Station. If he had indeed been bugged then Weidenstein might just be right. His last full sweep was performed two-and-a-half months before – the teams working on a quarterly basis – which would mean that surveillance had begun within that period: That would fit in with Max's theory of an MI5 operation mounted against them.

Adeane let thoughts of betrayal touch him as he made his way quickly to his British sports car. His country had betrayed

76

– and still was betraying – their greatest friend and historical ally. The British, not unreasonably, were taking action. As America would. He tasted bitterness, hating the thought of what could be destroyed – what had already been spoiled – but knew that in the final examination he must choose his country before his friends.

He drove at speed to Grosvenor Square, was stopped by the police and was rude to them, declaring his diplomatic immunity before accelerating off to reach his destination in a dangerously short period of time. From there he called Washington.

Weidenstein came on the 'safe' line, irritated by this interruption to a crucial meeting. He snapped a quick: 'Simon? What the hell?'

'Enemy action,' Adeane said.

'What?'

'Happenstance, coincidence . . .'

'Enemy action,' Weidenstein repeated then fell silent. 'Not ORACLE?' he asked, very quietly, apprehension tempered by fatalism.

'Not ORACLE. Not yet.'

'How did they hit him?' Weidenstein's pugnacious temperament overrode his relief.

'He's not dead.'

'They blew it?'

'They didn't try. They're hunting him. Little girls.'

'Talk straight!'

'He's supposed to have abducted a child. His face is splashed all over TV.'

Again a pause. 'Clever. They'll have to keep him in solitary with a charge like that. Takes him right out of the game and leaves ORACLE open for a hit. I should have realized that the Brits are too devious to go for three straight hits in a row. This way number three might just as well be dead. They'll get him when he's inside – lay it on some con – child-killers have a high mortality rate in prison.'

'Maybe it's true?'

'Maybe Gorbachev is Santa Claus. Wait.' Adeane heard the receiver hit wood. He waited. 'Simon? Meet me at Ruislip Air Force Base, Ruislip, Middlesex.'

'I know where it is, Max. Time?'

'I'll pull the fastest thing the air force have flying.'

'SR-71, based on Beale AFB, California – it hits Mach Three but you'll waste time flying to Beale. Try and get on the next Concorde out of New York.'

'And hang around civil airports while the Brits are moving in on ORACLE? With what we've got going here I can ask for anything. Moving a Blackbird from California to Washington is nothing.'

'All right. I'll drive down to Ruislip and book into their bachelor-officers quarters. Wake me when you arrive.'

'Forget the drinks in the officers' club and an early night in their BOQ, you've still got work to do for a few hours yet. We're going to need help.'

'The Company?'

'No way. I'm not about to widen the circle of knowledge on this. CIA asks too many damn questions before they decide to haul ass!'

'A few days in the US, Max, and you sound like a real American.'

'I *am* a real American. What about you Simon? You still too much in love with the British to stop them dead?'

'I'll manage.'

'Don't just manage. Commit. We have to take action now to make certain that our channel to Moscow continues. They've just lost three agents which means they're jumpy. They'd have reasoned it out already. They know it must be the Brits.'

'Or us.'

'Not us. Deep down they believe our relationship with the British is sacrosanct. They'd never credit us with moving independently.'

'Maybe they'll lift ORACLE themselves?'

'Never. With the material Moscow believe they're getting they'll never sanction a lift while ORACLE can still operate. Remember Philby? They left him drunk, broken, under suspicion, suspended – not even on the fringes of anything resembling secret – in the hope that he'd get back in. They were right – he did.'

'What do you want me to do?'

'Get a message to ORACLE. Tonight. I want the whole family out of that area. I want them somewhere they can be protected. Use crash procedure HARTFORD. Call the clinic to back up. Then get on to the Company for the real estate. They'll have a suitable property – somewhere in the country – clear ground on all sides. Tell them Max Weidenstein is sick, they'll be pleased, maybe they'll give you the keys gift-wrapped. But call ORACLE first, there'll be preparations to make.'

'Moscow won't understand. They'll hit the panic-button.'

'Sure Moscow will understand. ORACLE is a woman. When women are running scared they run and hide, hoping it'll all go away. That's exactly what they'll think she'd do – that's why it's got to be the whole family. No woman leaves her family behind when she's terrified. Sure Moscow will understand.'

'You've worked out all the ends, Max.'

'If I haven't ORACLE's dead – and we won't be invited to the funeral.'

'Do you want a team on ORACLE tonight?'

Weidenstein considered this for some moments. 'Too risky. Right now, I'd say her cover is more important than her life. If we jeopardize her cover she's useless to us. I don't believe the Brits will move tonight.'

'She'll be the one taking the risk, Max.'

'She's well paid. We're all in the risk-business. Only the operation counts. Do what you can with the Company, I want that safe-house by tomorrow latest. Meet me at Ruislip – and don't be asleep, you can sleep when ORACLE is protected.'

The line whistled shrilly then hummed continually through three octaves which meant the call had been terminated and the frequency changes were operating blind.

Adeane moved to a computer terminal and requested the information he needed, then lifted a different telephone and dialled. His call was answered first by a small boy who insisted on putting his father on the line.

'Actually it was *Mrs* James I wished to speak to,' said Adeane. 'Mrs Rhoda James?' His accent was perfect upper-middle-class English.

'One moment. Who shall I say is calling?' asked the some-what nasal male voice.

'Mr James, this is John Hartford. *Hartford*,' Adeane

repeated, which was the code-word their agent would recognize for extreme emergency. 'Doctor John Hartford actually.'

'Doctor? Do we know each other, Doctor? Is there something wrong? I don't recall seeing your name at our usual practice?'

'Your wife will explain, I'm sure, Mr James, but please, will you put her on the line. Tell her Doctor *Hartford*.'

Adeane could sense that the man was still holding the receiver, bewildered, and remembered from the file that the husband was a banker – a bank-manager – in one of the local clearing-banks and the analysis in his file showed him to be well short of a strong character.

'Darling! Rho?' a muffled voice came down the line. 'There's some chap who says he's a doctor. Says you'll explain? Explain what?'

Adeane seethed silently. Get off the damn line. Say *Hartford*. Tell her *Hartford!*

'Yes?' asked a puzzled female voice, low, almost contralto, and perfectly controlled.

'Mrs James? Hartford. Doctor Hartford. You remember your last examination with me in London? A special request. A *referral*.' The second code-word meaning listen, don't interrupt and agree with everything said.

'Of course, Doctor. I'd almost forgotten. Don't tell me you've actually found something wrong with me?'

God she's cool, Adeane thought. I certainly wouldn't be in her shoes.

'Actually, Mrs James, I would seriously consider taking some time away from the demands of your job. I feel you should do this right away, although you did explain to me that your position was very demanding. To be honest, our tests did detect a heart-murmur which, although not, should we say, critical at this time, would do well to be watched. Protected, so to speak. Some time in the country, peace and tranquillity – that sort of thing.'

'I see,' said Rhoda James, sounding serious now. 'But you know we're virtually in the country here, Doctor Hartford. Peter, it's all right! I'll tell you in a minute. Sorry, Doctor, my husband doesn't know about all this.'

'I thought not. Well, I honestly don't think that being near

80

your place of business will be any help at all, Mrs James. The weight of responsibility will still be there – that really is no solution. A complete change of scene is what is needed. In fact a colleague of mine has a house in the country which by happy coincidence is vacant right now. He's on a sabbatical in America and I know would be delighted to have someone living in the place – keeping the mice and rabbits down – while he's away.'

'That sounds wonderful. Is it vacant now?'

'I'll make arrangements. I needed confirmation from you. You should move in *immediately* – then we can decide on the treatment for your condition. Take your family with you. It's important, under the circumstances to have them around you.'

'Ah, well . . . I really don't think my husband will be able to come, Doctor – Peter shut up! He's a bank-manager you understand and right now he's got his auditors in. There really would be no way I could persuade him – or expect him – to neglect his position because of my health.'

'The children, then? I think the children would be good company for you. It would not be a good idea for you to be without someone you're close to in a fairly lonely location.'

'Yes, the children, of course. They'll be very excited. I'll make all the arrangements tonight. We'll travel by car – I have my own. Will you give me the address, Doctor, please.'

'I wonder if you'd mind calling my answering service in the morning, Mrs James – I don't have it right now. Tomorrow they'll give you all the details, route, everything. There'll be someone there to meet you – our senior consultant. Leave all arrangements to me.'

'Oh thank you so much, Doctor Hartford. It really is nice to have someone so concerned about me. I'll have to inform my superiors at work of course – but that should be no problem when I explain the circumstances. I presume you are able to supply some sort of note – I'm a civil servant you see and government departments are rather formal about these things.'

'Consider it done. In the post, first thing in the morning. To your immediate superior?'

'Heavens no! He's far too grand. The personnel department – you have the address?'

'On file, yes. First thing in the morning. And of course we're concerned about you Mrs James. What else could we be. You're a very valuable patient.'

'I'll call your answering service in the morning then, I believe I've got the number somewhere. Thank you so much for all you're doing, Doctor Hartford. I'd better break the news to my brood now. Goodbye.'

Adeane replaced the receiver then moved to yet another phone, an instrument with an oversized base, coloured green. There was no dial, just two recessed buttons.

A CIA night-desk man came on the line instantly with a flat drawl. Simon Adeane sighed and lit up a cigarette. It took a few minutes before he actually spoke to whom he really wanted and by that time his cigarette was burned away. He lit another and imparted the sad news that the old Silver Fox was not as well as he could be so would the Company be its usual co-operative brotherly self and hand over the keys to one of their nice safe holiday homes suitable for a sick man who was a security problem?

No, the Company had no safe-houses vacant at that time – business was pretty damn good – but if that devious bastard Weidenstein really needed somewhere in a hurry then he was welcome to shack up with an ex-Company man who'd gone native in some forest. New Forest – pronounced 'Noo'. Good guy – once. 'Nam did the job on him. No longer operational, thank Christ, but still a liability. Paints, and hides out watching animals and birds. Birds for Chrissake! Not hunting, watching. A trip-wire man. Happened to a whole bunch out of 'Nam and Cambodia. That was all that was on offer – perfect for Weidenstein – no one could get within a hundred feet of the house without him knowing. The guy had got the place rigged – really rigged! Take it or leave it. There was nothing else on offer.

But maybe this guy would refuse? Adeane asked, playing the all-American boy.

Not a chance. He couldn't refuse. The Company gave him the house as a settlement but that didn't mean they couldn't use it themselves when they wanted. That was the deal. Always was, always would be. The Company looked after you, you looked after the Company.

82

He'd take it, Adeane said. What choice did he have – barring going out, finding something himself and renting. Which would take too long and would be entirely insecure. It was one thing for the CIA to know the address – quite another to approach an estate agent without previously establishing cut-outs.

Adeane took the details.

'What's his name?' he asked.

'Wilder, Declan Wilder. Weirdo. Good guy once, though.'

'Maybe he still is?'

'Too far gone from the real world,' came the humourless reply.

Adeane put down the instrument and made arrangements for Rhoda James's call in the morning which by standing arrangement would be made from a public call box.

Then he drove to Ruislip, already certain that Weidenstein would not be pleased by the inclusion of an ex-CIA, burnt-out Vietnam Special Operations veteran in the operation.

There was, however, no choice. It was either Declan Wilder or nothing. So business was good for the Company. Maybe he should cut his losses and cross the Square? Maybe. But not yet. ORACLE was still an ongoing ticket to higher places. Max knew that, and Simon Adeane was still available to ride on that high-powered express.

William Salisbury, the man known to Cade as 'Brock', also saw the charcoal drawing of Gerald Parminter's face on the Channel Four News on Thursday evening. But unlike Simon Adeane, he was far from being alone.

'Dreadful!' the Prime Minister exclaimed. 'I simply don't know what this country is coming to when a child is abducted in broad daylight from outside her school. It's no more than another form of terrorism. Where will it end?'

Salisbury, like Adeane, was dumbstruck.

'Are you all right?' the Prime Minister queried, concerned, her shrewd eyes fixed on him. They were in her private apartments and she was sitting on a comfortable, patterned sofa, a slim file laid on top of the red box balanced on her knees.

'Tiredness, Prime Minister. We've all been overdoing things, trying to foresee and counteract the problems this accord with Dublin is sure to pose.'

The Prime Minister raised her eyebrows wearily. 'I know, but it simply *has* to be done. There really is no other solution. This must succeed. Ireland takes up so much time – time that can, and must, be spent on other things.'

'We're doing our best, Prime Minister.'

'Of course you are. Of *course* you are. We all are.' Her eyes moved back to the large television set. 'Gloucester,' she remarked, seeing the police telephone numbers. 'I just hope that this evil man doesn't turn out to be employed at GCHQ. So many are around that area.' She passed the file back to Salisbury but retained the red box. 'I should think an aberration – a perversion – such as this must show up under positive vetting. The questions are very searching but I'd still feel far safer if we could establish a lie-detector programme.'

Salisbury tucked the file under his arm. 'True. But until we're able to read minds we can never be totally certain of anyone.'

The Prime Minister arose, smoothing her skirts. 'I would not wish to live in a world where we could read each other's minds. Can you imagine the kind of thoughts I would pick up from the opposition benches!'

Salisbury forced a polite smile from his lips and left the apartment. Downstairs, he made his way to the Cabinet Room and arranged for briefs to be laid out for that evening's meeting on the new proposals for Northern Ireland.

As he was leaving he was faced with the Home Secretary and the Secretary of State for Defence who had just arrived.

'I hope there are no thorns among this bed of roses, Salisbury?' said the Home Secretary with a grim twist to his mouth.

'None you would not expect to be there already, Home Secretary.'

The Defence Secretary made no comment, wearing his usual stone-faced expression above his costly striped Savile Row suit. The standing jibe among Number 10 staffers was that he reserved his smile exclusively for Tory Party conferences and then it split his face in two. His blue eyes, however, never smiled. Glass, some wag had once remarked. He takes them out at night and polishes them. Just so that he could beam at the Americans, whom he believed were God's gift to the world, or possibly even gods themselves. He nodded, but his eyes looked right through the Deputy Co-ordinator of Intelligence.

Salisbury carried on past the two cabinet ministers heading for the Cabinet Office. There, in the privacy of his own office, he made a telephone call on the direct line to the Security Service, MI5.

'Henderson? Good, I've caught you. I wonder if we could get together this evening? Yes it is important. Something the Prime Minister will be concerned about. Shall we say eight-thirty? No, not at Charles — let's make it the Club then we'll have a chance to get something to eat. Very well, nine then.'

Across the city, in his office at Charles Street, Colonel Elwyn Henderson, the officer in charge of liaison (K7) between the Security Service (MI5) and the Secret Intelligence Service (MI6) replaced the secure line telephone and frowned. He had not seen the news on television but had he done so, he would instantly have recognized the face of Gerald Parminter as being the same man whose photograph and personal details were at that moment locked inside his briefcase.

Had he also known the reason why the police were hunting for Gerald Parminter, his expression would have deteriorated to one of deep consternation, for as a former agent-controller he knew very well that field-men who were already under stress through clandestine activities could tip completely off the rails if faced with sudden personal trauma.

'Harlow' like 'Brock' knew that their chosen executioner had once had a daughter aged six who had vanished on her way home from school one sunny summer afternoon, only to be found some three weeks later horrendously mutilated after being sexually assaulted and tortured.

'Mercifully, she was quite dead,' reported the police chief-inspector to the cameras, his feelings crushed under the flat statement. But in an angry, muttered aside he added: 'The bastard killed her for three weeks, if I get him I'll take a lifetime.' He was reprimanded for this unprofessional comment.

Little Amy Cade's killer had never been caught; and her father, with his prisoner's pallor and haircut, standing discreetly shackled in borrowed civilian clothes by the small graveside, had never fully recovered. Nor forgotten.

Colonel Henderson left Charles Street immediately, disturbed by Salisbury's insistence on an unscheduled meeting but completely unaware of the far-reaching consequences their conspiracy would soon bring about.

He passed a news-vendor whose display board announced: 'US President's Star Wars Problem.' His eyes fixed venomously on the face of the ageing American President on the front of the newspapers but he did not stop to purchase a copy. He had no intention of reading blatant lies, nor had he time to delay. His meeting with Cade in Soho was vital. The operation had to be expedited. Henderson had his orders.

At nine-twenty that Thursday evening William Salisbury, alias 'Brock', sat opposite 'Harlow' at their club in St James's Street, London. Despite the fact that they were surrounded by fellow members of the secret world they spoke in hushed tones. No one remarked on this; it was an accepted mode of behaviour.

Salisbury explained rapidly the reason for their crash meeting. His co-conspirator was aghast.

'He'll go off the rails,' Henderson blurted, aghast.

'Lower your voice. The main problem right now is whether Blue can target him at all. The man is bound to be on the run – God alone knows where he might be? And if the police do get him I have a strong suspicion that he'll crack totally. Spill the lot. KGB, NSA – everything.'

'If he's the one. We don't know which one of the four the Americans are using.'

'Does it matter? All four are KGB recruits – and we don't want *that* in the wretched papers. And you know damn well it doesn't have to be only one of them. Washington might have bought the whole network. They're capable of it – and they can afford it. And God knows it's worth it to them,' Salisbury added, viciously.

'Have you seen the evening papers? They're leaking information about setbacks to their programme. Front page. Official from Washington.'

'Of course they are. The longer the Russians think they've got problems, the further they move ahead. We're all going to wake up one morning to find their defence "umbrella" up there and opened – but you can bet your knighthood, and mine, that when the storm breaks the only targets it will cover will be those owned, leased or actually in America. Greenham Common, the SAC bases, all the little Americas in Britain will be protected – but you can write off London, Birmingham, Manchester and the rest. They can't protect the lot, so they'll protect what's theirs. You know what'll happen, Henderson? All those wretched creatures at Greenham, all the CND wailers, are going to rush headlong for all the Yank bases to try and immobilize them and they'll all survive. Talk about the meek inheriting the earth!'

'Blue will go right off the rails,' Henderson repeated, disregarding Salisbury's view of the future. 'I tell you, after what happened to his daughter he'll go for Number Three even if the police catch up with the perverted devil.'

'That would suit our purpose very well.'

'It certainly would not. The very last thing we want is an assassin half off his rocker making one-man raids on police stations.'

'They'll probably have to kill him – knowing his capabilities. They'll check his record and put it down to blind revenge – and a disturbed mind. He's good enough – and motivated enough – to succeed with the kill. We'll have to find someone else for Number Four.'

'You don't know?' Henderson said, astonished. 'Grey hasn't told you? You haven't spoken with him since your call yesterday?'

'Not spoken, no. What's wrong?'

'He called me after your call to him. He was disturbed. Thought you might be considering slowing down the programme. I understand you expressed that view?'

'I said that possibly our time-scale was too tight. Too many deaths in too short a time. That's reasonable, isn't it?'

'Grey isn't feeling reasonable. As far as he's concerned there's too much being given away by the Americans – too many of our own secrets. In my opinion he's right. He told me to accelerate the operation. Ordered me to.'

'Accelerate?'

'Blue has everything. I've passed over the details on Four.'

'When!' Salisbury exclaimed.

'Today. That's why I arrived late. I made contact with Blue on the way here.'

'But that's against all our agreed procedures! He gets one target at a time and destroys the details – any more is sheer madness. If he's picked up with the file on Four the police will call in the Security Service. You can't get that information out of a telephone book for God's sake, it comes off classified files! From Five's own computer. And they'll start looking inward – checking who pulled that information recently – they'll go back as far as they want. *You* know what they're like. Grey's gone mad. I know he wants to get back at the Yanks – we all do – but Jesus!'

Salisbury's furious murmurings had drawn attention to their table. He glanced around quickly then leaned forward. 'We have to do something. Blue has to be stopped from going for Parminter. Recall him!'

'You know perfectly well that that is quite impossible. The arrangement was that we had no knowledge of how he operates. That side is up to him – and safer for us incidentally.'

'It's not too bloody safe right now.'

'There was no way this situation could have been foreseen. We had no idea – nor, I should imagine, had the KGB or NSA – that Number Three – *don't use his name again* – has an unsavoury appetite for little girls. Even if we *had* we would probably still have used Blue – despite his past. He was the perfect instrument for the task. We needed patriotism and loyalty – and a certain sense of grievance against the Establishment. He had all three in abundance. I repeat, this could not have been foreseen.'

A steward brought food to the table but both men ignored the steaming dishes.

'So what are we supposed to do? What are *you* going to do? You pulled the information? You'll be questioned. If they decide you're involved they'll break you. There's a limit to anyone's heroism, Henderson.'

'In which case it will be your turn – then Grey's.'

'When that comes out the government falls with him – and a lot more besides. Try the "Special Relationship" – then

88

NATO. No one will trust anyone. We'll have the socialists in the House within a week – with a landslide majority – with the hard left, the Trots, ready to start jerking their strings. Goodbye Washington, hello Moscow.'

'It was because we feared the government could not withstand either the exposure of a spy-ring in GCHQ of this depth, or a crippling feud with the Americans that we took this course of action. I did, certainly,' stated Henderson.

'Never mind that now. We must decide what to do. Blue's possible reactions –'

'Probable,' Henderson interrupted.

'All right, *probable* reactions are the cause of all this. He must be stopped, and I don't care how.'

'Grey's order to pass on the details for Number Four are the cause. Blue is – or will be – the effect.'

'Christ! this is no time for an exercise in logic. Blue has to be stopped.'

'All we can do is wait. If Blue goes for Three and the police kill him in the attempt then information on where he'd been operating from – his vehicle and so on – will be reasonably easy to get hold of. We must make sure we get there first.'

'And if they get him alive?'

'Then we will have him killed. At least we'll know where he'll be.'

'What if he succeeds in hitting Three and gets away? You said yourself he's capable of doing that.'

'In that case he'd be a murderer. A hunted man. In the end the police will kill him – or we will.'

'The police must not be allowed to find the file on Number Four,' Salisbury breathed.

Henderson lifted his fork and prodded at his food. 'Even if they had the files they would find it difficult to prove anything – without Blue's co-operation. Basically it boils down to Blue being removed. But for the present we'll let him run. He may well succeed in dealing with Four.' Henderson laid down his cutlery. 'This fish is completely cold.'

Salisbury stared at his co-conspirator, realizing he had misread Henderson. The fish was not the only thing that was completely cold.

*

89

Cade rode into the yard of the Sullivan farm late on Thursday night. He stowed and covered the motorcycle then went into the house.

Lettie was sitting at the kitchen table, the local newspaper between her elbows, her fists pressed into her cheeks, her eyes glinting with anger – but for once she could not let her tears flow.

'What's up, Ma?' asked Cade. 'Hey, what's the matter?'

'Beast!' she hissed through clenched teeth.

'They should hang 'em,' said Will Sullivan, seated opposite, an ancient pipe unlit in his gnarled hands.

'They should do worse than that!' Lettie snapped. 'They should castrate them – like they do animals.'

'Who?' asked Cade.

'Filth like this one.' Lettie slammed her hands on the newspaper and turned it around, ripping the front page in her fury. Then the inevitable tears flowed.

For a brief moment, Cade's surging memories denied him the clarity of mind needed for recognition – but when it came, the roar that was caged inside him made his entire body shake although no sound passed his lips.

Lettie was on her feet. 'Will, the boy's sick!'

Cade could not hear her.

They placed him in a chair, leaning over him, Will Sullivan trying vainly to force his head down between his knees for they were certain that his colour was a sure indication that he was about to pass out.

'He's sick, Will. Call Doctor Perkins. Will!'

But Will Sullivan had perched himself on the scrubbed table above Cade with one comforting hand on his shoulder. 'Make some tea, Let,' he ordered gently, moving his hand to Cade's head and letting it rest there. 'Take your time, son,' he said.

There was no response from Cade.

'That's what happened to yours, wasn't it? Hold your head up, lad, she's gone now, nothing will bring her back. We've just got to hope that this little mite is spared. Nothing you can do about that. Nothing any of us can do.'

'Except pray,' said Lettie, placing her tray of tea on the table, still tearful.

Cade lifted his cropped head. 'I've done all the praying I'll

90

ever do. I prayed so hard I believed that God was sitting right there in front of me – dragged down from wherever he was. He did nothing. There was nothing he was ever going to do. My kid was being tortured and God sat there watching me, listening, and he did nothing. Forget God, Ma. I did. A long time ago.'

'Drink your tea, son,' urged Sullivan.

Lettie tutted through her sniffles, shocked at Cade's view of her God.

'You're good people,' said Cade. 'The best. But I'm no good for you. I've stayed here for too long already.'

'You worry about all that tomorrow,' Sullivan replied.

'He can stay as long as he likes,' said Lettie

'No one said he couldn't. There's plenty of work – and a sound roof over his head.'

'He's hungry,' Lettie announced. 'All that cycling about and no hot food inside him.' She turned to her stove. 'Kept some hot, just in case.'

'I'll wash up,' said Cade. 'Thank you. Both of you.'

They sat by him as he ate in silence, the newspaper surreptitiously thrust under a cushion by Lettie. At the end of his meal, despite both their objections, Cade went back into the barn saying he needed to complete some work on the camper.

Inside the stable he removed the bulky package that 'Harlow' had given him earlier from the Triumph's panniers and took it into the barn.

Switching on the Volkswagen's interior lights, he seated himself in the rear and unsealed the package. There were two sealed envelopes inside. He opened the one marked with the number three in thick felt-tipped pen; ignoring, as he had done with the previous two folders, the underlined instruction to destroy after reading. He still considered the contents of each – however incriminating – to be a form of insurance. Cade knew from bitter past experience that political considerations might well dictate that he be sacrificed. This time he would not let that happen.

He studied the photographs of Gerald Parminter and confirmed that the drawing on the front page of the newspaper was of the same man.

He stared out at the great open door of the barn and the

night beyond. 'You go the hard way,' he murmured.

He was still there when first light spilled onto the straggling grease-stained straw on the barn floor. He was not asleep, nor had he been.

He was waiting.

Chapter Five

It was late afternoon in Washington when Max Weidenstein finally squeezed into the cramped observer's seat of the monster Lockheed SR-71A high-altitude supersonic reconaissance aircraft.

The midnight-blue, twin-tailed, delta-winged monster had been waiting for almost an hour, its two Pratt and Whitney J58 afterburning bleed turbo-jets hot from false starts brought about by White House indecision.

Max Weidenstein was even hotter.

Previously he had waited in the base commander's office, a slow burn building, his pugnacious temperament barely held in check. Finally when the decision came – not by telephone but instead by courier in a White House limousine with wailing outriders as escorts – the heat inside him flared.

The slim envelope bearing the presidential seal of office contained all that Weidenstein might wish to know – written by the hand of the President, in ink, with no other copy in existence.

Weidenstein demanded a secure line to the White House but the courier informed him that the President would not take his call. Nor would the Defense Secretary, presidential advisers or anyone else close to the President whom the NSA London station security chief wished to name. The courier informed that he merely delivered messages; he did not make policy, nor would he wish to. And yes – emphatically – the President's decision was final and he had been ordered to pass on those very words.

So there it was, carefully chosen words in blue ink which set him loose into the wilderness bearing the sins of others higher than he, making him the classic scapegoat. At that moment Weidenstein truly felt the persecuted Jew, finally understanding his parents' never-forgotten fears.

However, he could save himself, wrote the President in his final vaguely merciful paragraph. Weidenstein should confess his sins to those whom he had sinned against and aid them in any way possible to recover, to give recompense and – perhaps – let them gain from his actions.

In other words hand the operation over to the British, thought Weidenstein. Keep the 'special relationship' alive and try to persuade them that what had been done was for benefit of both rich and poor cousins alike. The past was bad but the future could be brighter. In other words: It's over but not necessarily dead so save the operation and maybe your career with it.

Weidenstein allowed the massive thrust of the Blackbird's power to force him back into his seat. Then the needle nose lifted to the near-vertical, the blue-black monster almost becoming a rocket. So what's a little more pressure matter when you're already clamped in a big squeeze? thought Weidenstein as his vision clouded with the increasing G-force.

Before the huge aircraft hit the limit of its soaring climb, the telephone was ringing in London at·10 Downing Street.

The time was ten-fifty and the Prime Minister, for a change, had retired before midnight. She sat up in bed, the inevitable stack of red cabinet boxes on the carpet beside her, the coverlet weighed down over her thighs by folders containing cabinet papers. She decided she needed stronger reading spectacles, her ability to focus was deteriorating again.

'Damn job,' she complained to her husband who had not yet settled for the night. 'It's ruining my eyesight.'

'But you love it,' he remarked with a smile.

The telephone interrupted her work. She lifted it and raised her eyebrows. 'Very well, I'll take it up here,' she said and switched to another instrument. 'Mister President, how are you? No it's perfectly all right, I was working.' She laughed. 'No thank you, my own workload is quite enough.' She listened, puzzlement crossing her face. '*Hamlet*? Yes, I think I know my Shakespeare. Why do you ask?' She fell silent for many minutes, her expression becoming set. Occasionally she looked at, but did not see, her husband. Finally in a voice of iron she said: 'I appreciate your candour, Mister President. However this is not a matter which can be resolved on the telephone. Certainly I'll see your man the moment he arrives.' She replaced the receiver.

'*Hamlet*?' queried her husband, attempting to brighten her mood after what had obviously been a difficult conversation: he was well used to those. 'I understood that the only quotation he has to his name is from "The Shooting of Dan McGrew"?'

She cast him a look which he knew meant serious business – or trouble.

'An aide must have found him a suitable quote,' she said, bitterly. ' "I have shot mine arrow o'er the house and hurt my brother." '

'Oh dear. That sounds ominous.'

'It's worse than ominous. It's disastrous. God save us from government officials and departments who think they know best. Why do you think *we're* elected in the first place?'

'To serve them, my dear. You should have learned that by now. I assume this means you will be staying up?'

'I have no choice. You go on to sleep.'

'I certainly shall my dear,' he replied, watching her dress.

As she prepared herself, she reflected bitterly that there could not have been a worse moment for such a crisis.

Not only had she to fight a general election shortly with policies which had only half-succeeded but she had also to counter a growing power struggle within her own party. If what the American President had guardedly told her was true, then even her most powerful ally was – or certainly had been until that moment – arrayed against her.

She could, in the next few days, be fighting for her political life.

The Lockheed SR-71A Blackbird swooped down to the tarmac at the USAF base, Ruislip, just before 2 a.m. in the opening hours of Friday morning, its titanium skin hot enough to cause a severe burn after having reached a temperature of

300 degrees centigrade at its cruising speed of Mach 3.

Simon Adeane was waiting for his superior by a glowing hangar in a restricted area prepared for the top-secret aircraft. The deep exhaust noise from the tail-pipes of his pristine E-Type Jaguar convertible was obliterated by the shattering sound of the Blackbird's colossal twin turbo-jets as the plane taxied toward him. The needle nose of the jet dipped as the pilot applied his brakes, the great satanic airframe lurching forward over the set-back nose wheel.

Max Weidenstein had already spotted the classic British sports car and was emerging from the aircraft even as the engines wound down.

He slammed the door of the low car and said: 'Drive.'

Adeane slipped the clutch and headed for the main gate of the base. 'Grosvenor Square?' he asked, saving his attention for the road as he sensed the suppressed wrath of the small man beside him.

'Downing Street. Fast as you like.'

'They've pulled the rug in Washington?' Adeane asked, knowing the answer.

'We're going to Auntie to get our knuckles rapped.'

'And ORACLE?'

'The Brits get her. Maybe, if they're so disposed, they'll let us stay in the game.'

'*Why?*'

'Because that's the way it is. It's called political expediency. I call it something else. Can't you drive any faster?'

'I've already been stopped once tonight – last night.'

'We've been breaking worse laws than speeding,' Weidenstein growled.

'What about Washington – and Meade?'

'You met a politician willing to take the blame yet? Meade? Well, there's maybe one or two who'll figure Miami isn't so bad a place. Hush money can buy a good few comfortable years in the sun.'

'Shit,' muttered Adeane.

'And we're in it.'

Weidenstein settled lower in the bucket-seat and closed his eyes. 'Some flight,' he murmured. 'Expensive.'

'Washington paid.'

Weidenstein opened one eye wearily. 'For the last time. Wake me when you reach Number Ten – and don't bust through the barrier, the Brits only want one excuse to waste us.'

Adeane pressed his foot down further, relishing the pull from the engine's twelve cylinders, feeling reckless enough at that moment to outrun any police-patrol which might try to stop them. He reached Whitehall quickly, without incident – apart from a near scrape with a lane-drifting truck which Weidenstein snored through – and took the roads to the rear of the Prime Minister's residence, parking the E-Type in Horse Guards under the hard eyes of two Special Branch Protection Squad officers.

Weidenstein groggily brought his exhausted mind and body back to the demands of reality as the two armed officers detained them briefly, calling in by radio for confirmation of the information on their passes and also for verification of the Prime Minister's readiness to see them at that strange hour.

Under escort, in silence, they were taken via the spies' and tradesmen's route into the presence of the woman whose decision could destroy them and the complex ultra-secret disinformation operation they had been running for years.

'I think you had better sit down,' said the Prime Minister, addressing Weidenstein by his work-name which the President had given to her. She enquired coldly on the need for Adeane's presence.

'This is my deputy, Prime Minister,' said Weidenstein before accepting her invitation. 'He is conscious of the entire operation and I've been ordered to pass on the content of this meeting to him when it is over.'

'Then he may as well hear it the first time.' She turned and sat at her desk, her shrewd eyes fixed on the two Americans with open distrust. 'I gather you are the gentlemen who have been passing classified information to the Russians. *British* classified information, that is.'

'I have been in charge of the British end of the operation.'

'Oh please!' she interrupted, rudely. 'I'm not in the mood to hear the blame being shifted from here to there and probably back again. In good time we will find out who is ultimately responsible and the matter will be dealt with officially – and ruthlessly. All I wish to hear at this precise moment is just how much damage has been done – and what you propose might be done to minimize it.'

Weidenstein sighed and spread the palms of his hands. 'Minimizing any of the damage, I can't promise. Of course certain codes can be changed but that is up to you and your people, Prime Minister. But if you do this you will alert Moscow to the fact that you know that they know –'

'Oh that weary phrase! I'm intelligent enough to foresee the ramifications.'

Weidenstein shrugged. 'Then you also foresee that the vital disinformation we have been feeding the Russians will be cut off. If you change codes suddenly it means you have broken their network.'

'The one you failed to advise us of. I presume it is still operating?'

Weidenstein glanced at Adeane who was sitting very upright in his chair, deeply respectful of his surroundings and the woman whom he was facing. He seemed to have distanced himself from the matter under discussion – an observer only and plainly not involved.

Weidenstein rubbed the back of his neck. 'Ah well, this, if you will, is the problem – the catalyst which has caused our operation to be revealed to you by the President.'

'Please come to the point. I'm not one of those people who find spies distasteful. I understand, more than most, the need for them and also, in general, the very good and vital work they do, but quite honestly, I do find the tortuous routes you people take in your explanations quite tedious.'

Weidenstein nodded. 'Certainly, Prime Minister. Two of the KGB network are dead. One accident, one suicide. A third member is being hunted by your police at this moment for the alleged abduction of a female child, presumably for sexual purposes. Your Security Service is responsible for all these events.'

Adeane had found one part of the ceiling which deeply concerned him.

The Prime Minister's neck, above her single strand of matched pearls, had coloured, the fire ascending to her face. 'Would you repeat that, please,' she asked, her fury barely restrained.

'Surely,' Weidenstein replied. 'MI5 has executed two of the KGB network and have framed the third with a crime which will ensure that he's kept in a close custody while they move on the fourth. Number four is our agent. Ours now. Originally Moscow's.'

'I don't believe a word of it.'

'Believing, Prime Minister, has to do with faith, which can be a very blurred area. You have faith in your Security Service, you believe in them – but don't let it blind you to the circumstances at issue here.'

'If my, our, Security Service is responsible for these "events" – as you choose to call them – then I, most certainly, would know something about it. You can have little idea about how this Government operates, or you would not have made such absurd accusations.'

Weidenstein rested against the back of his uncomfortable, upright chair, pulled a handkerchief from his crushed suit and rubbed his stinging eyes. 'I'm sorry, I've had a very fast and hard flight from Washington. I'm considerably jet-lagged.'

'I too have gone without rest. I have no sympathy for your condition. I demand an immediate explanation – or a withdrawal and an apology. I shall be reporting this entire conversation to your President. He can deal with you as he sees fit.'

'Oh he's done that already,' replied Weidenstein with a humourless smile. 'Prime Minister, you are a lawyer – for the sake of argument will you listen to what I have to say? Hear the evidence – circumstantial though it may appear to be – before you dismiss my case? Without prejudice?'

She leaned forward and lifted a pencil, holding it poised above a loose-leafed note-pad.

'Please, nothing written down,' Weidenstein requested.

'Very well. Without prejudice.'

Adeane had switched his gaze from the safety of the ceiling, sensing that his superior was weaving his cunning way under the defences of the tough woman behind the desk. If she had been a fat complacent hen, he would have pronounced that the Silver Fox would have had her throat within moments; but he knew that she was far from being that. Adeane was more than interested in the outcome. His future depended upon it.

Max Weidenstein put forward his 'case', explaining the American disinformation operation in total – as he had been instructed to do by his President.

He took time over the motive, emphasizing that the Russians had their own experimental programme for a space-based advanced-technology defence-system running for as long as the American effort in that direction.

Also, how Moscow Centre had successfully targeted 'Silicon Valley' in California and had stolen the technology of the future from under American noses, applying it instantly to their own programme.

Then, he revealed how certain influential, and alarmed, persons within the American Establishment had felt that if they could not, effectively, counter the Soviet spy machine, then the only way to beat it was to use that machine themselves.

To give the Russians what they wanted.

Not the whole truth. But certainly part of the truth.

To pass on all the failures, even invent a few more – and exaggerate them.

Moscow *wanted* to believe America was suffering failure. They would half-convince themselves, given selected information – or, in reality, disinformation.

Then, as time moved along, to give the disinformation more bite, America could pass on occasional successes – but only those successes the Russians would themselves have within a calculated time-period.

And, while all this was being done, the American effort to safeguard the future would be surging ahead, building the dream that, one day, would make them unconquerable. And, naturally, her allies would benefit too.

The men of influence had had their way and America was now ahead of the Soviet Union. Well ahead and – possibly – unstoppable. She was no longer being robbed blind by her enemy.

The KGB had effectively been put to sleep.

'But someone, Prime Minister,' said Weidenstein, in closing, 'someone on your side of the water, has uncovered what we have been doing. We cannot prove how – nor does that really matter. What does matter, is that this person – or persons – let us assume within MI5, because they would have access to the relevant classified information and the means and personnel to carry out such an operation, has also discovered – or perhaps guessed – that we were allowing the flow of British secrets to continue to the Russians, via the double-agent we now run inside GCHQ. I mean, of course, genuine British secrets, used as collateral to back up our disinformation. Anyone can be induced to believe a lie if you associate it with verifiable truth. Even the Russians.'

The Prime Minister was leaning forward. A fraction more pressure and her pencil would have snapped between her hands.

'Your President,' she said, coldly, 'has already advised me as to how the Soviet Union were duped into believing your disinformation.'

She laid the pencil down, then looked directly at Weidenstein. 'After such a confession you still expect me to believe your theories regarding our Security Service? Why must it be a British action? Why not the Russians themselves? They may no longer believe your disinformation? They may suspect that you've turned one of their agents? If that were the case, then the entire network would become suspect – instantly. The Russians are ruthless, they would be more likely to kill off these spies than we would. It's not our style.'

'I raised that point,' Adeane put in, deferentially.

'Did you?' asked the Prime Minister, glancing over at the previously silent, rather English-looking – in a studied way – younger man.

She instinctively distrusted Adeane, viewing him as some sort of infiltrator; an enemy in British uniform, sly and waiting to strike.

Which was precisely why Max Weidenstein had wanted Simon Adeane in the room with them. He had guessed that the woman before him would not, in her present quite justifiable temper, see an Anglophile, but instead an American spy with British cover. And, in contrast, he Weidenstein, would be a thorough Yank, with a mixed ethnic background – but that was normal in America nowadays. She would see a brash but tough fighter out to prove his point. Clever – but blunt. So probably honest. Well, as honest as intelligence men could be.

101

Weidenstein, compared with the handsome, rakish Adeane would be the one she would finally trust. Or so was Weidenstein's conviction.

She was speaking to Adeane: 'So you thought it might be the Russians, did you?' She turned to Weidenstein. 'And you discounted it?'

Weidenstein shrugged his narrow shoulders. 'Oh, certainly I discounted the theory that they might kill their own people. The KGB have taken years – twenty, in one of the cases – to place, develop and establish their agents' careers. Why destroy a lucrative, and crucial, operation on the basis of unproven suspicion? If they are prepared to do that it would surely mean that they have other networks inside GCHQ – more productive and better placed. Do you want to believe that, Prime Minister? I can tell you, I certainly don't.' He waited, allowing her time to consider this unwelcome suggestion.

He continued: 'It is possible that other KGB agents exist at Cheltenham or at GCHQ out-stations, but my belief is that this network is the one that matters, the one best-placed to supply the Russians with what they want. Our agent, the most senior of the four, could not be better placed, and that is why I am certain that the KGB have no suspicions and did not kill their own agents. Nor do I believe in coincidences when they come in threes and all concern members of the same spy-ring. I believe, without doubt, that it is your people. You may not like the idea, and perhaps you won't face it right now, but believe me it will grow on you.'

'Perhaps you might convince me if I knew where your agent is placed?'

'May I take the Fifth on that?' Weidenstein asked, half-smiling.

She was deadly serious. 'The Fifth Amendment has no place in British jurisprudence and, most certainly, you have incriminated yourself already. You could be charged with spying against this country – operating a spy-ring within our most sensitive organization – and go to jail for thirty years.'

Weidenstein seemed to shut down, locked totally within himself; then admitted: 'Our agent, formerly a Moscow Centre paid operative, was turned by me after being offered an inducement she could not refuse. Her code-name is ORACLE and she is the personal assistant to the man with more power than anyone else in the entire organization. I mean, of course, the Director-General of GCHQ. The others were all of lesser importance, though of great value to Moscow, naturally. It isn't so surprising, Prime Minister – read your intelligence reports on the West German Service.'

'I don't need to,' she answered, quietly, her voice no longer steely but unsteady. 'I'm familiar with the details.' She fell silent, letting the full import of Weidenstein's revelation sink in, feeling at once desperate and defeated.

At last she lifted her eyes from the desk. 'I should imagine that you have some proposal? People in your profession always do. I suppose that is why we pay you.'

Weidenstein seemed infinitely weary. 'Proposal? Prime Minister, the only proposal I have is that we don't do a thing. *Nothing*.'

'That's quite impossible. Under the circumstances, out of the question.'

Weidenstein began to rise from his chair. 'Then I must leave you to do what you have to do.'

'I haven't finished!' she snapped. 'What is gained if we do nothing? America gains, certainly. Your operation continues as before – less the dead agents – but we, the British, only continue to lose?'

Weidenstein resumed his seat then spoke carefully. 'If the Russians could be made to believe that their three agents were the victims of some plot either by MI5 or some reactionary group within Five – and that this plot failed to uncover their best-placed agent . . .?' He paused.

'Then ORACLE would be doubly valuable to them,' put in the Prime Minister. 'Possibly even better established. The Security Service – or whoever is behind this – overlooked her, so therefore her position would be very strong indeed. What is the interval between positive vettings? Five years? If she's due for one right now it would seem certain that she would sail through it – and if she's recently been vetted that would give her a number of clear years to continue spying.'

'She's just been vetted,' said Weidenstein. 'Which gives both the British and American Intelligence Services plenty of time to co-operate in feeding Moscow whatever disinformation our respective governments want them to believe.' Weidenstein studied his manicured hands. 'Of course the circle of knowledge would have to be extremely limited, with the highest clearance for those involved.'

The Prime Minister glanced at Adeane. 'Apart from your deputy, yourself and me who else knows of the existence of ORACLE?'

'That is a question that, now, only the President can answer. But only the three of us here are aware of ORACLE's position inside GCHQ. Her identity of course you can get by lifting that 'phone.'

'I have no wish to know her identity. In some ways I wish I did not know as much as I do already.'

'You asked, Prime Minister,' Weidenstein reminded.

'And I threatened you, yes, I'm aware of that. The question is, who else needs to know?'

'Does anyone?'

She looked up sharply from the doodle on her pad. 'I don't run the country by myself! There is the Cabinet. Naturally I would not wish to inform every member of it – but certainly I must inform some. This is not just an intelligence operation you know, it is also a political conspiracy involving two allies. And that, I am sure I don't have to tell you, could be political dynamite in mischievous hands. If this ever leaked out I dread to think of the consequences.'

'That is exactly the problem our President faced after my superiors agreed that the operation was under attack by your people and went to him with the story. That is why he called you and why I am here before you now with the full facts.'

She wore a deep frown. 'The worst problem I have to face is that I may have to inform the Leader of the Opposition. Possibly even the leaders of the Alliance party. You do realize that – God forbid – if we lose the coming general election that any incoming Prime Minister will have to know the facts. *All* of the facts.'

'With respect, Prime Minister, the most immediate problem you have to face – perhaps even worse – is that there is the British conspiracy to be dealt with and only you are able to deal with it without blowing the entire operation. A conspiracy formed from within your own Security Service and carried out, possibly, for the most honourable, and most dangerous of reasons – patriotism.'

'Though perhaps not entirely without the added motive of political gain,' she said quietly, almost to herself.

'Only you can deal with the problem,' Weidenstein repeated. 'But I urge you, whatever you do, please do it after deep consideration.'

'Everything I do is after deep consideration,' she replied, rising from her chair. 'I presume you have certain plans of your own that you will implement? I don't wish to know them, you understand, I just want your assurance that there will be no surprises facing me in my morning newspapers during the run-up to the general election.'

'All you need to know is that ORACLE will be secure and kept above suspicion. As of this moment she is preparing to take some sick-leave – don't worry, her destination is in this country. The Russians will not view this as suspicious. In fact they would expect her to set herself up for a quick defection if the need arose – they'll be as disturbed by all that has happened as we are. Though, of course, they'll expect her to stick with it for as long as she can.'

'I'd like the details of that location.'

'I don't think that's very wise, Prime Minister.'

'Let me be the judge of that.'

'I haven't made a firm decision on the location yet,' Weidenstein stalled.

'Then do so – and let me have the information immediately. In person. Now, what about the man who is supposed to have abducted the child? His face has been on television? How can MI5 have arranged such a thing? It seems improbable.'

Weidenstein looked directly at her. 'MI5, as you know, Prime Minister, are capable of arranging anything. What is improbable is that Moscow Centre have been running a mole for over twenty years who is an active pervert. They would not risk it. A man with those appetites would be open to arrest and some rough questioning every time he had the urge. He could be broken too easily.'

'Perhaps blackmail was the method used to recruit him in the first place?'

'My information is that it was not. He operates on an

ideological basis. Any payment he gets is chicken-feed. No, blackmail it wasn't.'

The Prime Minister paused. 'You believe I should do nothing at all? Leave it alone? Let them get away with it?'

'That's right. In the long run – for our mutual interest – it might be safer.'

'I thought so. Thank you for being so candid, though on balance, I wish this entire episode had never begun – whatever the benefits. No doubt we shall be in contact – at a distance.'

'Only through the results of ORACLE's work. Otherwise you'll never see either of us again – hopefully.' Weidenstein hesitated, as if undecided about uttering his next words.

'Yes?' the Prime Minister prompted.

'A warning, Prime Minister. The main mover behind the killings has to be well-placed and of some influence within your establishment. If I were you I would be extremely wary of those closest to you. I believe that someone in Washington – I have no idea who – decided that the ORACLE operation was too damaging to the relationship between our two countries and leaked information to a person of influence here.'

'Are you implying that someone in my Cabinet is responsible?'

Weidenstein nodded gravely. 'It seems highly likely.'

She arose from her chair but did not offer her hand. 'I shall expect that address later today.' It was an order.

As they retraced their route out of Number Ten, Adeane murmured quietly, 'You turned her around, Max.' The relief in his voice was obvious.

Weidenstein shook his silver head. 'What else could she do? She's not on the strongest political base right now. If she loses the election then the next British leader we try to nail to the cross might not be so willing to accept the vinegar sponge.'

'Five will kill Parminter. You knew that. Why didn't you tell her? She was ready to face the worst.'

'She knows it already. What she has to decide is, does she really want to stop them?'

Outside on Horse Guards Parade, it was morning and the police had towed the Jaguar away. Adeane moaned.

'I told you the British aren't gentlemen,' said Max Weidenstein.

Chapter Six

Constable Philip Jones had been a fully fledged member of Gloucestershire Constabulary for less than one year. He was young, bright and exceptionally tall, touching six feet four inches without his regulation shoes.

PC Jones was a gentle person whom children called 'kind' whenever he had cause to encounter them in the course of his duties; his height astonishing yet pleasing them.

That Friday morning, had Jones been told that he would voluntarily give up his chosen career he would have smiled, then said, firmly: Never!

He found little Susan Franks, face down, tiny arms and legs cruelly roped behind her arched back after he had been dragged to the spot by a near-hysterical woman who had been exercising her Sealyham dog in the area.

Like the child, whose blue face was evidence enough of asphyxiation, his lungs could neither draw nor exhale breath. He could not remember what to do, his intensive training forgotten.

'She's still alive – for God's sake do something!' shrieked the woman. Her dog too was affected, leaping up and barking at both his mistress and Jones. Then it pushed its nose at the scraps of clothing left on the still form.

Jones lashed out with his polished shoe at the animal.

'Don't do that!' the woman shouted.

Jones dropped to the ground beside the child, his knees sinking in the sodden mud. 'She's dead,' he said.

'She was alive just now! I saw her breathe. You could have done something.'

His hands seemed uncontrollable, yet somehow he managed to take the small penknife he always carried from his pocket. He attacked the ropes, his breath coming in grasps, his mind blessedly reminding him that he was not supposed to cut the knots.

He heard through the haze the woman shouting: 'Call an ambulance. Use your radio.'

Wet grass by the small discoloured lips appeared to shiver. The ropes were soaked and the small blade seemed useless. The woman pushed past him and heaved the child over, her mouth going for the blue lips.

'Cut the ropes! She has to be on her back,' she ordered.

Blessedly Jones succeeded. Still shaking, he made the call on his radio.

'Don't disturb anything,' he said when this was done.

The woman had stopped, sitting shoulders slumped, half-sobbing, her face smeared with mud, tears and saliva. She hit Jones in the face, knuckles clenched, harder than any man had ever hit him, dislodging his helmet completely.

'*Now* she's dead,' she said, suddenly calm.

Her dog was bewildered, whining then growling.

Jones could not look at the child. 'You're sure?'

She did not answer, clutching her dog close, murmuring to it. The child lying between them could have been a broken doll.

Finally, when the ambulance and more police began arriving, she stood up, her clothes ruined. 'I'm sorry,' she said, seeing for the first time the blood on the young policeman's face where her ring had split the ridge of his nose.

Jones seemed unaware of the wound, he appeared oblivious of all that was around him.

The woman was picking at the mud on her clothes as she turned to the wailing sounds and running men. 'She's dead,' she told them when they reached the scene. 'She lived for a few moments. She's dead now.' Then she broke down and another officer led her away to the ambulance.

'See to the dog,' someone ordered.

An ambulance man was leaning over Jones while all the procedures for a murder investigation began. 'Come on, mate,' he said. 'Better come with us.' But PC Jones was immovable. 'She was alive,' he murmured.

The ambulance man shook his head. 'Look at her, mate. She was never alive when you found her.'

'I saw her breathe.'

'People always think that. Don't let it get to you. Nothing you could have done – nothing we can do either. The bastard's really done her. It's up to you lads now.'

Jones shook his head but allowed himself to be pulled up and taken away.

'First time?' the ambulance man asked a police officer nearby.

'Looks like his last. Some can't handle it. The poor sod's going to have to accompany the body to the mortuary, have the next of kin identify it to him, then do it himself for the pathologist, and one more time for the coroner. Rule twelve, First Officer at the Scene, worst of the lot. Looks like he's in no shape to carry out the other thirteen. They're down to us.'

'Hope you get the bugger who did it,' said the ambulance man.

A Scenes of Crime Photographic Officer was already photographing the body *in situ*, with close-ups of all wounds, both in black and white and colour, then moved away to 'fix' on the film the scene of the crime itself and the approaches to it. He worked efficiently, without apparent emotion, none of this new to him. After completing his duties he left to arrange copies for the Senior Investigating Officer, the Incident Room and for the Murder Squads.

The Senior Investigating Officer had already arrived and had taken charge, making his assessment of whatever additional manpower and equipment might be needed. He called one of his officers over to him.

'Body and air temperatures taken?' he enquired.

'All done, sir.'

'Preliminary message out? Log started?'

The officer nodded.

'What about that constable who was first on the scene?'

'In the ambulance, sir. The woman hit him. Probably hysterical.' The officer looked away, offering no further information.

109

'He'd better pull himself together quickly. We're going to need him.'

'Any word on the bastard who did it?'

'Usual mixture of calls. There's a couple of real possibilities being checked out right now.' He turned toward the ambulance. 'I want that young constable taken to the mortuary with the body – he has to face life's harsher realities if he proposes to stay in the job. You carry on, I'll get onto Division about an incident room.'

The small, abused, covered body of Susan Franks was finally removed from the scene. Every police officer present was relieved. While it had remained there it clouded their judgement and attacked even the hardened sensibilities of the Murder Squad. In their book there was no worse crime they could be faced with.

Constable Jones later chose to face life's harsher realities in a different role: he resigned from the force and – perhaps to assuage his guilt, real or imagined – trained and qualified as an ambulance service officer.

Unfortunately – the collection of evidence apart – the police efforts in the hunt for the child's killer were wasted as, at six-thirty-five that evening, Gerald Parminter, dishevelled from sleeping rough, with face and hands lacerated – and upon a later full medical examination his genital organs also – walked painfully into Cheltenham Police Headquarters and admitted that he was the man responsible. His voice was so low and querulous that he was made to state his business twice. Two civilians within earshot in the reception area – one a father of two, the other aged sixty-nine – caught the second pronouncement and attacked him on the spot before being forcibly restrained and ejected by other officers.

By eight o'clock that evening, after being driven under escort to the Gloucester Incident Room he began making his statement of guilt to the detective sergeant and detective constable who were assigned to interrogate him. Within one hour, in the full flight of confession, he admitted to numerous other charges of harassment and indecent assault involving small girls, although vehemently denying killing any of these. Before long the forensic department had confirmed through their tests that the fragments of skin found under the tiny nails

110

and between the teeth of Susan Franks proved Parminter's guilt quite conclusively.

To the astonishment and cynical disbelief of the two officers, Parminter then gave as his reason for his perverted compulsions the mental strain of being a Soviet agent for the previous twenty years, currently active inside GCHQ Cheltenham. His interrogators, wisely taking no chances, decided that they would summon their local Special Branch representatives. However, before that, aware that their suspect could only be interrogated for six hours before the provisions of the Police and Criminal Evidence (PACE) Act came into force, ruling that they would have to halt and provide their suspect with rest and refreshment while a senior officer reviewed his custody, they took an unwise decision. They agreed that the best thing to do was to press on hard themselves to secure the final elements of evidence immediately, in case the rested man later decided to retract everything he had confessed. That had happened to them before.

'So she fought you all the way, Gerald? Took bits out of you. Tough little kid, eh? Her mother said she'd fight. Stubborn. Little tiger apparently. So how'd you do it in the end? Come on, you said she stopped breathing 'cos you had her face down when you did the business. Now you know, and we know, that that didn't happen 'cos the marks on her throat tell us otherwise. You *want* to tell us all of it, Gerald, you'll feel better afterwards, I promise you. Wasn't your hands, was it? Fingers leave bruises which are easily recognizable and they aren't there. So what did you use? A pair of your wife's tights – you go for that do you? Used ones?' All of this the CID detective sergeant spoke very close to Parminter's face, never letting the frightened eyes shift from his own.

'I don't like that sort of thing,' Parminter answered, fast, almost a whisper, an expellation of breath.

'So that's not your style. So what is, then?'

Parminter glanced at the detective constable who was leaning against a wall of the interrogation room, playing the softer one of the two.

He nodded his head, apparent concern on his face. 'May as well tell us, we know the rest. What's the point of holding back? It only means more strife.'

111

'It was a fan-belt from my car. I always keep a spare – ever since one broke on the motorway when I was going to see my controller. I missed the meeting and the fall-back – he thought I'd gone over. I thought they'd kill me. I want to see someone from MI5.'

'Sure, Gerald. We're going to get around to all that but first we want that fan-belt.'

'In your car, is it?' asked the detective sergeant, coming back into it. 'In the boot? Under the seat? Or did you chuck it?'

'I buried it.'

'Buried it where?'

'I can show you. I don't know exactly – if you drive me I'll show you.'

'It's dark, Gerald. It's night outside. How d'you know you'll find the right place? We don't want to be messing about in the mud for hours.'

'There's a lay-by – up near Great Witcombe where there's that Roman villa. I stopped there and slept a bit. I had to. But I buried it first, close by, in case a police-car woke me up and asked me questions.'

'You were lucky then, we always wake people sleeping in cars. Could be sleeping it off, couldn't they? Drunk.'

'I don't drink,' Parminter retorted, almost indignantly. 'It would be insecure.'

'For your spying?'

'Of course.'

'What do you say about finding that lay-by right now, Gerald? Look, we drive there, just the three of us and a driver, dig up the fan-belt, then you can talk all you like to the Security boys? You can have a meal and a rest before they get here.'

'I'm hungry now. I'm tired too.'

'How about a sandwich in the car – to tide you over.'

'What about tea?'

'Tea now, then a sandwich in the car. How's that sound?'

'All right.'

'I'll see to it,' said the detective constable.

They were out of the station inside fifteen minutes after logging out their suspect and finding another uniformed constable free to ride up front with the driver as insurance. Their

112

route developed into minor roads and countryside quite quickly, the constable grumbling because he had almost reached the end of his shift.

'So you're on overtime,' said the detective sergeant in the back, Parminter squeezed between himself and his colleague.

'There's a motorbike following us,' said the driver.

The detective constable turned in the rear seat.

'One of ours?' asked the uniformed constable.

'We didn't ask for an escort,' said the detective sergeant. 'How long's he been there?'

The driver's eyes were in his mirror, tracking the single headlight. 'A while.'

Now the detective sergeant turned. 'Slow down, let's have a look at him.'

The engine note changed. Parminter had become agitated.

'Settle down, Gerald,' said the detective sergeant.

'It may be my people,' Parminter blurted. 'They won't want me answering questions.'

'Oh, you mean Moscow? You think they've got one of their satellites homed in on Gloucester nick? Be your age Gerald, they've got better things to look at. You know, missile sites, Polaris, that sort of stuff.'

'He's been on the telly tonight,' said the constable in the front. 'Nine o'clock news. Cheltenham reckon that one of the blokes who did him over when he gave himself up made a few quid by 'phoning the TV and the papers.'

'Go faster!' Parminter almost shouted.

'He's matching us,' said the driver.

'Put on the lights and pull over,' ordered the detective sergeant.

'No!' yelled Parminter.

'You're in a police-car, Gerald, with four coppers. Settle down.'

As the car halted, blue lights flashing, the beat of the motorcycle engine grew then was upon them, moving fast.

'Pull him in,' the detective sergeant ordered and the car leapt forward, making ground quickly despite the narrow road. The police driver blipped his siren and lighted his stop sign. The motorcyclist drew over to the side of the road.

'There you are, Gerald,' said the detective sergeant. 'You're

113

even getting to see a bit of police work first-hand. Apart from your own problem, that is.'

Someone in the car chuckled.

'Go see to him,' the detective sergeant told the constable.

'What can I have him for? He wasn't speeding.'

'Suspicious behaviour on a public highway. Whatever you like. You just want to see his licence, don't you?'

It was very dark with no houses in the immediate vicinity. The car's headlights held the rider in their beams as he sat astride the motorcycle, not turning back but searching inside his leather jacket, presumably for his papers.

The constable strolled forward, his movements made to seem jerky by the strobe-effect caused by the swirling blue lights. He stopped beside the rider and saw the black automatic held in the left hand, flat against the leather jacket, blocked from backward view by the stocky body. The rider wore an out-of-date protective helmet with leather sides and a heavy chin-strap under the pudding-basin dome. The constable was reminded of a photograph of a World War Two dispatch rider he had once seen. A dark scarf masked the rider's mouth and nose under the helmet but his words were utterly clear:

'The one in the breech is dum-dummed. It isn't meant for you so don't be a hero.'

'Oh shit,' murmured the constable.

'We walk back to the car, you behind me like everything's normal. They won't see the gun but it'll be ready. You do anything and I'll kill you. Now ask me for my licence.'

The constable blinked, then cleared his throat, his fear evident. 'Can I see your licence?'

'Tell me to take it out of the wallet.'

Again he cleared his throat, the saliva dried up in his mouth. 'Will you take it out of the wallet, please.'

'Look at it then ask me to accompany you back to the car.'

The eyes under the peaked cap went down to the licence obediently. A piece of paper had been stuck over the details.

'Keep the licence in your hands where they can see it, now ask me.'

The constable stared blankly.

'Ask me to come back with you. Do it!'

'Uh, will you accompany me to the police vehicle, please?

114

You're supposed to switch off the engine.'

'No. Let's go.'

Jack Cade dismounted, lowering the stand first, then walked·toward the bright beams and the flashing blue lights, the constable a little behind him to his left. The driver had his window down and his head protruding. 'What's the problem?' he asked then saw the Browning come out from beneath the unzipped leather jacket.

'Switch off,' said Cade and heard the slight rise of the engine note. 'Don't try it!' His arm had gripped the constable, pulling him in close, the automatic digging deep into the uniform tunic. 'Chuck the keys out as far as you can.' The engine note ceased leaving only the slightly uneven beat of the old Triumph as the only sound in the night air.

Parminter was sobbing, doubled over between his two escorts.

Cade said. 'Straighten him up.'

'No,' said the detective constable, seated nearest Cade in the rear.

The police radio came to life and they all looked toward the sound – except Cade.

'Was that your call-sign?' he asked the driver.

The officer looked into Cade's eyes and decided against lying. 'No.'

'Pull out your mike – all the way.' ·

The driver tugged at the cord. It was stronger than he expected.

'Both hands,' Cade suggested, then when it was done said, 'Chuck it.'

Parminter was howling, a muffled, wet sound, down low from the floor of the car. A foul stench came from him but no one commented on it.

'Straighten him up,' Cade repeated.

The blue lights on top of the patrol-car continued to swirl, giving Cade's figure an unreal quality, and perhaps the men in the car felt this for they sat unmoving, like unwilling participants in someone else's nightmare.

'Please!' the uniformed constable uttered, as the Browning jabbed harder at him.

The detective sergeant leaned forward and down to get a

better look at Cade's eyes. He hesitated only momentarily then dragged Parminter up by his hair.

'No!' his CID colleague shouted, tugging at Parminter

'He means it. It's this bastard or us – and if you want to chuck your life away for this scum then you go ahead.'

Parminter was almost upright and struggling. The Browning swung inward and blasted, the ejected casing striking the roof lining. The interior of the car reeked sharply of cordite and the smell of burning. Parminter stared at his lower abdomen, speechless and dribbling, on that razor-edge between shock and agony. The zip-fly on his trousers was smouldering. He shrieked with a sound more animal than human, projecting himself forward almost into the front seats, vomiting.

The detective constable, white and beaded with sweat, repeated 'Jesus!' over and over.

Cade began pulling the uniformed constable toward the front of the car.

'Please no!' the man blurted, misreading Cade's intentions.

'You're all right,' said Cade.

Parminter's demented shrieks continued from inside the car. Cade fired one round into the patrol-car's radiator which erupted with released steam then, his forearm clamped firmly around the constable's throat, placed a round in each front tyre.

'I need time,' he explained in a tight voice to the half-choked man, then led him toward the motor bike.

One rear door of the car flew open and Parminter leapt out, either by his own volition or thrown. From the off-side the detective constable dropped onto the road and was sick. The detective sergeant stepped slowly from the vehicle, his eyes fixed on Cade and his hostage as if debating some action but turned to Parminter who was lying on the grass verge doubled over, head touching his knees, screaming for release. His lower back looked like a red pulp.

'*You fucking dum-dummed it!*' the detective sergeant roared.

'*He goes the hard way!*' Cade shouted back, for the first time losing his cold balance.

The detective sergeant kicked at the ground then at the car. '*And we're stuck out here to listen to him die!*'

116

Cade heaved his hostage away and leapt on the bike, the detective sergeant running at him hard – but it was a futile gesture. The officer ran until he collapsed to his knees then buckled over to all fours, sucking in air, the motorcycle only a sound in the distance. He got up and began walking forward, there was no point in going back, there wasn't a telephone behind him for miles.

Jack Cade had seen the news of Gerald Parminter's unexpected appearance at Cheltenham police headquarters on television. Couched in careful terms, the news item simply stated that a man had approached police there, claiming responsibility for the death of Susan Franks. The foray in the station reception area was mentioned only as an incident which had taken place at the same time but no connection was confirmed excepting that the man in question was involved.

Seated with both Sullivans in their comfortable living room, he had watched impassively while listening intently for every detail, but little more was forthcoming. Cade knew police procedure very well from his time in the Special Air Service Regiment and was certain that Parminter would be transferred to Gloucester where the crime had been perpetrated to be interrogated by murder squad detectives.

He announced that he felt like a late-night spin on the Triumph and, after listening attentively to Lettie Sullivan's pleas to be careful and her brother's aside of 'going bloody bonkers over a piece of machinery', set off fast for Gloucester. When he arrived, with the eye of an expert he chose the best watcher's position and settled down for a long wait. In his past, he had been renowned for his ability to withstand the immobility and boredom of covert static surveillance; quite simply, he just switched off.

For once in his life he had no plan, simply the very firm intention that Parminter must die at his hand – with the maximum amount of pain. The means was inside the leather jacket, a little tight and long in the arms, which had belonged to Lettie's dead, illegitimate son. It had taken no more than five minutes, before leaving the farm, to unclip the flat stainless-steel box from the underside of the camper, brush off the accumulated dirt which concealed it from everything

117

except the most searching examination, and remove the 9 mm Browning automatic and two magazines — one of these containing jacketed rounds and the other soft-nosed lead bullets. He had then dum-dummed one of the lead rounds, pumped it into the breech, then fitted the jacketed magazine in place.

He watched numerous patrol-cars exit the station but none contained the pattern of occupants he was hoping for: three in the rear and probably two up front — the rear seat passengers almost certainly wearing civilian clothes, his target in the centre. There was no way he could be certain that Parminter would be taken from the station that evening but he thought it probable that he might be escorted to his home to assist in a search of the house — and Cade knew that address from the information Harlow had given him.

He was beginning to consider the unwelcome possibility of more drastic action the next day when a patrol-car emerged with the configuration of occupants he was watching for. He moved fast to reach the Triumph, almost losing the patrol-car because he was staying far back, fully expecting them to head toward the A40 and Cheltenham. Their unexpected route threw him and he had to catch up quickly, perhaps getting too close at times, but he quickly realized that they were probably heading for where the murder had taken place, or somewhere where Parminter had hidden vital evidence.

The events which had followed seemed unreal to him, a dream, satisfying yet disturbing, which, when he finally returned to the farm, left him feeling stranded without purpose in a surreal world. He parked the motorcycle, then sat on the floor of the disused stable in the straw, wondering if he had tipped over the edge of sanity. The risks he had taken were enormous — his training should have rejected them out of hand — yet there he was, shaking and hazy, but nevertheless *there*. And it had been done. He realized that he was disappointed. He was experiencing the flat, purposeless, feeling of anticlimax. His Amy was still dead, and a man who was both child-killer and traitor was probably still lying curled around his exploded abdomen, miles from nowhere, screaming for someone to finish him. So what? Amy was still dead. If he had no purpose now, then he may as well be dead also.

'You all right?' asked Will Sullivan, his torch capturing

118

Cade on the cobbled floor. He wore pyjamas tucked into his gumboots and a battered sheepskin coat across his shoulders. His shotgun was in his arms, unbroken.

Cade looked up straight into the beam, then turned away.

'Had a close one?' Sullivan flicked the beam at the Triumph, surveying it for damage. 'You look pale enough for a corpse.' The torch moved back.

'I've done something. I used the bike. The police could come here, they'd have seen it – it's one they'll remember.'

'Oh-aye? Knocked someone down?'

'Nothing like that.'

'What then?'

'Better you're out of it.'

'I thought you were a rum one first time I set eyes on you. All that foreign fighting. You on the run then? That why you came here? Used us?'

Cade's head was down.

'We deserved that, did we? The lying to?'

'No!' Cade's head came up sharply. 'I came here to get the van off the roads. I stayed because I wanted to.'

'Maybe I don't believe that? Maybe you took advantage all along. Especially of my Lettie. She took to you and you knew it. The motorcycle – she let you use it – more'n she's done for anyone in my recall. You tell me what you've done lad and maybe I can stop the urge I have to hurt.'

The beam was fixed rigidly on Cade. 'They'll come here – you're better off not knowing.'

'I'll be the one to decide. You just say what has to be said.'

'I killed a man. He deserved to die.'

'You make your own laws?'

'The law would have gone soft on him.'

'Aye, nowadays it does that – but it's still the law of this land. This man – how'd he wrong you?'

'He killed a child.'

Sullivan's chin lifted. 'Ah, that one. Did it for your girl, did you? He the one who killed her?'

Cade shrugged.

'How'd you do it?'

'I shot him.' Cade reached for the Browning inside the leather jacket and laid it on the straw between his legs. He

119

squinted into the beam of the torch, catching the oiled glint of double-barrels. 'Is that thing pointed at me?'

'Roughly your direction. Where'd you get that? Lifted it when you got demobbed?'

'More or less.'

Sullivan fell silent, shifting his position so that he leant against the door-frame. He crooked the gun over his arm and lit his battered pipe. It was the first time Cade could see his face behind the beam. The eyes bore dull resignation.

'You reckon they'll trace the motorcycle? Registered a long time ago, y'know. Not taxed, never been off this land. Not since the boy died.'

'They'll track it down in the end.'

'Oh-aye, they've got those computer machines to do all the work for them. Not too long before all our brains dry up, I reckon. Better stand up, lad, I don't like a grown man to be on the ground like that – not seemly. Just you push that weapon over with your foot.'

Cade obeyed. 'So what now?'

'Well, lad, it's her that I worry about really. She's going to break in two if she sees the police coming to cart you off. Still thinks there's hanging. Better she doesn't see that. I reckon you should get in that foreign van and drive off this land – then you can go and lay your troubles on some other folk. That's the best thing all around.'

'I'll go now.'

'Not just yet. What else you involved in? You came to hide here before you killed that feller tonight.'

'I can't tell you that.'

'You've told me enough to put you away already.'

'This is beyond the police.'

'Nothing is beyond the police, son – they're the law.'

'Sometimes the law lies to itself.'

'You into something political? Only politicians can hide their lies behind the law.'

'Just don't ask, okay. Stay out of it.'

Sullivan studied the hard man before him. 'Aye, reckon I'll do that. That van of yours working now?'

'It's working.'

'Then you'd best be off.'

Cade pulled himself up.

They walked across the yard, Sullivan behind, and into the barn.

'You have everything of yours, then? Nothing left inside the house?'

Cade nodded and started the Volkswagen's engine. Straw swirled around Sullivan's upright figure: he lifted his hand to his face to protect his eyes then waved Cade backwards. In the yard he came up to the window and handed Cade the Browning. 'Maybe what you did tonight was wrong – maybe in this soft world it was right. Lettie would say it was right – probably I would too – but our opinion doesn't make the law, does it? It's only powerful people get to make that. I'll tell you something, son, you're straight, I can see that – so could she – so I don't mind saying, go well. I don't wish you harm – no matter if you deceived us. You just remember, if you're doing something for those powerful folks who make the laws then bend them for their own purposes – maybe even break them – then it's easy enough for them to break you too. Keep that in mind. You best be off now.' He slapped the side of the camper and Cade looked directly into his eyes for a few moments then nodded.

'I'll remember. Tell Lettie . . .'

'I'll tell her you decided it was best to go back to your wife. She'll be pleased with that. Thinks life's a storybook – full of happy endings. 'Cept her own.'

Cade pressed the accelerator and was gone.

Will Sullivan walked back into the stable and moved the motorcycle into one of the two disused stalls. He stopped, took his sheepskin coat from around his shoulders and thrust his arms into the sleeves, buttoning it against the night chill, then hefted a pitchfork from a corner and began covering the Triumph with straw.

Gerald Parminter took some time to die. The police later calculated that from the time the detective sergeant had located a telephone until the arrival of an ambulance, and almost enough patrol-cars for a major disaster, the time elapsed had been a few minutes more than three-quarters of an hour. Which gave Parminter that period, plus another twenty minutes, before he expired – a surfeit of life he would gladly have passed over, had he been given the option.

'Right, recriminations later,' stated the Senior Investigating Officer, one Felix Aske, a CID detective inspector. 'The most promising factor is the motorcycle used by this assassin. The driver of the patrol-car, who apparently has an interest in classic vehicles, swears that it was a Triumph Bonneville. Says he used to ride one in his early days. This one appeared to be in perfect condition. Maroon. I want a check made on every machine of that type and colour in Gloucestershire and the surrounding counties. Given that the first the killer might have known of Parminter's detention was on the nine o'clock TV news, I doubt very much that he could have travelled to the point at which he struck from much further afield.'

'Why not try Moscow, guvnor?' suggested the dishevelled detective sergeant who had been in charge of Parminter's interrogation, his jacket and trousers still stained with blood and other body fluids.

'Special Branch are looking into this supposed Russian connection, DS Nash. And I'll thank you to omit the sarcasm. If you had taken more notice of your suspect's admission to being an espionage agent for a foreign power – and his concern regarding possible hostile acts against him by them – we might at this moment have had a double result: convictions for the assault and murder of a child – and espionage.'

'Come on, guvnor? They'll say anything when they're in the hot-seat. You've heard the lot in your time.'

'I would not have taken a man who had just confessed to twenty years of spying for the Russians out onto the streets, at night with no escort, until I had spoken to and had clearance from a representative of the Special Branch. Nor for that matter should you have done. Isn't it about time you and DC Morris got out of those soiled clothes? Do you realize what you smell like?'

'Like shit,' said the detective constable. 'Feel like it as well. We should have done something.'

'Oh yeah? What? Had our guts blown out as well?' asked Nash.

'That's enough, Nash. I said, recriminations later. Let's get the blighter first, shall we?'

122

'Bleedin' Charles Bronson,' muttered Nash. 'I wondered how long before the effing Yanks turned someone over here into a vigilante.'

Aske seemed interested by this. 'So you don't think it was political?'

'Political my arse. Guvnor, this was *personal*. I looked right into his eyes. Believe me it was personal.'

'So, someone who knew Parminter?'

'Not that kind of personal. Personal like in revenge.'

'A relative of a child Parminter could have attacked previously? All right, I'll go with you on that line. Get records to search out details of previous assaults on young kiddies – start with the recent ones where a relative could still be angry enough to kill – again Gloucestershire and then the neighbouring counties. Maybe we can tie the motorbike to a relative.'

Two men in plain clothes entered. One said. 'He was for real. The house gave us enough to have him inside for forty years. The lot! Short-wave receiver, tape-recorder, subminiature camera – even a nice briefcase, leather job, handtooled – complete with false bottom. Shame we had to rip it apart, could have done with it myself. Oh yes – those things in his wallet – little pads printed like a grid? One-time pads, standard Soviet issue. Someone should have got a bit curious when they spotted those, shouldn't they?'

'We're not all James Bond,' said DS Nash to the Special Branch officer.

'Not all that good at straight police work either, I'd say.'

Nash rose quickly and menacingly.

'That's enough of that!' Aske snapped. 'Thank you for the information. We'll see to our end and leave you with the politics.'

The Special Branch officer shook his head. 'This one gets kicked straight at the Security Service. We're out.'

Aske seemed curious. 'They're involved already?'

'They've taken over.'

'It must be serious.'

'Serious? He worked inside GCHQ. You can't get more serious than that.'

Aske nodded. 'Well, I expect you've still an interest in the killer. He might be political.'

'Definitely.'

'DS Nash sees him as a revenge killer. Relative of the murdered child or some other Parminter might have attacked.'

The Special Branch officer raised his eyebrows, glanced sideways at his colleague and smiled. 'Your average dad with a 9 mm Browning, cool as you like, takes out a patrol-vehicle and scares four cops shitless? So much in command of one hell of a hairy situation that he doesn't loose off any extra bullets except one dum-dum soft-nose for the suspect and three jacketed rounds for the vehicle? And that's a story all by itself. That must be one hell of a father some kid has got out there. Better get him in to train some of our lads. If you ever catch him without losing half the division.'

'So where would you start looking?' Nash put in acidly – but interested.

'Where they train people to perform that well in that sort of situation.'

'Back to Moscow again.'

'Not necessarily. There's a whole regiment of them not a million miles from here.'

'Hereford? The SAS?' Nash queried, incredulously.

'Correct. Any one of them could do the job with their balaclava helmets on backwards.'

'Get on to it, Nash,' Aske ordered. 'Fathers of children up to the age of, what, fifteen? After that they're women nowadays.'

'Plenty before that,' commented the second Special Branch officer.

'Start with those men with the youngest children. Doesn't have to be a direct involvement of course, could just be someone who decided to do something and was expert enough to have pulled it off. We want the names of men who were off base within the hours in question and solid back-up for their movements. Don't forget the motorbike, it's distinctive. Someone ought to try the motorcycle clubs. DC Morris, you get moving on the civilian side. However unlikely it might seem, there is still the possibility that a man out there was desperate enough – and perhaps disturbed enough – to have carried out the killing. We'll leave the political side to the Security Service.'

Aske gave the two Special Branch officers a grateful nod. 'Thanks for your help. We really need it.'

124

'How much heat are you getting from upstairs?'

Aske looked grim. 'Any more and I'd ignite.'

Nash said, 'I'll get moving, guvnor.'

The second Special Branch officer shook his head. 'I think it might save a lot of time if I pointed out that there's no way that DC Nash is going to be allowed carte blanche with SAS personnel records. They won't give him anything that way. You have no name, which means Nash will have to view all the service records of the Regiment's strength, present and past. I can promise you they won't allow him to do that, not without clearance from someone at the top. And I don't mean the Chief Constable. *The* top. SAS personnel records are classified as military secrets.'

'Then we'll go to the top,' said Aske, tightly. 'This is a murder investigation with espionage involvement. That means we can claim Defence of the Realm. We'll get those records.'

'That's the way, guvnor,' said Nash.

'That's not the way, sir. Members of the SAS are a protected species. You'll get tied up in red tape and blocked by stalling until you're so pissed off you'll give up. There's a right and a wrong way of dealing with the SAS. The wrong way is how you're approaching it now. You want a sight of their records without an identity to go on? Forget it. But if you want a favour – a chat say with their CO or someone who'll co-operate – well, there's a better route.'

'Which is?' Aske asked, not pleased by the thought of having to resort to unofficial channels.

'Okay, first you instigate a search with Criminal Records – just to show you're following procedures. Give them a profile – they've got computer-headings to narrow the field – then while they burrowing away you ask one of us to call our colleague at Cheltenham who, in the line of business, is on drinking terms with the SAS Unit Intelligence Officer at Hereford. If they're talking at the moment we get him to arrange for DC Nash, or whoever, to get into Stirling Lines and discuss the problem nice and friendly.'

'We're not after favours. This is police business. We have the right to pursue our enquiries by all possible means.'

'It's worth a try, guvnor,' put in Nash.

Aske considered for a moment. 'Well, perhaps, if it's going

to save police time, we could ask Cheltenham SB to help out.'

'Right,' said the first Special Branch officer and left with his colleague.

A chief-superintendent walked in, his face displaying his mood. 'I hope there's some action going on around here,' he snapped as they came to their feet. 'I've just had the Chief Constable on the 'phone and he wants me to let you all know that losing a prisoner in custody – permanently – is a crime he would recommend the death penalty for.'

'We're following every avenue, sir,' said Aske.

'Well, I hope for your sakes you get onto the bloody highway damn quickly. This incident has all the hallmarks of a political hurricane – and they usually destroy a few careers when they really get going. Find that killer, *and soon*, before we're all part of the great unemployed!'

Cade knew that the road blocks would be out, securing the county borders. He felt certain that he would be allowed through them without problem, but the VW camper might still be on the computers as a suspicious vehicle. He decided to play safe and found a field with a five-bar gate and drove in, tucking the van against the tall hedgerow. In the dark the van was invisible and he did not intend to be there much after first light. If the farmer was a really early riser, and caught him, he would admit to trespassing, say he was worn out driving and thought it unsafe to leave the van in the narrow country lane. He would have to talk his way out of it. Anything was better than facing a bunch of suspicious coppers who had just had one of their prisoners gut-shot.

He stretched out on the cushions in the rear of the camper, hands behind his head, and stared through the window at the stars. Back in Oman, in the seventies, he would lie on his back in some jebel watching the night sky for hours but never with the feeling of being small and vulnerable which blanketed him now.

'So get on with it,' he murmured aloud, then thought: There's no going back, there's only going forward. See to Number Four and it's all over. Then hit the road and keep on going. Maybe he would go back to the desert and the mountains. Why stick around? England – he never thought in terms of Britain – had blown it. It was like him: a good past turned rotten, a lousy present and a bloody shaky future.

He reached down to the locker for the second file in the envelope Harlow had given him. 'That's the last two,' Harlow had said. 'Get it over with and get out – quickly. And no mess, please.' That's a laugh, Cade thought, a picture of Parminter *in extremis* in his mind.

He used his small pencil-torch to examine the second, sealed, file. The beam picked out the usual three identifying photographs of the target, full-face and both profiles. The woman was very attractive despite the official, non-smiling poses. Reddish hair, a full mouth and deep eyes. *Alive*. In her thirties, but young.

Cade closed the file and his eyes.

After a while he re-opened both and began reading until finally, deeply troubled, he replaced it in its hiding place and tried, with little success, to get some sleep. In a brief dream he saw himself killing Maurice Blaikley's mother.

He awoke to the sound of hammering on the roof of the camper and jerked himself upright.

The heavy rain made the dawn sombre and dark but one glance at his watch told him that he had overslept for far too long. In haste, he drove the van out of the field, slithering wildly in the loose soil. On the hard surface of the lane once more he floored the accelerator, forgetting the open gate, and headed for London.

The Prime Minister received the report on Gerald Parminter on Saturday morning just after her usual meagre breakfast. The Security Service officer who gave her the news of Parminter's proven involvement in espionage left Downing Street holding the opinion that she had accepted the alarming revelations more with resignation than alarm. He was, however, convinced that she had been deeply shocked by the unexpected, and possibly professional, killing of the GCHQ spy. In the event he did not pass on these observations, fully aware that in his profession there were often wheels within wheels and he had no intention of being run down by any of them.

After the MI5 officer had left, the Prime Minister began placing telephone calls to those people she had chosen to advise of Weidenstein's revelation. She was glad that it was the weekend and that Number Ten was quiet with only the usual skeleton staff on duty. When this was done she called William Salisbury, remembering that his superior, the Co-ordinator of Intelligence to the Cabinet Office, was in Northern Ireland that weekend.

Salisbury wasted no time in getting to Downing Street from his Kensington address, his usual high confidence shattered. He had himself made a telephone call before leaving his home but this did nothing to lift his spirits. Grey had confirmed that he too had been summoned.

He found the Prime Minister in the Cabinet Room, at the centre of the long table, under the painting of Walpole above the fireplace. Unusually she was without any of the red dispatch boxes which seemed so much a part of her, having only a note-pad, sparsely notated. Her mood was distant, preoccupied, even guarded, which did nothing for Salisbury's already frayed nerves.

Quickly she passed on the Security Service's findings, adding wearily that it was she who had voiced the fear to Salisbury that Parminter – although at the time she had not known his name – was employed at GCHQ. Then she said:

'How long can we keep the espionage factor away from the media?'

'We can't, not entirely. Parminter was an employee of GCHQ as you feared, Prime Minister. The media will have that news by lunchtime – if they haven't got hold of it already. The story of his killing has been on the morning radio news – no mention of his job, just referring to his confession to the murder of the child. But the dam won't hold – you know what they're like once they sense scandal: if they can't find it, they'll invent it.'

'I want you to arrange for a D-Notice on the reporting of any aspect of this case which does not involve the murder of the child.'

'The editors will fight it – once they have the GCHQ connection they'll not let go.'

'The Security Service are currently carrying out an investigation – use that to hold them back.'

'I'll try.'

'How long before we can get a reasonably accurate assessment of the damage done by this dreadful man?'

'If Parminter were still alive, Prime Minister, it might be relatively easy – assuming he would have been willing to co-operate – but now that he is dead the Security Service will have to go back a long way. Twenty years, you said, according to his confession? To be quite honest I think it's unlikely that we'll ever know the full extent of his treachery.'

'Perhaps time will be an advantage in this case. Politically.'

'Yes, Prime Minister.'

'Do you believe that the KGB engineered the killing?'

'Who else, Prime Minister?'

'I've talked with the Chief Constable of Gloucestershire. His men are working on a theory that the killer was highly trained –'

'Which would confirm KGB involvement,' Salisbury interrupted.

She gave him a look of annoyance. 'Let me finish. He pointed out that Hereford is relatively close to Gloucester.'

'The SAS? That's ridiculous!' Salisbury could feel cold sweat prickling his body. His shirt felt chill against his skin.

'Why? They may be highly trained but some are also fathers, brothers, uncles to children. The police believe that the motive might be revenge. They are in contact now with Stirling Lines to see if any of the Regiment's strength have been close to or directly connected with a situation involving assault or murder of a child.'

'I see. Well, it is a theory.'

'And a plausible one.'

'I don't agree Prime Minister. The men of the SAS are trained *not* to react under stress. That is what makes them the best in the world.'

She fell silent and tapped her pen on the cabinet table for a few moments. 'Perhaps you're right – but I wonder if anyone can guarantee the reactions of any human being who has lost a child in such a terrible way? I doubt very much if my own thoughts would not, at some stage, be very dark indeed.' She stood up and smoothed the skirt of her navy blue costume. 'I've summoned members of the Inner Cabinet for a crisis meeting this morning. If you receive any new information from the Security Service I want to be told immediately. You may interrupt the meeting if it is essential.'

Outside the Cabinet Room in the cheerless ante-chamber, Salisbury, to his astonishment, was confronted by the waiting figure of Simon Adeane.

'What the devil are you doing here?' he demanded. 'This is highly irregular.'

Adeane appeared thrown. 'When I saw you come out I thought you'd just been briefed. Urgent message for your leader as promised at last night's meeting – don't ask what it is because if she hasn't briefed you, I can't tell you.'

'I see. Look, sorry if I was abrupt, had to cancel plans for the weekend – my wife was not amused, thinks I've got another woman. I have.' Salisbury tipped his head at the double doors. 'How about another lunch on the US Treasury soon?'

Adeane gave a wry grin. 'If we're still allowed to fraternize.'

Salisbury frowned but did not pursue the American's curious comment. 'You'll have to be in and out damn quickly, she's expecting the heavy end of the Cabinet any second.' He walked out, leaving Adeane by the double doors, and wondering with increasing trepidation, what, exactly, was going on?

A dreadful realization began to spread through him. Max Weidenstein was controlling the British end of the American betrayal. If that were the case, how was the Prime Minister involved? The ramifications were too hideous to contemplate. And Grey had been summoned! In a moment of panic which he barely brought under control, Salisbury seriously contemplated clearing his desk and running. He soon realized that he had nowhere to run to. Ironically, if he were one of the network, he thought, he could defect.

Then he remembered Cade and thanked God he was not.

Chapter Seven

The Prime Minister sat at the great coffin-shaped cabinet table, in her usual place, under the ornate clock on the mantelpiece. On her right sat the Cabinet Secretary, arguably the most powerful man in the realm and certainly the best-informed. Opposite, were seated the Foreign Secretary, the Home Secretary, the Lord Chancellor and the Secretary of State for Defence.

'I'll get right to the point,' she began tersely. 'At eleven o'clock last night I received a telephone call from the American President. He informed me – without details – of a clandestine operation being run in this country by their National Security Agency which had just been revealed to him. He told me that he was sending me the London-based controller of this operation to give me full details. I met him in the early hours this morning and what he has told me will make it quite clear why I have called this meeting. Quite simply our greatest ally has betrayed us and has been doing so for some time. These are the facts: Up until this time we have been led to believe the American Strategic Defence Initiative, the so-called 'Star Wars' system which we have given our backing to on the basis of receiving manufacturing and research contracts ourselves, has been in a very early, and failure-prone, experimental stage. This is simply not true – SDI is well advanced. Also, we were informed, when the concept was originally discussed, that this space-age defence system was one option available and emphatically not the central point of any future defence policy. It now seems that they are concentrating their major defence effort on SDI.'

The Foreign Secretary broke in: 'This explains the Soviet hard-line stance on SDI. Presumably the KGB have uncovered American intentions? But I'd hardly call this news a betrayal – the Americans are not bound to reveal to us the full extent of their forward defence planning.'

'Let me finish. As we are aware, the KGB have concentrated their efforts on the advanced technology of the system. With this in mind, certain powerful men in Washington – without the President's knowledge – formed a plan to nullify the Soviet Intelligence effort. Or in the words of the man I met last night: To put the KGB to sleep. This they have done most successfully. Unfortunately at great cost to ourselves.'

Her words were received with silence, her ministers' familiar with her temperament and none seeming prepared to interrupt again.

She continued: 'A long-term disinformation operation was planned by this small but powerful Washington cabal. The prime objective needed to implement it was the recruitment of a senior Soviet agent operating in a highly sensitive post who could be turned against her masters.'

'Her?' blurted the Lord Chancellor, involuntarily, his thick eyebrows raised high.

The Prime Minister ignored the interruption. 'They were supplied with the names of a deep-penetration network by a senior KGB officer who defected to the Americans around two years ago – a defection we were not informed of.'

'It seemed they've informed us of very little, Prime Minister,' said the Defence Secretary, cuttingly, his colleagues surprised by his rashness.

She agreed with a tight nod. 'All their efforts were aimed at the one member of this network whose recruitment to the Soviet cause was motivated by financial gain. I know that it would appear that sucn an agent would be the least trusted by the Kremlin but the fact of the matter is that she – yes it is a woman – is so well-placed that the results of her spying could not be ignored. Her lack of sound ideological commitment was dismissed – her product outweighed this. Once the woman was bought, it was imperative to the Americans that the disinformation she passed on must be believed. To achieve this it was essential that her product did not drop either in

132

quantity or quality. In other words she should continue to supply her masters in Moscow with nothing less than her previous established output.'

'Dear God,' murmured the Foreign Secretary, 'she's one of our people.'

'One of our top people,' admitted the Prime Minister. 'The agent in question is the personal assistant to the Director of GCHQ.'

'Shades of West Germany,' muttered the Home Secretary, heavily.

'Dear God,' breathed the Foreign Secretary.

'So the Russians have our codes, our frequencies – everything?' asked the Cabinet Secretary.

'They have a great deal. At this stage I cannot confirm just how much they know. Washington are going to inform us as soon as they are able.'

'Prime Minister,' said the Defence Secretary. 'Surely the amount of damage must be very limited. GCHQ is so closely connected with the American National Security Agency that the Americans would be damaging themselves if they allowed too much to be passed on.'

'A point I considered, but I was informed that the degree of information-sharing was pared to a level which would stop any real damage being done – as far as the Americans are concerned, that is. Our information was not subject to such monitoring I regret to say.'

'I'm reassured by the fact that the President was not involved,' said the Defence Secretary. 'If he were the crisis would be monumental.'

'With respect, Defence Secretary,' said the Cabinet Secretary, 'your pro-American feelings must not allow you to underestimate the gravity of this situation. Whether the President is involved or not, does not dismiss the fact that irretrievable damage has been done to our national security. I have advised for a long time that the American President does not have total control of his Administration. Their system is not based on collective responsibility as ours is; because of this, the President may well be unaware of a power-group making and implementing independent decisions right under his nose – the FBI and CIA under Kennedy are proven examples – but

133

nevertheless an aware President should make it his duty to be on top of these matters.'

'We're not here to discuss the merits or de-merits of the American system of government,' said the Prime Minister testily, cutting short an extension of the long-standing disagreement between the two men.

'Of course, my apologies,' said the Cabinet Secretary, glancing sharply at the Defence Secretary who shrugged his broad shoulders.

The Home Secretary grabbed the chance to speak: 'Presumably the President has given orders to have this operation terminated?'

The Prime Minister looked down at her pad but found nothing there which could save her from giving the only answer possible. 'No,' she admitted, then raising her voice, cut short the inevitable protests. 'The question we are here to answer is whether it will be to our advantage to let this operation continue? Please listen to what I have to say! Damage – *considerable damage* – has been done. Of *course* it has. But it is possible that now we have full knowledge of the facts we could make use of this disinformation channel to the Kremlin ourselves. Perhaps we can reverse, or at least minimize the damage.'

'How on earth can that be done, Prime Minister?' asked the Lord Chancellor.

'That would be up to the Secret Intelligence Service. The SIS have people whose entire lives are geared to fabricating disinformation. They should at least be given the chance to use this woman themselves. God knows the Russians and the Americans have been using her long enough.'

'I'm not sure I would trust a whore who has sold herself twice over already,' muttered the Home Secretary.

The Prime Minister frowned disapprovingly. 'Whatever description she might deserve we must only address ourselves to the question of whether or not we wish to use her. For obvious reasons I would prefer that decision to be taken only by those present in this room. I don't believe that circulating this information further will serve any purpose whatsoever.'

The Cabinet Secretary turned to her. 'Constitutionally, this is extremely dangerous ground. Forgive me, Prime Minister, but if your party lose the coming general election then the incoming Prime Minister will have to be informed of the full facts. He may well feel, after hearing them, that this is not a legacy he would wish to accept. He might indeed decide to reveal the matter to the House.'

'Defence Secretary?' queried the Prime Minister, seeing him lean forward in reaction to these words.

'I would say that any Prime Minister – of whatever party – would be in no position to make political capital from this issue.'

The Cabinet Secretary snapped back angrily: 'I did not suggest it would be done for political capital! Conscience alone is sufficient reason for such a disclosure. Safeguarding the defence of the realm is another.'

The Defence Secretary laid his hands on the long table. 'I was going on to say that there is, perhaps, a greater issue at stake here? Perhaps even a greater conspiracy? Has no one considered that the Kremlin might *know* that such an operation is in progress and chooses to do nothing about it?'

'To what end?' asked the Cabinet Secretary, archly.

'I must admit I don't follow you,' agreed the Prime Minister.

The Defence Secretary settled back in his seat. 'Whether or not the Russians believe the present lack of advancement in the SDI programme might well be academic. In any event, the actual implementation of such a high-technology defence umbrella must be years off. It is simply not possible for the Americans to be so far advanced that they could begin placing the hardware in space within the next decade. The logistics – which my staff have studied in depth – dictate this. And I am discounting research, physical testing programmes, etcetera. The loss of the space shuttle is another delaying factor. I submit that the Russians may be after a more immediate prize.'

'Which would be?' questioned the Prime Minister.

'The destruction of Anglo-American relations. The end of the so-called "special relationship". Prime Minister, if you were forced, you would have to admit that one overriding reason for not immediately demanding that this operation be halted, is the fact that we would then have to arrest the woman in question and of course the rest of the spy-ring. Which would of course mean a trial and subsequent public exposure of the

135

entire plot. Soviet and American. The public outcry and the resulting political furore would be such that it would destroy our relationship with the Americans for a very long time indeed.

'In realistic terms, the rift might be healed by time – but mutual trust would no longer exist at the same level between our two countries. My point, Cabinet Secretary, about any incoming Prime Minister not being in any position to make political capital out of this issue is based on this argument: his position would be no different to the one we find ourselves in at this moment. This secret would pass from government to government, and like Pandora's Box, none would dare unlock it.

'Now, I don't enjoy prophesying doom but the reality here is that on the one hand the Russians stand to gain heavily if we clash with the Americans – while on the other, the Americans have us over the proverbial barrel. From now on, unless we decide to let the Americans have their victory, America will be able to control the British government – any British government – whenever that government decides not to follow Washington's line.'

They all stared at the Defence Secretary as though he were as unstable as a bomb placed in their midst.

The Foreign Secretary broke the prolonged silence: 'Are you implying that Washington may have planned this deliberately?'

'Not necessarily with this outcome in mind, no. But one does not have to own a brilliant mind to realize that such a hold could be possible under these circumstances. Let us say that perhaps this secret cabal in Washington were forced – it does not matter how – to reveal their disinformation operation to an unsuspecting President. Let us also say that certain presidential advisers – who would *have* to be given the full facts – looked at the overall picture. That's what they're there for. They would soon realize that here might be the perfect way to put the overly proud, vain, lurching-towards-socialism-British in their pockets for as long as they hold the key to their Pandora's Box. Their disadvantage and embarrassment over the issue becomes an immediate advantage – *long term*. And Russia loses in every way. If they continue to believe American disinformation, they lose. If they do not and we don't break with America, they also lose.'

The Prime Minister leaned inward to him and asked, quietly: 'And if the Russians decided to reveal that the Americans have turned one of their agents and have been using her for their own benefit whilst damaging us at the same time?'

'Who would take their claims seriously, Prime Minister? They've cried wolf too often in the past. The Americans would accuse them of lying and trail out details of all past Soviet disinformation exercises, perhaps even exposing their recent defector and have him tell the "truth" behind the Kremlin's claims?'

The Cabinet Secretary was studying him with heightened interest. 'Prime Minister, would the Secretary of State for Defence mind telling us where his well-publicized admiration for the Americans is at this moment? It seems extraordinary that someone who has gone out of his way in the past to uphold American policy and indeed to give it open support in Cabinet and Parliament, should suddenly discover that their thinking could be quite so devious?'

'Not devious,' replied the Defence Secretary. 'Pragmatic. And not hostile. They may have done what we have done over and over again throughout our history – that is, taken hold of an advantage with both hands when it has presented itself. And as far as my feelings toward the Americans are concerned? Well, let's say that all alliances are subject to review in a realistic world. We always have a choice of enemies.'

The Prime Minister said, steadily: 'You speak as if you are certain that the Americans have spotted this advantage and have already decided to use it. If you have any inside knowledge of what is going on here, Defence Secretary, you had better let us have it – immediately.'

'None whatsoever, Prime Minister. All I have done is to put forward an hypothesis. Nothing more.'

'So you have no suggestions as to how this situation might be resolved without further damaging results? Other than going along with the American operation from now on? No ideas on how to deal with your "Pandora's Box"?'

The Defence Secretary looked directly at her. He could have been alone with her in the room. 'If the matter were solely in my hands, Prime Minister, I would find a way to get hold of the

137

key to the box and throw it down the deepest pit I could find and bury it for ever.'

She settled back in her chair. 'Well, gentlemen, which course of action are we to follow? Do we throw everything into the hands of the people – and the media of course – or use this disinformation source for ourselves?'

'The first course of action is out of the question,' stated the Foreign Secretary. 'We could not allow such a rift between ourselves and the United States. Such an action would leave us in disarray. We must use this source to our own advantage.'

'I agree,' offered the Home Secretary.

'I also, I'm afraid,' said the Lord Chancellor.

'Defence Secretary? asked the Prime Minister. 'Your view?'

'From my side of Whitehall, the view would be bleak indeed without American commitment to our defence capability.'

'And your advice, Cabinet Secretary?' she asked, turning.

'My position is extremely difficult, because as things stand I shall certainly have to serve whoever is the next Prime Minister – though thankfully at my age no subsequent one – but in the short term, perhaps while SIS uses this disinformation source and we can weigh more fully the advantages or disadvantages of this horrendous situation, I would tend to advise that this matter is not put before the country at this moment in time.'

The Prime Minister arose. 'Very well. I shall inform the President that, at present, we shall not be revealing their treacherous actions – though I'll leave him in no doubt as to our feelings on the matter – and that we shall avail ourselves of their disinformation operation whenever we so choose. Of course the flow of genuine secrets must stop instantly. If the Russians have our codes then we will have to use this to our advantage. This was done very successfully during the last war so there's no reason for it not to succeed now – especially with all our technological advances in this field. Naturally I shall keep you informed of all developments.'

She bade her ministers goodbye, then, as if as an after-thought, called the Defence Secretary back from the Cabinet Room exit as the others departed.

'An unconnected matter,' she said. 'We may as well deal with it now. It won't take long.'

As she did not sit down, he too remained standing before her.

'Were you aware of three deaths involving members of GCHQ over the last nine days?'

He nodded. 'The first was a domestic accident, the second suicide and the third a shooting, last night, while the victim was in police custody.'

'But you did not consider that these deaths were worth mentioning during the meeting? GCHQ being uppermost in our minds at this moment?'

'As I recall, Prime Minister, you did not broach the subject either. Yet I assume from your initial question you had the facts before calling the meeting?' He placed his red leather-bound cabinet dispatch box on the table, reading from her note-pad – though upside down – a list of all those present at the meeting. His name bore a question-mark beside it.

She continued: 'You don't consider these – coincidental – occurrences have any bearing on what we have been discussing?'

'Should they have, Prime Minister?'

She paused. 'If you were in my position right now – and who knows, perhaps in the not-too-distant-future you may well be – would you feel that a more direct course of action might be advantageous . . . both politically and, dare I use that very unfashionable word . . . patriotically? You are, like myself, very much a patriot. Also a former, highly distinguished soldier. Perhaps, for the sake of the country, you could be tempted to take the soldier's option?'

'May I say, Prime Minister, that the historic position you hold should be protected from certain levels of decision-making.'

'An odd viewpoint. A Prime Minister is appointed to take decisions.'

'Not necessarily all. A sniper in the field with the enemy in his sights does not go to his most senior general and ask for a decision as to whether he should pull the trigger. He trusts his own judgement and does his duty as he perceives it at the time.'

'And of course his general would never know if he pulled the trigger or not?'

'There would be no need for his general to know. In any

139

war, as long as the enemy is defeated – and is seen to be defeated – the object is secured. The means are incidental, he cannot be concerned with every shot fired.'

'By *object*, I presume you mean victory? Or perhaps peace?'

'I mean that the protagonists retire and the *status quo* is restored. That, in realistic terms, is the only absolute conclusion in any war.'

'Would you hold the same views if an armistice were close?'

He smiled. 'I believe military history has proven that any armistice is only compromise brought about by the weakened position of one side or the other – thereby ensuring that one of the protagonists must lose. To win, you must defeat the enemy – which means you must stop dead his capability to destroy you.'

Under the hard cover of her note-pad was a cream-coloured envelope. She removed it and held it out, unopened. 'I believe you were looking for a key? Someone handed this in this morning. Perhaps it might fit your box?'

His eyes were steady on her face. He took the envelope. 'Thank you, Prime Minister, that will save me searching.'

After he had gone she sat down in her chair and surveyed the Cabinet Room, wondering how much longer she would be privileged to view it from that or any other position. Her sense of history was profound and she savoured the moment with pleasure – marred only by trepidation for her future.

How would she be viewed by history? As the Prime Minister who secretly allowed Britain to become the mute slave of American power? Or as a disgraced politician who used her position to sanction cold-blooded murder?

How stupid I am, she thought. Either way, no one will ever be allowed to know.

Cade reached Central London by mid-day that Saturday morning, one hour after the meeting of the Inner Cabinet at 10 Downing Street finally came to an end. He found a public telephone box in St John's Wood and called the emergency number he had been given, which as he had previously checked, was for that area. The number rang continuously without reply so he drove off in the camper to find somewhere where he could eat. In a small cafe he fed well, stopping halfway through his meal to use the pay-phone on the wall, again without result. He thought about trying the answering service – the normal procedure he had used throughout – but did not want to take the risk of being put off. Cade was determined to see Harlow or Brock and tell them his decision immediately. He paid his bill, then walked along the Edgware Road until he found a call-box which worked. This time his call was answered by a voice he did not recognize. The man informed him there was no one called Harlow at that address.

Cade said: 'Tell whoever lives there that this is Cade.'

The man, who by now Cade had decided was a servant, told him to wait and left the 'phone. Cade hung on for a long while, pressing in another coin as he held the receiver, impatiently looking around at the crowded road. A youth, dressed outlandishly and wearing make-up approached the call-box and waited impatiently.

'Don't say anything on this line,' said Colonel Henderson. 'Where are you?'

'Harlow?'

'Damn it, man, where are you?'

'Edgware Road, just outside Kilburn. Look, I don't want to do the last one, okay? Not a woman. Find someone else. You should have warned me.'

'Listen to me! It's important that we meet.'

'You won't change my mind. I won't do a woman.'

'All right! But don't say any more on this line. There are matters we must discuss, but not over the telephone. We can help you.'

Cade became wary and fell silent. The youth rapped on the glass with a studded shoulder-bag.

'You need help,' said Henderson.

'I can handle myself.'

'Cade, I assure you we're behind you in this. We'll back you all the way. Look, come here – to my London address – my home. Surely that proves we're willing to stand by you.'

'Come to your home?'

'Yes. Come now. Have you something to write with?'

'I can remember.'

Henderson gave him an address in St John's Wood. 'Leave straight away,' he said when he was done.

Cade put down the receiver and stepped outside, his mind churning.

' 'Bout time,' said the youth. 'Blew you out, did she?'

Cade looked at the painted face then down at the effeminate clothes.

'Bloody degenerate,' he said to his face and parried the blow from the studded shoulder-bag. The youth swore, falling heavily with the impetus of the swing. Cade walked away, the obscenities following him.

It took him twenty minutes to find the address Henderson had given him, a tall Edwardian house almost hidden from the street by high, green hedges. Both sides of the road were lined with cars, one of which pulled out, leaving just enough space for the camper. He switched off the engine and turned in his seat surveying the road back to the house for five minutes. He thought about the folders hidden in the back, knowing that they were both incriminating and insurance, half of him wanting to give them back the other half certain that he should retain them in case they decided that he was expendable. He got out of the camper and walked toward the house, the folders remaining hidden.

The front door was opened by a fit-looking man in his late forties whose bearing screamed British army and appraising eyes said bodyguard – despite his butler's clothes.

'I'm expected,' said Cade.

The man nodded and led him through a tiled hall to one of the doors which led off it. Henderson was inside, an iced drink in his hand.

'Thank you, Murray,' he said as the servant closed the door. 'I'm glad you came,' he said. 'Whisky? Or something else?'

'Whisky's all right.'

'You realize that half the police forces in this country are searching for you?'

'For someone. They don't know who I am.'

'You attacked a police car and shot their prisoner. Their pride is severely dented. They want whoever did it very badly indeed.'

'I'm getting out.'

'I think you'll need to – but I feel you might not want to quite yet.'

'I said I'm getting out. Forget the woman, I'm not going to do the job on her. Definite.'

'I'd like to persuade you otherwise. She is the worst of the four. The damage she has done far exceeds what the rest have accomplished all together.'

'So do her yourself. Use your own people. It's only one hit – you can cover that.'

'As we said in the beginning, the risk of leaks is too great. Leaking sensitive information has become the fashion these days as, no doubt, you've read in the newspapers.'

Cade shook his head. 'You people can do anything. You'll have to take the risk.'

Henderson passed over a generous measure of scotch, waiting while Cade took a mouthful gratefully. 'I think you needed that,' he said.

'I'll drink it, then I'm off.'

'There's some information I have which is of personal interest to you. We had it right at the beginning and were prepared to barter it for your services. As things turned out you were willing – for all the best and admirable reasons – to do what we asked without us having to bring it up.'

'You had nothing on me that you didn't tell me you knew. You read out my background like it was "This is your Life".'

'Please sit down, I'm not trying to blackmail you – that would be foolish.'

'It would be bloody stupid. Look I'm off, all right.'

'Cade, I can get you the identity of the person, persons, who tortured and killed your daughter.'

Cade put his glass down on a low table. 'Then you'd better tell me.'

'Wait. If it's in your mind to extract the information from me, please discount the idea. I said I can get you the information – but it will not be released to me until you complete the task you agreed to perform. I am deeply sorry that we have to deal with you in this way but there is no other choice in the matter. The life of the woman – a traitor to her country for no more than greed – must be extinguished. You cannot begin to understand how important this is – for your country which you love dearly as you've already proved. In exchange for her life – after it is done – I will ensure that you receive full details on your child's murderers.'

Cade shook his head and picked up his drink, swallowing it in one gulp. 'You don't know anything. This is just a try-on.'

Henderson moved closer and poured him another measure. 'I can tell you this much. You killed four youths in Northern Ireland who were undoubtedly involved with the INLA – not the IRA as you believed. This is a fact that one of MI5's informers has verified. There is no doubt at all. You were sentenced to a term in prison because . . . shall we say that your action rocked the boat at a particularly sensitive time – politically speaking. The political right of the IRA were moving, cautiously, towards a settlement with us, perhaps settlement is too strong a word, let us say an accord, which entailed their holding sway over their powerful left-wing comrades-in-arms. Your action undermined the position of those we were dealing with and a sacrifice had to be made on our part. You were that sacrifice.'

Cade sat deathly still, his knuckles bone as his fingers, clamped around the thick tumbler, tightened. 'Who butchered my daughter?'

'This much I can tell you. Two members of the Irish National Liberation Army kidnapped your daughter while you were serving your prison sentence at Winchester. They raped, tortured and finally murdered her. One of the two was – and still is – a paid informer to MI5. He reported what had been done in complete detail, pleading that he had had no choice but to go through with it. He had to obey his orders or questions might be asked about his total commitment to their cause. You know perfectly well what that might mean to someone in that heinous organization.'

'Names,' Cade demanded.

I don't know them. Nor do I have clearance to get them. Only someone of extremely high position could acquire those identities. The informer is very valuable to MI5 and every effort is made to protect him. My own position is not without power but even I am not allowed access to his identity.'

'But you know someone who can. Someone who wants the woman dead.'

'That is correct.'

144

Cade swallowed his drink. 'You get the names, I'll finish the woman.'

'After she is dead.'

'No chance. Get them now. I'll close her off first – that's the deal. I won't let you down. The other is personal. I'll do those two bastards when things quieten down – in my own time. You tell that to your man.'

'He may not believe you.'

'Make him believe me. That's my price and I want it up front.'

Henderson walked around his antique desk and sat down, staring at the telephone.

Cade lifted the receiver and gave it to him. 'Do it,' he said.

Henderson dialled, his eyes on Cade's fixed face. He waited, then said: Grey? There is a problem. Blue is-here with me. He refused to deal with the woman so I had little choice but to bring up the matter of the two identities. He wants them immediately. He has agreed to complete his task – but not until he knows the names. Very well.' He held out the receiver. 'He wishes to speak with you personally.'

Cade took it and a voice said: 'What you have already done was done well. Do I have your word that you will complete what has been started before you do whatever else you decide is necessary? Time is of the essence here.'

'Like I told him – when it's finished I'll deal with my personal business. I just want to be sure I'm not being conned, okay?' Cade listened then said: 'He wants you.'

Henderson took back the receiver. After a few moments he said: 'Very well,' and replaced the telephone.

'I know that voice,' said Cade.

'Perhaps you do,' Henderson answered, walking around the desk to kick a Persian rug aside on the parquet floor. Underneath was a sunken safe which he opened. He looked up at Cade. 'Please don't do anything hasty, there's only a file inside, I assure you. Your file.'

Cade nodded.

Henderson extracted the file and from inside took out a postcard-sized photograph. He held it out.

Cade stared at the beaming face of his daughter.

'On the reverse,' instructed Henderson.

145

Cade turned the shot over and saw two names and an address in London written in pencil. 'You had them all the time,' he accused.

'I'm sorry, I couldn't make the decision myself.' Henderson leaned over the carved desk and took an envelope from a drawer. 'Number Four is no longer at the address we gave you. In here is the new location. I must warn you that she will undoubtedly be protected, although our information is that they will be trying to keep everything looking normal.'

'How many?'

'We have not been told. All we know is that her people have arranged things so that her position is not compromised. Obviously they are more than a little disturbed by recent events so they'll want her out of harm's way for the present, but at the same time they have to make certain she can go back to her position at GCHQ without suspicion falling on her. We have no idea what type of situation they've set up, only the location, which you'll see is fairly remote. I suspect you won't find this one as easy as the others.'

'That's my problem,' said Cade, taking the envelope. 'How good is your information?'

'Perfectly sound. The directions you have in there are accurate, they were passed on to me this morning and we're certain that there will be no change in location. Remember this: she'll be guarded but almost certainly her guards will be under cover. I'm afraid they might be expecting you – or someone like you.'

'Like I said, that's my problem.'

'When it's done you may find you'll need new travel documents – or perhaps money for expenses. I'll make arrangements. Contact me in the usual way.'

'We'll see,' said Cade.

After Cade had departed, Henderson called the same number he had telephone earlier. 'Blue's gone,' he said.

'I believe he'll do it,' said the Secretary of State for Defence. 'You'll ensure that your informer will be warned to expect him?'

'Of course. They'll be ready.'

'It's the only way to cover ourselves. A necessary action.'

'It's essential,' Henderson replied.

146

'Incidentally, he'll have to move very fast. The SAS are complaining because the police are trying to go through their personnel records. They've been onto my people for a ruling. You know how the Regiment reacts when outsiders want to look through service records. I don't think that in the case of murder we'll be able to hold the boys in blue off.'

'I've told him to act immediately. With the impetus he's now got to finish it quickly and get on with his own vendetta, I'm certain he won't waste any time at all.'

'How about opposition? Will he be able to handle them?'

'I don't believe that the entire Guards Armoured could stop him now.'

'Wrong nationality,' corrected the Defence Secretary.

'From the look in his eyes I don't believe that that would make any difference at all,' said Colonel Henderson and finished the call.

Chapter Eight

Simon Adeane's E-Type Jaguar was running hot as it sped through the trees of the New Forest, nearing the end of the journey from London. His eyes dropped anxiously to the temperature gauge but he kept his foot pressed hard on the accelerator.

'So what do we know about this Company drop-out?' asked Weidenstein, waking for the first time since Adeane had delivered the envelope containing the address of the CIA safe-house where ORACLE would be kept to the Prime Minister.

Adeane's temper was short after his night without sleep. 'Wilder's not a drop-out. He may have his problems but from what the Company told me he's one of the best they've ever had. He's not the only one Vietnam screwed up.'

'I know the background. Post-traumatic stress-disorder. Trip-wire men. They live alone in the wild using trip-wires to warn them of any intruders. They learned from the enemy how to protect themselves.'

'Wilder especially. He was heading up Special Forces teams intiltrated into the North and Cambodia under CIA control.'

'So what kind of work did he do for the Company? Physical or political?'

'The kind which usually ends up with dead people.'

'Ah, political!'

Adeane turned and caught Weidenstein's smile. 'Wilder's a trained silent killer, Max – and disturbed mentally – I doubt if he'd appreciate your humour.'

'I'd say he'd appreciate it more than most. He saw the system at work.' Weidenstein grunted. 'Maybe I mean failing. So what did he get out of the war apart from a disturbed mind?'

'Silver Star and Bronze Star with V.'

'No wounds?'

'No one mentioned Purple Hearts. Maybe the Company doesn't count them.'

The road turned sharply and dipped at the same time causing Adeane to fight the steering-wheel.

Weidenstein tightened the buckle on his seat-belt. 'Does he live inside the facility?'

'Mainly out of it, they said.'

'Neighbours? Locals?'

'The nearest people live on a camp-site – two miles west according to the Company.'

'Other properties?'

'Farther still. The nearest shopping area is around six miles away.'

'Transport?'

'He doesn't need it.'

'He walks six miles for the groceries?'

'He could – but he doesn't. Lives off the land, normal with his kind.'

Weidenstein turned to watch the trees flashing past in a blurred green stream.

Adeane said: 'Maybe he won't be there. They can't live with other people around.'

Weidenstein shook his head, his gaze still on the scenery. 'If the Company told him to be there, he'll be there. You've never worked for the CIA. I have. They know more about pressure than the KGB has yet to learn.'

'They'd use pressure on a disturbed mind?'

'How do you think Wilder's mind got disturbed? Who kept putting him back into the jungle? You know what we have here? A conditioned rat who got to love the maze they played him through. Then the maze was handed back to the Vietnamese, so the rat was lost, bewildered, directionless, because the guiding walls were no longer there to show him the way. Right now he knows too much to be allowed to run loose so they've caged him up and he accepts the cage because he feels

149

safe. He probably likes it. They'd have called him last night and told him we'd be coming. At first he'd have told them to forget it – then they'd have said: okay, welcome to the real world. He'll be there.'

'What happens if he tells them Max Weidenstein's brought a woman and two children with him?'

Weidenstein stretched his short legs. 'You wouldn't believe the number of people in our business who have secondary families existing quite happily on foreign territory. CIA fieldmen are notorious for it. I knew one who had four homes going in different countries at the same time. He loved it, thought no one else knew. They like to believe they have secrets beyond the secret world.'

'So ORACLE and her children are your secret?'

'That's how we play it. They'll think they have something over me – which will please them.'

Adeane braked. 'We take this turning. The cottage is a quarter of a mile into the forest.'

Weidenstein peered over the long bonnet at the deteriorating track winding deep into the forest. 'Say goodbye to your exhaust pipes.'

The low sports car bottomed-out repeatedly accompanied by Adeane's curses until finally, with the deep note of the exhaust unchanged, it lurched into a small clearing with a timbered two-storeyed cottage at its centre.

A man sat on the stone doorstep, his head down as if examining the earth at his feet.

Adeane left the car under the trees rather than risk the uncharted grass of the clearing.

'Wilder?' he enquired as they drew close.

'I stay, okay?' said the man, barely raising his head. 'I do the watching. Maybe you won't see me but I'll be there. There's food – tinned – I don't need it. Anything else you'll have to bring in yourself. There's one freezer and a TV. Maybe they still work, I don't use them. Two telephones, one straight the other rigged for Company business. Sure I'm Wilder. Who else would be living out here?'

The entire speech was delivered flat, devoid of expression, he might have been a house agent churning out a well-worn pitch. He stood up and was not as tall as Adeane had been expecting – then he remembered that height was no advantage to a jungle fighter and that this lean, tense man was one of the best.

Wilder's wide tawny eyes, oddly bright as though back-lit, narrowed as he straightened with the penetration and distrust of the rebel. There was a familiarity about him that Adeane struggled to place, searching his excellent memory – even recalling the faces of his own two brothers – but none would fit. Much later it came to him, but even then it was not the haunted, young-old face which brought recall but the loose, awkward movements of his body: an older James Dean with long light brown hair streaked with grey. He wondered whether the grey was caused by age or trauma and decided on trauma after calculating that his Vietnam service would give him a present age around the mid-thirties or possibly younger. Twenty going on forty, Adeane thought, wondering how many years had been lost in between.

'Who needs the R&R?' Wilder questioned.

Weidenstein answered: 'I do, but I won't be around much.'

'You staying?' This asked of Adeane.

'No.'

Weidenstein said: 'There'll be others, arriving soon, a woman and two children.'

Wilder's eyes flicked toward the trees. 'That makes things difficult.'

'We've brought plenty of supplies,' Adeane reassured him.

Wilder scanned the clearing. 'Feeding them is no problem. Keeping them safe is. If I have to cover four then there may come a time when I have to lift my eyes off someone. That way you lose people. You'd better speak to the Company.'

'This isn't a Company operation,' Weidenstein said.

'So you're who?'

'I'm someone the Company would prefer to keep safe. That's all you need to know.'

'The woman and the kids? Your family?'

'Something like that.'

'You bringing in your own help?'

'I'd prefer not to. I want to keep the profile low on this. Do I need my own people?'

'What are you expecting?'

'I hope nothing. This place isn't known.'

'If it's blown how will they come? In the open or the other way?'

'What makes you think anyone will come?'

Wilder's smile made his creased brown face seem absurdly young. 'People who need safe-houses have a serious reason for not feeling safe.'

Weidenstein nodded. 'If they come it won't be in the open. A team. Probably at night.'

'Victor Charlie,' Wilder said, distantly. 'VC. That's how they came. Team of three, in the night, and cut your balls off.'

'Another time,' Weidenstein said. 'You'd better learn to forget it.'

'In the dark it's the same.'

Adeane moved toward the door. 'Let's get inside.'

Wilder led the way. The interior of the cottage was gloomy with the musty odour of an unoccupied dwelling. The furniture was covered by dust-sheets in all the rooms with only the narrow kitchen seeming to be in use. The sink had one used plate in it and on the pine table lay a US Army issue bedding-roll.

'You sleep in here?' Adeane asked with a grimace.

'When it's wet,' Wilder replied.

'Get rid of the dust-sheets and air the place,' Weidenstein ordered but Wilder was already outside the kitchen door and heading for the woods.

'I'll do it,' Adeane said.

The sound of a car horn, blown twice, reached them. Weidenstein reached inside his jacket and a snub-nosed Smith & Wesson .38 revolver with a concealed hammer appeared in his right hand.

'He heard the car,' Adeane said.

'Way before we did. Maybe we've got ourselves a bargain. You go out to her, I'll cover from the window.'

Adeane opened the front door and walked into the open toward a small red hatchback. There was no sign of Wilder but Adeane could almost feel those bright eyes observing every movement he made.

Adeane opened the door, looking immediately into the rear.

'Max wanted you to bring the children. I told you that on the telephone.'

She stepped out of the car, lowered her sunglasses and appraised the cottage. 'I hope there's constant hot water,' she said, pulling her mouth down. 'Domestic strife loomed large after your call. It took me an hour to convince Peter I wasn't having an affair, and even then he had his doubts. This morning he insisted on speaking to someone at the "clinic". Your girl is good, charmed him right out of his shiny-bottomed pin-striped trousers. He loves a sultry female voice. Her accent threw him but she told him she was Canadian, clever girl. You came over ultra smooth on the 'phone – he didn't like *you* one little bit. Where's Max?' She was wearing a head scarf which she untied then shook loose her thick auburn hair.

'Inside,' Adeane said. 'Where are the children?'

She started toward the house. 'With his mother. I'm sorry but he insisted on it. He's very concerned. Said that if I'm supposed to be having a complete break the children should stay with him – which of course was impossible – so his mother stepped into the breach.'

Weidenstein had opened the door and stood inside in the gloom.

'No children,' said Adeane.

'Inside,' Weidenstein ordered.

'Sorry, Max,' she said. 'Simply not possible. It was me alone or nothing.'

'Husband problem,' Adeane explained.

She bent down and kissed Weidenstein on the forehead. 'I've never seen you dressed for the country, Max. Very rustic. What happened to the silk suits?' She tossed the light raincoat she carried over the bannisters then handed Adeane her keys. 'There's a case in the car, would you mind?'

Weidenstein led her into the beamed sitting room and she raised her eyebrows at the covered furniture then pulled a dust-sheet off a settee and flopped into it, wrinkling her nose at the dust she had raised. For the first time, fear touched her eyes. 'Max, I'm scared witless. What's going on? Who's killing them?'

Weidenstein chose to sit on an armchair opposite her,

153

ignoring the cover. 'You don't believe in coincidences either?'

'Not when I could be one of them, thank you.'

'We have no actual knowledge of who is behind the deaths – but I'm assuming the British. MI5. Either official or unofficial.'

'Then speak to someone and get it stopped.'

'That's been done – but there's no guarantee – that's why I want you here, safe.'

She looked out of the grubby windows. 'This is safe? We're in the middle of nowhere! I don't see anyone who looks remotely like a bodyguard.'

'Listen to me carefully. You've got a fine brain – so use it. Your position is precarious –'

'I'm well aware of *that!*' she snapped.

'You have to remain cool and see this through. The Russians must believe that you've arranged this yourself because you feel threatened – a springboard in case you feel you have to jump. That's why it's important to have the children here.'

'Can't be done. Peter is pig-headed and he won't shift.'

'Have you contacted your controller?'

'Without speaking to you? Of course not.'

'When is your next drop?'

'Next Friday. Local cinema, last performance, ladies' loo upstairs.'

'One week. We should be able to wrap this up in that time. They must not start to think you've crossed over.'

'Why should they? I've gone away for a few days. I've done it before. Last February. I stayed with my sister for three days. They don't watch the house. That would be stupid.'

'Maybe they don't need to. They may have agents inside GCHQ who we don't know about – they'll know you've not been into work. The personnel office would be a prime target for them.'

'You're right of course. Actually, with my position, there'll be gossip anyway. Especially with that heart condition story. There are plenty of conniving women in the Puzzle Palace who are after my job. They'll view my supposed illness with glee.'

'Good, that will work for us. What we have to show here is a completely open situation. You've had tests – documented and verifiable through the London clinic. All that is arranged,

154

bought and paid for as part of our long-term contingency plans, so that side will hold up. This house is a CIA facility but there's no way that anyone can find that out.'

She became alarmed. 'I've given this address to personnel at Cheltenham – I had to, it's standard procedure. If the Security Service are behind all this they're going to dig deep. They'll look for a connection between "Doctor Hartford" and the listed owner. They probably have this place listed as a CIA safe-house on their computer.'

'The Hartford connection will be verified. The Company don't even tell *us* what properties they own – never mind about the British. This place is safe, believe me. The problem is that we have to make it appear straight.'

'The problem, Max, is that I'm supposed to be a sick woman and you've got me stuck out in the middle of nowhere with the nearest doctor too far away to do anything about it if I keel over. Come on Max, you're not even convincing me – never mind Moscow or the Security Service!'

'You're not supposed to be dying. You've had tests which show you need a rest. Time away from pressure. We had to move fast – maybe too fast – but this location fits what we need. Cheltenham security is not going to come all the way down here to check on you. They'll check out the clinic, maybe, and they'll keep in touch with your husband, but that's all. You're too well established. *You* know what you are – but they don't. All they want is to have you back.'

She lit a cigarette and Weidenstein noticed the tremor in her long fingers. 'Perhaps I don't want to go back, Max. Perhaps, deep inside me, I can't take any more. I've drifted too far away from my husband, and my children are turning from being babies to little people without me noticing. I can't get involved at home any more – I push them away. I suppose it's because I daren't get too close in case I lose them.'

'You won't lose them, Rhoda. I promise you that.'

'No one can keep that sort of promise, Max.'

'We need you to continue. I can't tell you how important you are to our forward planning.'

'What about my forward planning? I want to live and enjoy a complete life.'

'A few more years and you will be able to. Have you any idea

155

what you're worth? How much hard, tax-free currency we've got on deposit for you?'

Rhoda James looked at him with tired eyes and sighed. 'Money, Max. I should have been satisfied with what I had.'

'What you have is half a million dollars – and growing as we sit here.'

'And I can't touch it. I live on a civil servant's salary plus a bank manager's salary – oh, quite well, thank you – but secretly, I'm half a millionaire! Except I can't spent it. I'm still young, Max. Thirty-four. That's an age when a woman wants to spend what she's earned. I want an expensive sports car instead of a middle-market hatchback. I want clothes that other women can't afford. I want to live in the sun basking by a pool that comes with the villa that I own. I want all of it *now* – but I can't have any of it. When I'm forty it'll be too late. Can't you understand that?'

Weidenstein stood up and walked to the window. 'Sure I understand. But remember this. We bought you off the Russians. You let that happen because we offered you more. No ideological crisis, just hard cash – and plenty of it. You accepted the deal – and the risks – and the delay before you were able to touch the money. You were told then that the road would be hard and sometimes bitter, and always lonely. Now you're really feeling how bad it can be. No one in this world gets half a million dollars for an easy ride.'

She threw her cigarette into the empty fireplace. 'I just needed to get it out of my system. Of course I'll carry on. I'm hard, Max, I have to be to do what I do, but not that hard that I can't see what this is doing to me.' She stood up and pulled off her jacket revealing a good figure covered by a lightweight wool sweater. 'Let's make this place livable,' she said and began folding the dust-sheets.

'I'll have to leave soon with Adeane. It isn't secure for us to be around. There's someone here to protect you. You'll find he's not very sociable but that's not what he's here for. I'd better warn you that he's . . . well, not what you'd expect.'

'What is that supposed to mean?'

Weidenstein struggled to find an acceptable description for Wilder. 'You remember the hippie era?'

'Of course not. I'm a sixteen-year-old virgin – if those exist any more, poor things.'

'Like that. Long hair, jeans, sweatshirt. No shoes.'

She laughed. 'Brilliant! What'll he do if they come for me? Put flowers in their guns?'

'Forget what he looks like. He's good. There isn't one inch of ground around here he doesn't know – or have covered. A regular bodyguard wouldn't be much use in this terrain. He's trained for just this kind of situation. But you don't ask about that. He's likely to want to stay outside – it's his way – but try to keep him as close to you as possible even if he kicks against it.'

'You can be certain I'll do that.'

Weidenstein gave her a knowing look. 'You remember that trip you made to Baltimore two years ago, when Moscow wanted you to get inside Fort Meade.'

'Shut up Max.'

'Just reminding you.'

'You mean warning. All right, so I had a fling. I know it was highly insecure but it happened. It was blind funk and you know it. I needed a man and one was available, it was as simple as that. And I did what Moscow Centre wanted – and, incidentally, what your people wanted, so to hell with your moral judgements. Don't worry, I'll make sure he keeps his eyes and his mind on my body – in the professional sense of course.'

'This time, if you get scared you call Adeane. He's acting as field-man. He'll be close but not too close. You'll get a call from him with a contact number when he takes position. I've already told you that this place is secure – Wilder and Adeane are insurance, that's all. Trust me. You feel the need to speak to me, you call Adeane first. Wilder uses the Company line – you keep away from it.'

'Wilder's the bodyguard?'

'Wilder, Declan. Do what he tells you.'

They had moved out into the hallway. Adeane came down the stairs.

'I've checked the place over. It's bugged – no problem, standard CIA issue. Voice-activiated recorder and back-up, in the cellar – now deactivated.'

157

'They've bugged their own safe-house?' Rhoda James asked.

'The Company bug their own bugs,' Adeane replied, without humour. 'Ask Max, he's an ex-Langley man.'

Weidenstein made no comment, stepping outside onto the path. 'Are the supplies inside?'

'Done,' Adeane said. 'Wilder's gone back to the trees – and don't ask me to go look for him. I'm not taking one step out there unless you walk in front.'

'Wilder has his own ideas about security,' Weidenstein explained, seeing his agent's puzzlement. 'You might call it his Vietnam legacy. You go back inside and stay there.'

She watched them go back to the low sports car through the bay window of the cottage, her fear a tight knot inside her. There was a full liquor cabinet, every bottle still sealed. She selected cognac and poured herself a stiff measure, the tremor in her hands returning. 'Oh bloody hell!' she swore and swallowed half of it, grimacing as it burned.

She saw a figure flit through the trees then, impossibly, vanish. She fell against the nearest wall, her back pressed flat against it, barely breathing, her eyes wide and fixed on the trees although every part of her screamed for them to be closed. A noise came from the hall and her teeth bit into her lip shutting off the small cry in her throat.

'Where are the kids?' Wilder demanded, suddenly before her, his denims, bare torso and feet smeared with damp mud.

She shrieked and her glass thumped, unbroken, on the carpet.

'Shut up! I'm Wilder.'

She found herself laughing.

'Be quiet,' Wilder said.

'They're not here. I didn't bring them.' Still she laughed.

'What's so funny?'

She struck his face, hard; then again. He remained rigid. She bent down for her glass and refilled it, this time not pausing before she drank. 'You *shit*! You terrified me! Why the hell didn't you call out?'

'I never call out. Don't drink, I want you alert.'

She poured another, defiantly. '*You* stay bloody alert!' She

158

laughed again, this time in ridicule. 'Have you any idea what you look like?'

'Lady, I don't give a damn.'

'That is obvious.'

He stared at her, his face livid with the marks of her blows, his strange, bright eyes without emotion even as they drifted over her body.

She felt both revulsion and a sudden stab of intense physical desire and supposed that came from fear. She studied the man beneath the grime and saw an untamed animal locked in the body of a man, and the mixture was undeniably potent to her.

'I'm hungry,' she said. 'Show me where you keep food.'

'They stocked the freezer. I live' – he tilted his head at the windows – 'out there.'

'Now who'd have guessed that?'

'When you want feeding you fix it yourself.'

She put down her glass. 'All right, bad start. I apologize. I was just being stupid – and who would blame me faced with you. Sorry, okay? I was rude and I shouldn't have hit you. The children couldn't come.'

Wilder hunched his shoulders and stuck both hands in his jeans. 'Okay.'

'Wildgrave,' she said, studying his face and, more intensely, his eyes.

'What?'

'Wildgrave. A keeper of the forest turned hunter.' She teased with a half-smile. 'Cruel and profligate and addicted to the chase. A German legend. My mother was German, she told me that story just when I hit puberty – God, she didn't know what she was doing to an innocent half-fräulein. I've never forgotten it. You could have stepped right out of my lurid imaginings – except for the clothes of course. You have the eyes. Bright amber, like fire. So what do *you* hunt, Declan Wilder?'

'Anything that comes at me.'

'I thought so. Oh yes, I'll be safe with you. Clever little Max.'

'Head for Beaulieu,' Weidenstein ordered as the E-Type reached the main road. 'The Montagu Motor Museum. Find a hotel and check yourself in on the way. The first one, even if it's below your standards.'

'Why Beaulieu? It's in the wrong direction.'

'A meet.'

Revelation passed over Adeane's face. 'If the Company's providing back-up, I hope they know what they're getting themselves into?'

'I didn't say the Company were involved.'

'Contract?'

'Just drive.'

'I hope to God they know how to keep out of sight, otherwise Wilder might take them out himself. Did he know already? Or did you tell ORACLE to warn him?'

'I told her to make sure he stays as close to her as possible. Nothing else.'

'Wilder? He'll be out in the trees right now.'

'Now, I don't mind. Tonight I want him back inside. She'll see to that. The back-up will go to ground and remain static, well back from the house and Wilder's trip-wires. We've limited the knowledge of the house's location as much as we can – but if Five are behind this they won't have any trouble getting the information from personnel at GCHQ. In which case we'll be ready.'

Adeane swung around, sharply. 'You're trying to draw them out!'

'Watch the road,' snapped Weidenstein.

'I thought she's supposed to be irreplaceable?'

'She is.'

'Yet you're willing to risk her life?'

'Haven't you learned yet that in our business it's sometimes wiser to risk an agent's life rather than risk their exposure. ORACLE is targeted – we know that for sure – and she's going to stay targeted until we blow Five's operation or those in Five who're running it. The Prime Minister may be working on that from the inside – but we're at the sharp end. We can't get those who planned all this but we can certainly get the men they're using to carry out their plans. If their hit-team is taken out, they're going to have to put another together – quickly – and that means reorganization and a lot of rethinking. Which means taking risks. In our world, taking risks without a great

160

deal of calculated thought and preparation can be fatal. Someone in Five will have to ask for ORACLE's present location – and according to NSA's charter we have an information-sharing agreement with GCHQ, so if we really wanted to push it – and we will – we will ask, as concerned and involved partners, why the British Security Service is showing such an interest in one of GCHQ's senior employees.'

'But why should we suddenly be so interested in her ourselves?' Adeane questioned.

'Not just in her. We ask – as we do regularly – for an update on personnel employed by GCHQ across the nation who are under MI5 scrutiny.'

Adeane smiled. 'So we take out the hit-team and while Five are wondering what hit them and start recognizing, we check out who in Five wanted to know where she had gone?'

'Unless, of course, they don't need to check. Maybe we passed that information on ourselves.'

'*We* did? When?'

'This morning.'

'*The Prime Minister?* You're paranoid, Max.'

'Am I? She's on the rack and she knows it – no matter what inducements we offer for the future.' Weidenstein sighed. 'But I suppose, in the end we can't lose. If she decides to act against us and passes on the information to those behind this – which naturally means she knows who they are – then we will know she's done it, because Five won't need to ask where ORACLE is being kept.'

'Which means what, as far as the Prime Minister is concerned?'

'It means we have to destroy her.' Weidenstein caught his deputy's startled glance. 'Politically, of course,' he added.

The car-park to the Montagu Motor Museum was almost full.

'Drive around,' ordered Weidenstein. 'They'll recognize your car.'

Adeane complied. 'What are they driving?'

'Rented car. They'll have gone for something big, knowing their style. There, the Mercedes.'

'Cubans?' Adeane queried, seeing a tall string-bean of a man with dark Hispanic features step from the driver's seat then immediately re-enter the car. 'When did you arrange this? Not last night?'

'It's just a question of being prepared for all eventualities.'

'Washington? Before you had any idea how any of this would work out?'

'Take that space and stay in the car.'

Weidenstein got out and walked over to the big grey Mercedes, sliding into the rear seat. The two men inside sat smoking, one a cigar and the other a chain-lit cigarette. The interior was blue with smoke.

'Lower a window,' ordered Weidenstein. 'Are you equipped?'

The shorter man, negroid in appearance, was seated sideways. He lit another cigarette and spoke with it in his mouth, spilling ash. 'We got everything, okay? So how they go for it? Night or day?'

'Be ready for both.'

'Nice wheels,' commented the tall one, his accent betraying no ethnic origins. 'That an XKE? These Brit cars stay good, must be the metal.'

Weidenstein passed over a section of a map identical to the one Adeane had supplied to the Prime Minister which was now in Cade's possession, the only difference being that this one bore figures which marked out distances from various points on the perimeter of the clearing to the CIA safe-house.

The tall Hispanic turned to study it. 'The killing-ground clear?'

Weidenstein nodded. 'No cover, no obstructions.'

The heavier man curled his thick, negroid lips around his cigarette. 'Carnival ducks,' he said. 'They cross that, they're gone.'

'He means dead, not gone,' advised the Hispanic.

'Sure I do,' said the negro.

Weidenstein said. 'Ground rules. You fix two static posts and you hold position. No roaming. I want them brought down at long range, fast and silent. Our people inside the house don't know you're out there and it should stay that way.'

'What they look like? We don't want to make mistakes,'

said the negro with a chuckle. 'The ones inside?'

'One man, wears jeans, no shoes, long hair. Maybe a sweatshirt or nothing.'

'Fuckin' Rambo!' the negro chuckled again.

'The other one is a woman. You won't mistake her.'

'Good looker?'

'You won't be close enough to find out, the place is trip-wired, so stay back.'

'Who cleans up?' asked the Hispanic. 'Your people?'

'Just make the hit and get out. Disposal is arranged.'

'How long you want us to stay? Maybe no one comes?' asked the negro crushing out his cigarette and checking what was left in the pack.

'They'll come. You've got rations?'

'S-packs, no problem,' said the Hispanic.

'Clothing?'

'In the trunk, bought it this morning. Ex-army stuff. British. We'll dump it afterwards.'

'You'll be cold, don't fall asleep.'

'You crazy?' said the negro.

'And don't smoke. The man inside will smell it.'

'From where we'll be?' the Hispanic questioned.

'You'll be on his ground. You'll need all the advantages.'

'Bullshit,' said the negro.

'He chews gum,' said the Hispanic. 'We walk out? After?'

'Cover any traces then make your own way out. I don't want to know where you are or how you got there – just keep it legitimate.'

'We're hikers,' said the negro indicating their outdoor clothing.

'Just stick to the woods and don't hitch rides.'

'We confirm by 'phone direct with you in London, right?' asked the Hispanic.

Weidenstein nodded. 'Cain means affirmative, Abel negative. Nothing else.'

'Abel we won't need. If the word isn't Cain you won't hear a thing.'

'He means we'll be wasted,' said the negro, with a fat smile.

'Wait,' said Weidenstein and walked back to Adeane. 'Get back to your hotel and stay there. Call ORACLE with the number. Don't do anything without checking with me first.'

Adeane started the Jaguar's engine. 'I don't like being stuck down here, Max. And I don't like only knowing half of what's going on.'

'This is where you're needed. If anything goes wrong I want ORACLE out of there fast. You know all you need to know.'

'What about Wilder?'

'Wilder's the Company's problem.'

'You mean he's expendable.'

'I mean he's not our problem. They wanted him in — we weren't given the option.' Weidenstein walked back to the Mercedes. 'Drive,' he ordered. 'I'll direct you.'

Chapter Nine

Chief-Superintendent James Rand had read his morning paper that Saturday over a late breakfast. He was a trim fifty-year-old, greying in a distinguished manner and, at that time, between marriages, although his rugged looks and his status ensured he was still more than eligible. He sipped at his coffee and frowned at the story halfway down the front page. Something in his sharp mind told him that he knew the identity of Gerald Parminter's killer. The connection lay in the ruthless efficiency of the killer and Parminter's crime of child murder. He put the paper aside and searched his memory but no sudden flash of inspiration came to him. He gave up. Somebody else's cock-up he thought; he would not want to be in their shoes. It could happen to anyone; especially when *that* sort of crime was involved. Emotions run high and discipline can be impaired. He had been involved in similar cases when he had been a detective inspector. One had been particularly appalling, with the father serving a sentence for unlawful killing while serving in Northern Ireland, undercover, with the Special Air Service.

He snatched at the paper, read the story again carefully then made for the telephone. Quickly he traced the number for Gloucester Police Headquarters, gave his name and rank and asked to be put through straight away to the Head of CID. When the detective chief inspector came on the line he explained rapidly the reason for his call.

'I may know the perpetrator,' he continued. 'Cade, Alan John Cade, always calls himself Jack. SAS sergeant – or was – did time in Winchester prison, eight years reduced to four. His daughter was abducted then strangled – nine-tenths killed by torture first. I went to the funeral – being the officer in charge of the investigation – bloody terrible. I said too much to the press about how I felt and got dragged over the coals for it. Cade was emotionless throughout. We had the cuffs on him because of his capabilities – SAS and all that – but he was no trouble. Stood there like a damn marble statue. The only time I saw anything in his eyes was when his wife turned up – a real slag – then he looked at her and she may as well have died right then. Murderous – but icy with it, no temper, no physical reaction. I thought he was going to go for her and – to be honest – didn't want to be near him if he did. Anyway, he just stood there and killed her with his eyes.'

'Is it possible for you to get down here?' asked the chief inspector. 'I've got my DI on it and he could do with all the help he can get.'

'I'm sure,' said Rand sympathetically. He paused, thinking about the golf clubs waiting in his car. 'All right, I'm free for the weekend – just have to let my people know where I'll be then I'll drive straight down to you.'

'I may not be here when you arrive, but in any case you'll want to talk to DI Aske. Good man – a bit prim and proper, thinks the training manual is only one step down from the Ten Commandments, but very able. It's a pity you didn't call half an hour earlier, Aske and a DS have driven up to Hereford to try and get hold of the information you've just given me.'

'I could be wrong,' Rand said. 'It's only a possibility.'

'Of course, but right now we need something – anything – to give us direction.'

'I know the feeling. Right I'll get a move on.'

'I'll book a decent hotel for you – leave the bill to me.'

'I'll be with you as soon as I can, two hours at the most. The M4 will take me almost to you.' Rand put down the telephone, hurriedly packed an overnight bag, made telephone calls to Thames Valley Police Headquarters and to cancel his round of golf with his partner, then started his new Audi Coupé and headed toward his headquarters at Kidlington.

He considered the thought of being in on the hunt for a man whose possible motives he might – had he been in a profession which allowed such self-indulgences – have sympathy with.

166

But this man, whoever he turned out to be, was a cold, expert killer, who would undoubtedly be both difficult and dangerous to apprehend. Whatever moral judgement might be made about his actions, the fact remained that he was a murderer who, had the circumstances turned against him, might have killed the officers escorting Gerald Parminter.

No, he decided, discarding all sympathetic thoughts and jamming his foot hard down on the accelerator, he was glad he was in on the hunt. Rand would never know that at some point on his fast drive along the M4, a Volkswagen camper had flashed past his Audi the other side of the crash barriers heading toward London carrying Jack Cade to his final meeting with the man he knew as Harlow.

Lettie Sullivan was standing over her stove preparing her brother's lunch when she heard the sound of a motorcycle. Believing it to be Cade returned, she abandoned her cooking to rush to the kitchen door.

In the yard a policeman was removing his helmet, the sound of his radio taking over from the beat of the motor.

Lettie froze and slammed the door shut, peeping out through the net curtains, trembling.

The policeman dismounted and walked over to the farmhouse, rapping on the kitchen door with his gloved fist. Lettie did nothing. The policeman called out to her then came and looked through the windows, pointing at the door, but still she did not move.

'Oi!' she heard her brother call and quickly resumed her cooking.

The policeman turned from the window toward Will Sullivan.

'What're you after then?' demanded the farmer.

'Just some questions. Your wife wouldn't answer the door.'

'Sister. She's a bit deaf.'

'She looked straight at me.'

'Like as not you scared her then. What questions?'

'You used to own a motor-bike. Triumph. Long time ago. On our records we have information that it was registered at this address. The owner was involved in a canal accident. Drowned.'

'You just lower your voice, you'll upset her.'

'I thought you said she was deaf?'

'The lad was hers. She can't talk about it. Best move away from the house. Came like you did – the police at the time. That's why she's hiding from you. She remembers, you see. The motorcycle was sold – oh, a long time ago. Couldn't have it around could I? Not with her like she is. Near killed her.'

'Sold to whom?' asked the officer taking out his notebook and pencil to write.

Sullivan raised his thick eyebrows. 'How'd I know? Too long gone now. Just took the man's money and let him ride off. It was his then, wasn't it!'

'I'm sorry, but a motorbike of that description was used in a murder last night. I'll have to ask you to search for some record of the sale. This is a very important matter.'

'No good. I didn't write anything down. Cash is cash, isn't it.'

'That may be so, but there's no trace on record to show that the vehicle changed ownership. Nor has it been taxed for many years either. I have to ask you if you would give me permission to look around these premises.'

'This is my land, my property. You want to go searching, you bring the proper papers with you.'

'I can have other officers bring a search warrant, if that's what you want – but I should inform you that you're making things difficult for yourself.'

'Don't you worry about me, son. You get the papers you need, then maybe I'll allow you to search my property.'

'There's no maybe about it. That's the law. If I get a search warrant we'll have every right to take your home and these outbuildings apart.'

Sullivan's face grew livid. He turned and stormed to the front door, coming back out with his shotgun. 'See where I'm standing, son? Under my feet is my land and you're trespassing on it. This in my hands is *my* law. Now you just get on that motorcycle of yours and take yourself off to whoever sent you. Just you tell them that if they feel like stepping onto my land and breaking up my property they're going to have to get past this first.'

'Pointing a loaded gun at a police officer is a very serious offence. I take it that that weapon *is* loaded?'

Sullivan raised the gun and fired one barrel. 'You best be going now,' he said, fury in his eyes.

'I'll be back,' called the policeman, starting his engine and riding fast out of the yard.

'And I'll be waiting!' Sullivan shouted back, in manic anger. He stepped back into the porch and brought out two full boxes of cartridges and went into the kitchen. 'They're going to come and break up the house!' he told Lettie. 'Take it apart, he said. We'll see about that!'

Lettie had her hands over her ears after the blast of the shotgun but heard enough of his words. 'Why, Will? Why?'

'They want the motorcycle. They want the lad too. That's plain.'

'What's he done, Will?'

'He killed the man who murdered his child. Maybe he did right, maybe he didn't – but there's no cause for them to say they're going to tear down our house.'

Lettie began weeping uncontrollably but Sullivan ignored her. He marched to the telephone, dialled emergency and said: 'You tell your people that the Sullivans live and die on their own land. Hear that?' then slammed down the receiver.

'That's ambulance, Will, or the fire brigade,' Lettie said through her tears.

'All the same. All together to make people like us into nothing. We let who we want onto our land – like the lad – no one else sets one foot on our soil without permission. And that I'm not giving.'

'You'd better let them come,' she pleaded. 'They've got guns nowadays – its not like it used to be.'

'Aye, that's true enough – and sadder for it. We'll see them off, Lett, don't you worry. A landowner's still got rights. That's what this country is all about. You just get that lunch on the table.'

He sat waiting as she, trembling, put food before him. The sound of wailing sirens stopped them both. Sullivan stood up.

'You best get upstairs out of harm's way,' he said. 'Middle of the house, on the floor. Now!' he snapped.

Turning away from her he stepped out into the yard, the shotgun low between his roughened hands. He saw movement

169

in his fields: swift dark figures scurrying across his land and a fleet of police vehicles parked the full length of his long driveway from the road. From one of them a voice, heavily amplified blasted at him:

'Armed police! Throw down your weapon.'

He raised the shotgun and fired one barrel in the direction of the voice. The windscreen of the nearest vehicle, a dark-blue van, disintegrated. 'Get off my land!' he bawled, then raised the gun, pointing toward one of the scurrying figures. He fell back, not hearing the sharp crack of the weapon which had fired. Looking down he saw spreading blood over his jacket. He did not know where he had been hit. There was no pain. He was glad. He had never had the chance to show a wound off. All through war, when the young men he had known had come back showing off their wounds he had felt ashamed. They told him the work he was doing on the land was just as important as theirs but still he would have preferred to have a wound. Now it was all right.

He pushed himself up but fell back again. Bad, he thought. Odd it doesn't hurt? Maybe wounds don't hurt until they're getting better? He thought he heard Lettie wailing but then she always did weep. The dark figures were closing in fast now, like soldiers. He found he had amazing strength and ran toward the barn, dropping sickeningly in front of the door of the stable. Shuffling forward on his knees, doubled over, his head grazing the cobbles, he reached the tall split door and pulled himself upright. The top half was open and it took no strength to pull it past him. The figures were in the yard now and closing and the pain was beginning. He dragged the shotgun up then something hot thumped into his side but it did not stop him from pointing the gun at the piled-up straw and pulling the trigger.

Behind the straw the petrol tank of the Triumph caught the full blast and exploded, the straw igniting instantly.

One police marksman dragged the fallen figure away from the flames.

'It'll burn down before you take it apart,' Sullivan croaked, and died.

'You bloody old lunatic!' said the marksman and shouted: 'Somebody get the brigade!' but it had already been done.

His stop-off at Kidlington taking longer than he expected, James Rand arrived amidst pandemonium at Gloucester Police Headquarters.

'What the devil's going on?' he asked the desk sergeant as he produced his identification.

'Armed incident sir,' replied the sergeant sharply, eager to impress.

'Casualties?'

'One civilian, sir. The woman involved was unhurt. No casualties among our lads. The man died.'

'Any connection with last night's incident?'

'The shooting, sir? I understand that it was something to do with the vehicle used by the perpetrator. A motorcycle.'

'You'd better tell Detective Inspector Aske I'm here. Your Head of CID has informed him that I was on my way.'

'Detective Chief Inspector Murray has passed that on, sir. Mr Aske arrived himself barely fifteen minutes ago from Hereford.'

'Where can I find him?'

'Second floor, sir. I'll have someone show you.'

'I'll find it.'

Aske was sitting at his desk, using the telephone. Detective Sergeant Nash was pacing the room, a mug of tea in his hand. The local Special Branch officer, a detective sergeant named Simmons, was leaning against a tall filing cabinet.

Nash was complaining bitterly about their treatment at SAS Headquarters. 'First we had to get past some jobsworth called the Chief Clerk, then the bleeding RSM, then some glamour boy with a horsy accent who's the CO's assistant –'

'Adjutant,' corrected Aske, cupping his hand over the telephone. 'Details should be precise.'

Nash raised his eyebrows. 'Adjutant then. So we wait some more because the CO's probably chatting to the Queen –'

'But he gave you what you wanted?' Simmons interrupted.

'He gave the governor what we wanted. Me, I sat outside.' Nash tapped his shoulders. 'No pips, see?'

'Protocol,' put in Aske again. 'There's an accepted form in these matters.'

'The form was I sat on my arse half the morning,' muttered

171

Nash as an aside. 'All right, so I says to this adjutant: "You'd think we were effing Russians, or something." He says, real plummy: "You could be. They have people trained to impersonate police officers." So I asks, looking around like: "So when did World War Three start then? This morning?" He comes back with one of those toothy smiles his sort give you. "Didn't you know, old boy? Back in 'forty-six when the Red Army took a breather in Berlin." That's what he said, straight up. And you wonder why the bleeding Russians are paranoid?'

'They've got to see it that way, haven't they,' said Simmons. 'When they're not doing the action man bit for us, they're real soldiers. They've got to believe there's a war coming. No point in them being there if they don't believe that.'

Rand walked in through the open door. 'DI Aske?' he enquired. 'Chief Superintendent Rand. Thames Valley.'

Nash quickly put down his mug. 'On the blower sir,' he informed, smartening up. 'I'm DS Nash, CID, this is DS Simmons from the Branch. Local.'

Aske was on his feet, quickly concluding his call. 'DCI Murray told me to expect you, sir. Cade, Alan John, also known as Jack – like the Shakespearean character in *Henry the Sixth*.'

'Oh?' said Rand, putting down his briefcase.

'Rebel, sir. Pretender to the throne.'

'This one's real. I was there when they buried his daughter. Your rank at the time, if I remember correctly.'

'Quite a while ago then, sir.'

'Not so long,' Rand replied and caught Nash's rigid grin. 'So what have you discovered?'

Aske reached for a notebook. 'Commanding Officer of the Twenty-second Special Air Service Regiment at Stirling Lines – they've changed the name in case you didn't know, sir – could give me no information regarding any member of the Regiment who had ever had a child sexually assaulted, abducted or murdered.'

'In Cade's case he wouldn't know. Cade was no longer a member of the SAS when it happened. He was serving an eight-year stretch in Winchester at that time. Did four years – then someone decided he'd paid his debt. He was out on civvy street with a dishonourable discharge in his pocket to give him a new start. Hard man. Not like your hard-case villains, I mean *hard*, right the way through. If I had to face up to him I think I'd walk away. I *know* I would.'

'You're a big man, sir. Six-two? And fit,' Aske remarked.

'Cade is five-ten and he'd chop me down easily. If he is the man you're up against I'd prepare yourself for real trouble. By the way, this armed incident – the one today – connected with last night's murder?'

Nash said: 'Farmhouse, sir, in the Cotswolds. We believe the perpetrator was holed up there.'

'Close to the scene?'

'Could have been there quick enough. Used a motorbike.'

'I understand you've found it.'

'The old boy who owned the farm burnt down the stables it was hidden in. Blasted it with a shotgun. Covered with straw it was – place went up in seconds. Hit the tank I suppose.'

'Deliberate?'

'Must have been. One of our lads winged him – then he went straight for the stables and blew the bike away.'

'He's dead, I'm sorry to say,' put in Aske. 'Couldn't have been helped. He fired at one of our vehicles then aimed at an officer. Shotgun. He didn't get his shot off, our marksmen hit him, two rounds, upper torso.'

'You're sure he wasn't the man you're looking for?'

'No way,' said Nash. 'Too old, too stupid.'

'I was told there's a woman involved?' Rand enquired.

'Sister. Elderly couple they were. Old boy was a nutter,' said Nash.

'Neighbours told us they lived like recluses,' said Aske. 'Very old-fashioned. The incident seemed to have been sparked off by a young patrolman informing the man that he was going to get a search warrant.'

'Is that what the patrolman said? I mean, exactly those words?'

'That's what his report reads.'

Rand grunted. 'Old people who live that way – out of touch with the modern world – can react badly to the wrong form of words. They feel threatened. Though it hardly matters now, I suppose, however regrettable the death may be. Is the sister here – now?'

173

'Her statement is being taken down now by a WPC,' said Aske. 'Though I doubt if she'll get much sense out of her – she's in a bad way.'

'So would you be if you'd just had your brother – and lifelong companion – shot dead by a team of armed police. He was probably her only living relative. So what about the motorcycle? Enough left for identification?'

Aske nodded. 'Old Triumph. It has to be the same one used by the perpetrator. There's not too many of those around these days. It was too badly burned for fingerprinting but scene-of-crime officers are going over the farmhouse and outbuildings. I was speaking to them when you arrived, sir. They're ringing back if they find any prints which don't match the old couple's.'

'You've got hold of Cade's prints?' Rand asked.

'Computer facsimile from CRO. Very poor. DCI Murray arranged for them after your call.'

'Presumably he's tied up with senior officers right now?'

Aske and Nash glanced at each other. Simmons said: 'Parminter, the prisoner shot last night, was involved in espionage, sir. Worked at GCHQ, handling highly classified material. A Russian mole, long-term, we believe maybe as long as twenty years. We already have material evidence to support that. Code-books, recorder, short-wave radio – we've even got the frequencies he used. That's off the record, sir, the Security boys have put a gag on that side of it. DCI Murray is with them at present, sir.'

Rand sat on the nearest desk-top. 'Now that sheds a whole new light on the matter, doesn't it? Brings in the possibility of a KGB hit-squad to silence Parminter in case he spilled the lot. Bugger it! I wish your DCI had told me, it would have saved me a wasted journey.'

A telephone rang. Nash lifted it then handed it to Aske.

Aske listened, then replaced the receiver. 'One set of prints, not belonging to the deceased or his sister. All over the kitchen table, also in a bedroom and on machinery in the barn. There's traces of a vehicle having been kept recently in the barn. They think a van from the length of the wheelbase. No tyre tread because its cobbled inside but there's straw with indentations in it from wheels. Also a patch of oil. There are tracks in the

174

yard which they'll check out but they are certain that the farmer's vehicle – a short wheel-base Land-Rover – is not the vehicle that was parked in the barn. They've compared the prints they found with the computer facsimile of Cade's and they're cautiously optimistic but are not prepared to give a positive ID. I would hardly say your journey was wasted, sir. We need all the help we can get – any information you can give us.'

Rand got up and seated himself at the desk. 'Right, I'll be able to help with the prints when they get back here. In the meantime I'll tell you all I know about Jack Cade. Things you won't find on a computer. What I remember about the man – and I promise you it won't make you happy.'

A uniformed WPC entered the room: 'That's the best I can do, sir,' she told Aske. 'She's come to bits completely. Thinks that the man who stayed with them was her son – except that the son died when he was eighteen. Drowned. May have been suicide, though the coroner's verdict was Misadventure. I still can't get her to believe it even though I showed her the coroner's report.'

'Any description of this man?' asked Rand.

'Chief Superintendent Rand, Thames Valley,' Aske informed her. 'You may tell him.'

'Oh, er . . . no, sir. I mean she described her son. Well, a fair-headed youth – obviously her son as he then was. All she keeps saying is that he came back for his motorcycle. There's no way she'll accept that it was still there and got destroyed in the fire. Insists he left, riding it, the night before.'

'She described no other vehicle?'

'She did say he arrived by bus, but preferred his motorcycle and used it to travel up to London to see his wife to make up. She got very confused at this point. Definitely said "wife" then cried about some "poor little dead soul", but after she stopped weeping she couldn't remember that part at all. I assumed she was thinking about the dead youth.'

'Bus?' Aske enquired. 'Arrived by bus? There's no bus route which goes anywhere near that farm.'

'She definitely said he arrived by bus, sir.'

'Van?' Nash suggested.

'A minibus,' Rand corrected. 'If she was more or less a

recluse, a modern minibus would seem like a bus. Go back to her and ask her if her son – don't bring up anyone else, her mind won't accept it – *drove* the bus or rode in it? If he did drive it, was it kept in one of the outbuildings while he rode the motorbike? She told you he *preferred* his motorcycle which seems to indicate he had a choice available to him right there on the farm itself – not on a bus route. Try and get a description of the vehicle, however vague.'

'You were saying, sir,' Aske prompted, after she had left.

'Jack Cade,' Rand resumed. 'Fiercely patriotic. I saw his cell at Winchester – he was kept on his own because of his SAS background and what had happened in Northern Ireland. Pictures of the Queen, Queen Mother, the whole family. Framed, glass sparkling. The whole cell was like that. Polished, not a speck of dust anywhere, could have been his room back at Hereford. Even in prison fatigues he looked like a perfectly turned-out soldier. Shoes like mirrors, always remember that, asked him how long he took to do it. But by Christ he was no chocolate-box soldier. Tough as teak – but never flaunted it like some of your hard cases do when they get inside. The word in the nick was that you said anything against the Royals – or England for that matter – and if looks could kill . . . I saw that look myself – at his kid's funeral – he used it on his wife, apparently she used to let the girl out on her own when she had a boyfriend around. No trouble from Cade though. No violence. Absolute self-discipline. That's from the SAS, I suppose, you don't last long in that outfit if you can't control yourself.'

'I suppose it was his self-control that got him parolled,' observed Aske.

Rand shook his head. 'Political. I'm certain of it. He killed four men in Belfast. Armed, he said in court, though no evidence of any firearms other than his own weapon was admitted as far as I know. The case was reported in the press but it was still very hush-hush. He was on an undercover mission – driving at the time – when a car rammed him. He said they had weapons. He took out the lot before they got off one shot between them, he said – and I'm inclined to believe him. Four men – supposedly teenagers.'

'They mostly are over there these days,' put in the Special

Branch officer, Simmons. 'The IRA recruit younger ones all the time. Kids believing they're Dirty Harry.'

'Anyway, he was charged with Unlawful Killing. The four were supposed to be kids joyriding who lost control of their vehicle.'

'Did all four?' murmured Nash.

Rand nodded. 'That's worth remembering if it turns out he's the man you're after.'

Nash rubbed a hand over his face in memory. 'He's the one.'

'You were there? You'd recognize him?'

Nash shrugged. 'Helmet and scarf. Impossible to make a positive ID – but those eyes I'll remember till I die. Thought he was going to do all of us.'

'You haven't seen a photograph yet?'

'We've only just got back,' Aske said. 'It's in hand. DCI Murray arranged a runner with CRO.'

Rand opened his briefcase. 'I didn't realize that any of you were actually in the car.' He took out a newspaper cutting in a transparent envelope. 'I used to keep cuttings of all my cases,' he admitted with a deprecating smile. 'That's me at the funeral of Cade's daughter. The man between the two heavies is Cade – handcuffed, though you can't tell. We picked the biggest men in the Division for the job and I still don't believe they could have held him down if he'd decided to make trouble.'

'Got a glass, guvnor?' asked Nash.

Aske opened a drawer and handed him a magnifying glass.

Nash bent closer and covered the top and lower half of the grainy face with his fingers. 'He's the one,' he said, quietly. 'No question. Tell you what, I'm glad this is only a photo. You say that look was for his wife? Cameraman really got the moment, didn't he?'

'Cade had just lost a child he worshipped. There was no doubt in his mind where a lot of the blame for her death lay. He never said so, but it was plain to see how his mind was working. It made it worse that he was inside doing time when it happened, I suppose. It looks as though he's still looking for someone to blame.'

'With his background he must be a survival expert,' said Aske.

177

'That's right. In fact he lived rough for a while after getting out.'

'How rough?'

'Rough. And I don't mean squats or railway waiting rooms. Forests, marshland up in East Anglia, that kind of rough.'

'The funeral was the last time you saw him, sir?' asked Nash.

'No, my next sighting of him was when we raided a gypsy camp. They'd been thieving – or so local residents said. He got pulled in with the rest of them and got his prints taken. They should have been destroyed when he was cleared, but you know how it is. Luckily for you they didn't. I've brought copies your lads can compare with those taken at the farm. You know, I honestly thought Cade would make it all right after he got out, but I suppose the loss of the child put an end to that. I should have realized that he was never going to get over it.'

The WPC returned, knocking on the door and smiling. 'You were right, sir. Minibus. Dark green. All the wrong way round, she said. I couldn't understand what she meant at first but then she said he was working on it and the "motor was where the luggage goes".'

'VW!' Nash exclaimed.

'I thought that too,' said the WPC. 'Then she told me that the rest of the bus was the wrong way round too. The seats were sideways – not right for a bus she insisted because she'd been on a bigger one to London once – also the driver of that bus sat on the other side.'

'Caravanette,' said Rand. 'Left-hand drive. No registration I suppose?'

'No sir, sorry. But I did have a check made for any similar vehicle seen in the county and there is one on the computer. Stopped on the motorway by a patrol-car last Saturday – driver acting suspiciously, made a sudden turn off a roundabout, maybe seeing the patrol-car? Licence in the name of Alan John Cade, address Mill Hill, London, though not living there at present. Listed as having no fixed abode.'

'Got the bastard!' Nash exclaimed, loudly.

'Not yet you haven't,' warned Rand. 'Any other reports on the vehicle?'

'Sighted at Benhall, sir,' the WPC recited from her notes.

178

'The roundabout outside GCHQ. Very late the same Saturday night. He seems to have problems with roundabouts, he circuited twice, that's why they logged him. They're very nervy there.'

'It's not roundabouts he's going to have problems with now,' muttered Nash, rashly.

Rand gave him a thin dry smile. 'This is only the beginning,' he said, then looked up at the WPC with curiosity. 'The sighting outside GCHQ? That's definite. *Saturday* night?'

'Absolutely, sir. Apart from the double swing around the roundabout, they noticed his engine was noisy.'

'Definitely a VW,' said Nash slapping his palms together.

'Forget the vehicle,' Rand said, impatiently. 'It's the timing that's important. It's also wrong.' A frown appeared on his tanned face and he became very still.

'Sir?' Aske queried.

'Last Saturday?' said Rand. 'Last Saturday, Cade's vehicle was positively identified as being outside GCHQ – presumably with Cade inside it. Now, the child was abducted from outside her infant school when?'

'Thursday, the day before yesterday,' offered Aske.

'And her body found on Friday – yesterday. Correct?'

'That's correct, sir,' Aske answered, puzzled.

'And this man Parminter who confessed to her murder works for GCHQ? That is certain?'

'Verified by Cheltenham,' said the Special Branch officer.

'Watching Gerald's movements, wasn't he,' said Nash.

Rand raised his eyebrows. 'Was he? Does Parminter have a record for this type of crime? Does he have a sheet at all?'

'Clean, sir,' Nash answered, losing his brash self-confidence fast, though he could not follow Rand's line of questioning.

'So what was Cade doing in this area – and outside the extremely sensitive Government Communications Headquarters where Parminter worked – at least four days before Parminter abducted the girl? If he killed Parminter because he wanted revenge for his daughter's death, then who gave him the information that Parminter would be a suitable target? That he was a paedophile? Who, except some very official people, would have access to confidential material – any material for that matter – on Gerald Parminter? If you, DS

Nash, in a private capacity, began making enquiries about people employed behind the fences of GCHQ, all you would get is some very strange looks, then some very heavy questioning by some very serious people. Something is very wrong here. Like that old woman said to the WPC about the van – it's all the wrong way round.'

Aske had moved from behind his desk, his already listing world tipping further over. 'Are you suggesting, sir, that Cade could not have known about Parminter's perversions – and therefore he killed him for some other reason entirely?'

'What I'm suggesting is that someone – or some people – who have access to that information and have kept it from the police for their own reasons, may have pointed Jack Cade at Parminter *before* he abducted and killed the child. Or worse still, they did not know about Parminter's appetites at all and set him up to be killed – because they knew he was a traitor. A Russian spy. Now, if it's the latter, Aske, you could well be talking about much more than just murder. You're talking politics and very high government policy. If I were you I would check to see if there have been any other deaths involving GCHQ personnel recently because, sure as I've lost my round of golf this morning, where there's one mole burrowing under the greens there's a whole nest of them dug in there also.'

'Jesus, a network,' murmured Simmons.

'You can go now,' Aske told the WPC hurriedly. 'And don't repeat anything you've heard.' Aske's face was grey. 'There've been two deaths. Two others that is. One in Cheltenham, the other on our patch. The first last Friday, a bottled gas explosion. The second, last Monday, an apparent suicide, carbon-monoxide poisoning. The suicide note we found linked the two deaths: homosexuality. The suicide took his life because of grief.'

Simmons nodded in confirmation. 'Cheltenham SB brought in London because of the security aspects. Which brought in the Security Service. Everyone seemed satisfied. Not happy, but satisfied. Nothing we found linked the two men with espionage activities – not like Parminter.'

'They may have been better at their job. Somebody seems to have linked them with espionage – or they would still be alive. If I'm right.'

'If what you say *is* right, sir,' said Simmons, 'that could mean that Cade might be out there now, setting someone else up for a hit. There's no guarantee that there were only three members in the network.'

'None whatsoever. What can be checked though is to see if anyone employed by GCHQ in a sensitive post has taken unexpected leave of absence, because if I were a member of a hostile spy-network and saw it being decimated around me, I'd sure as hell head for the hills. Wouldn't you?'

Simmons said: 'I'll get on to Cheltenham.'

Rand stood up. 'Before any of you start doing anything, I suggest you ask yourself one question: How high are you prepared to go in your investigations? Because, if this is what my gut tells me it is, then you might well end up pursuing an investigation which could lead you all the way up to the doors of the Cabinet Room at Number Ten Downing Street.'

'Oh,' said Aske.

'Oh, indeed,' agreed Rand, replacing his cutting in his case and laying copies of Cade's fingerprints on the desk-top.

'You're leaving, sir?' Aske asked.

'You bet your pension I am. I've still got tomorrow to play golf and a job to go back to on Monday. I wish you all the same.'

Rand made his way down to the car-park and smiled with pleasure at the lines of his new Audi as he approached it. He entered the car and switched on the engine.

Well, good luck to them, he thought. But the hunter in him gave him the feeling that he was leaving unfinished business behind.

He touched the accelerator, hearing the purr of the engine become a muted growl and smiled again. Life was good to him; why should he complicate it with a case that was not his business and which stank of conspiracy? In his view there was nothing more certain to complicate a senior police officer's life than taking on a case with a background of political conspiracy. Yet, still he hesitated.

A hard rapping on the window cut into his deliberations. He lowered the electric window and a clean-cut, worried face peered down at him.

181

'Chief Superintendent Rand? Murray, Head of CID. Could I please have a word?'

Rand unlocked the passenger door as Murray walked around and stepped inside. 'Spotted the number plate,' Murray said. 'Thought it must be you.'

'I've given your man Aske all the information I have. It seems certain to be Cade,' Rand said, appraising Murray. They get younger all the time, he thought, and I'm no pensioner by a long way. Graduate entrance, stood out a mile. He took in the public school tie but could not place which one. Perhaps not one of the top establishments – but it all helped.

Murray leaned closer, conspiratorially. 'Something's going on.'

'Yes,' Rand agreed. 'Keep me out of it.'

'I need some guidance, sir. This is the first time I've encountered . . . this sort of thing.'

'I have – once. Nothing as deep as murder though. Burglary. We had a suspect and the case seemed to be sewn up tight. Then – right out of nowhere – came a hands-off directive. The suspect went free of course. Go on, tell me: you've been told to let Cade run?'

'How in heaven's name did you work that out?'

'It didn't take much brainwork. You've had two previous deaths involving GCHQ employees in this area. I've just discovered that upstairs. Parminter was number three which stretches coincidence too far. So the Security Service have worked out that they were hit by a person, or persons, unknown. Cade being one – perhaps the only one.' Rand switched off the Audi's engine. 'From Five's side of the street their only interest is the big *Why?* Well, the evidence found in Parminter's house definitely points toward the existence of a Soviet espionage cell. From my limited experience in these matters they rarely place one agent alone – they prefer to have back-up when they can. I understand their preference is four-man cells if they can manage it. So in this case, three are already down which means there may well be one more to go. The chances are that Cade will try for number four and if you hang onto his coat-tails successfully he'll lead you right to him – with the Security boys right behind. Sounds straightforward doesn't it? But in reality – to my nose anyway – the whole thing is bent.'

Murray fidgeted nervously. 'Bent how, sir?'

'Because from the rare, but enlightening, conversations I've had with the Security boys, the KGB don't kill off their agents when the going gets rough. They do everything possible to keep them safely in place but, if all seems lost, they lift them fast. All right, Parminter I can see them hitting because of the nature of his criminal offence: bad security, bad risk, so lose him. But the other two? No, I don't go for that at all. Do you know how the SAS took out a cottage full of IRA planners and bodyguards up on the border some four years ago? Domestic gas-cylinder, beautifully booby-trapped. Great things explosions: if you know how to use the minimal amount of the correct explosive, every scrap of evidence goes up with the bang. And carbon-monoxide poisoning? Well, get the victim drunk enough and he'll sit there and breathe in the exhaust gases because his brain and his body don't work any more, I'm not saying that Cheltenham CID, or yourselves, should have spotted any of this – you had no reason to suspect that the two original deaths were any more than they purported to be: one careless accident and one grief-induced suicide. There was no reason to extend your enquiries – and, with present day work-loads, little opportunity.'

'What are you trying to tell me, sir?' Murray persisted.

'This. If the Russians are not responsible, then someone else is.'

'*Who?*'

'There's your problem. Who could have worked out that the three dead men were all KGB agents? And long-term ones by the sound of it. Also, and here's where it starts to get bent: who gains by their deaths? Or to put it another way: who *loses* by their exposure, interrogation and trial?'

'That makes it political.'

'It surely does.'

Murray looked sick. 'But that might mean that the Security Service is involved themselves? *They* might want number four dead. And I've just agreed to let the killer run loose. If another spy is killed – and all this comes out – I'll be an accessory before the fact.'

'Of murder. Which is why I'm leaving.'

'Shit.'

183

'Quite.'

'What the hell should I do?'

'That depends on whether you wish to uphold the law and risk the wrath of the people who may be behind all this – or go along with the conspiracy and save your career. *Maybe*.'

'Why *maybe*?'

'Think. The government we have now may not be the same one which is in power in a few weeks' time. All kinds of nasties creep out of the woodwork when a new broom starts sweeping out the darker closets of a former administration.'

'What would you do, sir? In my place?'

Rand smiled drily. 'Sitting on the outside as I am, I can afford to say I'd go directly to the top and voice my suspicions. Blow the whole thing wide open. But if I were sitting where you are now . . .? Well, I'd play it long – and plead, later, if it blows wide open, that I did not have enough evidence to follow up my suspicions.'

'Play it long, how?'

'Track Cade down using routine police procedures but, knowing that the man is extremely dangerous, even a special case, keep all patrols well back. No direct approach if he is sighted, advise that considerable back-up will be needed, corner him but do not make any attempt – without pushing it much higher – to apprehend him. Wait. Play it long.'

'You mean create a siege situation?'

'Exactly. That way there'll be negotiations and questions will be asked for which there will have to be answers. That way you might get yourself off the hook and leave the Security Service – along with whoever else may be involved – swinging their legs in mid-air.'

'Thank you, sir,' Murray breathed, gratefully, though still far from untroubled.

Rand asked: 'Did the Security Service tell you that they'd uncovered the network recently or that they've been running a surveillance operation on it over an extended period?'

'I don't think they knew anything about it. They seemed bewildered – and very disturbed. It took Parminter's death to make them realize that something was going on. They're desperate to talk to Cade – but even more desperate to find out who else might be on his list. Why do you ask?'

'Just to try and work out how deep their involvement is – if any. I'd guess – going by what you've just said – that they know nothing at all and what they're doing is covering their backs. They're in deep trouble if a nest of Russian agents has been running undetected for years inside GCHQ. They'll do practically anything they can to stop that leaking out. That's human nature. Nobody wants to look a complete fool. Incompetence is just about the worst crime the head of any government department can commit. Civil servants can actually be sacked if their level of incompetence proves too embarrassing to cover up. If I were you I would not trust anyone at this stage. Play it long, Murray. And watch your own back all the way.'

'Don't worry, I will. Any suggestions as to where this man Cade might hide?'

'If he's after number four – or more – in the network, he won't waste time hiding – not after the way he came out into the open and did Parminter. He'll want to get it over with. I've told your team to check with GCHQ to see if anyone has taken an unscheduled holiday or is off sick for an extended period since this business began. Of course Five will be onto that as well but I doubt if they'll share their findings. They'll want to follow that alley themselves. I don't honestly believe that GCHQ will co-operate on that either, it's too sensitive. My advice is to accept that someone is feeding Cade information – and that the information is up-to-date. He'll be moving to where number four was headed. Knowing Cade he'll utilize whatever cover he can while on the road. No hotels for a start, he'll sleep in his vechicle – a VW caravanette apparently – but even that he may consider too risky. It depends on what resources he has and they may, if you're lucky, be limited. Put out a call to all divisions. Spread the responsibility as much as you can. He's used to living rough and he may well go to ground if he thinks we're onto him. One thing you can pass on: the last time he hit a hard patch he shacked up with gypsies. He could do it again – and they might hide him because he knows their ways and their language. But remember, you must advise that if he is located, no direct approach should be made until an armed unit has arrived. Cade is a crack-shot and a trained killer – and he won't give up without a fight, I can promise you that.'

185

Rand started the engine again.

'You won't stay, sir?' Murray asked, hopefully,

'It's your problem. If he comes on my patch that will make it mine. You have my 'phone number, call me if you need any more advice. I'll help if I can.'

Rand drove off, leaving Murray standing in the car-park, a disconsolate, slightly hunched figure. Glancing at him in the mirror Rand suddenly identified the public school tie he was wearing. It was not so minor after all. Well, it won't help you much in this, he mused. Nor will your degree. This was all about instinct and experience and neither of those attributes came with privilege or intellectual qualifications. They only came with living the job.

Chapter Ten

Cade had no illusions about his position. He knew he should turn the camper around and run. But still he let the miles roll by under the wheels, pushing his doubts away, for somehow it seemed that the only way left for him was to go forward. He had to continue believing that what he was doing was right.

He passed police vehicles many times on the journey down to the New Forest and on each occasion waited for the blare of the siren behind him. If it happened, would he pull over? he asked himself each time but the decision was not forced upon him.

He thought about what had to be done. Would he finish the woman without being killed in the process? Harlow had warned that there would be guards this time. Russians? Where from? The London embassy? Unlikely, if only because they would want to keep the woman's cover intact.

So they would use people not known to the Security Service: undercover agents, sleepers trained to kill. Which meant Spetsnatz. He had no illusions about their quality, the SAS had given him a healthy respect for this deeply-buried group of saboteurs and assassins. They existed, despite the ridicule poured on the idea by the peace movements – whom he despised as ostriches with heads buried in the sand at best, or at their worst, as traitors. Like the woman, he reminded himself, allowing the thought to settle and bring his blood up for the deed.

So how many? It was stupid – and futile – to think about that. The only way he would find out was by going in. He shook the thoughts from his head.

The forest was all around him now, closing in as the day began to die. He was exhausted and drained. He lit a cigarette and drew smoke from it gratefully, watching closely for the small left-hand track which would take him to the house. And the woman.

Not tonight, his training told him. You're not ready, you'll get blown away before you put one foot into the killing ground. He rolled the window down to throw out the cigarette and saw, in a quick flash, a jumble of cars and caravans set deep in the trees to his right.

He applied the brakes and turned the van around when the road was clear, leaving it at the point where flattened grass directed him straight into the trees.

He drove right into their camp and switched off the engine.

Men approached him first, as was their way with strangers, the women and children staying back but curious. He greeted them in Romany, using the dialect he had picked up during the year he had spent with another group who were working their way south from the cold north.

A good year that, he recalled. Not like the one before when no one wanted him after taking one look at his record. The gypsies then had asked no questions, save the ones they used to judge him by. He had savings and some of these he carried with him – so he was able to pay his way, which they had admired. They hated freeloaders and soon found them out; ejecting such men – or women – from their camp, usually with force. He soon found out that they never stole from those they had befriended.

He remembered how impressed they had been by his trapping skills and the way he could track anything completely undetected. He had shown them new ways to cover their own tracks when necessary and they, in turn, had shown him their hospitality. They had accepted him into their world while his own rejected him.

Excepting, of course, Harlow and Brock who, although much later, had given him back his self-respect, his pride and his battered faith in his own beloved England.

One of the group of men before him replied to his greeting and made a gesture which Cade returned.

'Come join us,' said the man in Romany.

'You honour me,' Cade replied and followed him through the gathering crowd to the place where they had made an oblong pit now covered in soil from which smoke escaped though there was no visible sign of fire. Underneath he knew would be wrapped meat – probably lamb – which would have been cooking slowly for most of the day in layers of stone, charcoal and earth. He was pleased that they were genuine Romanies and not one of the many bands of travellers who were no more than lazy drop-outs who preyed on society like pariah dogs. These were an honourable people whose culture could be traced as far back as ancient India.

Cade took a seat by a folding table with the man who gave his name as plain John, then, as was the custom, took his time appraising the cars and caravans which filled the camp, finally complimenting his host on the obvious good fortune that he and his people shared.

'We share our good fortune with those of our kind in need,' John replied formally, pleased.

'You trade well?' Cade enquired.

'Times are poor for the country. Much metal is discarded when people cannot afford to look after the things they own. We gather well and make good use of what others use badly.'

'This is the life,' replied Cade, using the phrase in their philosophical sense. 'Misfortune for some brings good fortune for others.'

'This is the life,' agreed John, with a gesture of thanks. 'You are travelling far . . .?'

'Jack,' Cade said. 'Not far. But my journey has been long and my destination one I must prepare myself for.'

'Your weariness is our pleasure. Where is this place you seek?'

'A few miles away. A house, in the forest. On its own.'

'There is such a house – through the forest, westwards. A man lives there, alone. A strange one. He lives in the house only when it is his choice. The young men have seen him running through the trees like a fox. He knows the way of silence. He wears no shoes and his clothes are poor – though he is young. He is, perhaps, damaged.' John tapped his sleek black head.

'There should also be a woman.'

John shouted harshly at the group around the smoking pit and two youths detached themselves. He spoke rapidly, losing Cade, then raised his thick eyebrows at their answer, which came with smiles brimming with innuendo.

'You are right. A woman came today – but first two other men came to the house in a car. A fine car.' He formed with his hands the low sweeping lines of the Jaguar. 'Not one that should be driven on forest tracks.' He smiled with pride. 'We see everything.'

'Where are these two men now?' Cade asked.

'They have gone with the car but the woman remains with the strange one.'

One of the youths made a gesture which was obviously sexual.

John laughed loudly. 'They would like to bring her here. The strange one will stay inside the house tonight, I think. He too has good luck.'

Cade reached inside his anorak and took out the photographs of Rhoda James, holding them out to the young men.

They nodded studying the photographs eagerly. One said: 'Yes, the same. You have others?' and mimed an exaggerated female figure with his hands.

John's expression clouded and he issued a quick reprimand then turned to Cade. 'This woman – she is . . . something to you?'

Cade smiled. 'She is not my woman.'

Relief came over the Romany's swarthy face. 'I thought perhaps . . .?' but he left his thoughts unspoken.

'She has not dishonoured me – but she is dishonourable. If she were in your camp she would sell your secrets to those who would use them against you.'

John made an odd, surprisingly loud sound with his tongue which both youths returned.

Cade asked: 'The men who left in the car? How were they dressed? For the forest or the city?'

'Not for the forest,' replied one of the youths, showing rotten teeth.

'Perhaps there are others. These will be dressed in clothes which make them like the forest.'

'Soldiers?' John asked.

190

'Not soldiers, but with a soldier's skills. If your people became too curious they might hurt them.'

'You also?'

'Yes, but that is my choice. That is why I must rest. First I must tell you this. The police may be looking for me. I must reach this woman before they start to hunt me. It is a matter of honour to me.'

'You will take her away from the house?' John enquired.

'If I can,' Cade lied. 'I have warned you of this so that you can choose if I stay in your camp tonight. I would not wish to bring ill-fortune on your people.'

John considered this, then said, firmly, 'You may stay.' He looked hard and long at Cade then asked: 'You have a cigarette?'

Cade offered his packet and took one for himself.

The Romany blew smoke then touched his forehead between his eyes where his thick eyebrows met over his strong nose. 'I have the gift,' he announced. 'Do you wish to know what I see?'

Cade hesitated, then dipped his head carefully.

'Between the strange one and you there is . . . something' – He hooked his hands together, the fingers locked tight – 'so. He and you are the same – brothers in the heart though much water separates you. The woman, she is . . . not evil . . .?' He made a snaking movement with his hand.

'Devious,' Cade offered.

'Like this, yes. You and the man . . .' he frowned deeply '. . . there is something very strong I cannot see clearly . . . but in some way you will give him the responsibility for a life. A child's life.'

'My child is dead. Her child? The woman's?'

'I cannot see,' said John, then paused. 'Perhaps it is better if you do not go to this woman. She will try to have her way between you and the man.'

'I don't understand?' Cade said.

John said, gravely: 'Seeing is a gift which is only ever half-given – except to some, who then wish they had not received it, for it is a gift bound with pain.' He arose. 'We eat now, then you must rest. Tomorrow, the road you take from here will make your decision for you.'

Cade sat with the gypsies, beside their leader, and told them of his year spent with the other Romanies which brought pleasure because they were known to John's group but the subject of the house and the people in it was not raised again. After the meal was over he was led to one of the older, wooden caravans and fell asleep immediately, all fears for the next day blotted out by exhaustion.

'I've put two steaks under the grill,' Rhoda James told Wilder as he returned from his prowling in the fading light. 'Please eat with me.'

'All right,' he said.

'They're almost ready. I'll bet you eat yours raw.'

He pulled a denim shirt from a chair and put it on.

'We're dressing for dinner, are we? You should have told me.'

'What's your problem, lady?' he asked, washing his hands.

'Oh, just a little nervy you know. I'm just *thrilled* to be in this predicament. Go on, tell me I must be here out of choice. I've made my bed so I've got to lie in it? Is that the pearl of folksy wisdom forming in that clam you call a mouth?'

'Don't work your hate off on me. Whatever you're into is your problem.'

'I was given to understand it's also yours.'

'I'm here to protect you – that's where it ends.'

'It's not hate, damn you, its sheer body fright.' She banged the plates on the table and filled them. 'Feeding time,' she snapped.

They ate in silence and afterwards she lit a cigarette.

'They'll kill you,' he said.

She smiled. 'Has anyone ever told you that you're a real pain in the arse?'

Wilder laughed – to her amazement. 'I didn't think you were capable!' she exclaimed, mockingly.

'I've never heard anyone say *ass* that way before.'

'I suppose you think British women don't use words like that either?'

'I've heard worse.'

'In your sheltered existence? Come on, you've opted out of the rat-race and you've got no real idea of what's going on in

192

the real world out there. Grow up, join the rest of us poor sufferers. Okay so you've got a nature-fixation – you love trees – so become a tree surgeon. Don't hide behind them for the rest of your life.'

'Go to hell, lady.'

'And stop calling me *lady*, damn you, the name's Rhoda – and if you're really going to stay in the house tonight you can call me Rho.'

He stood up. 'I'll check the perimeter then I'll be back.'

'Where do you sleep? In the woodshed!'

'Right here – but tonight I'll sleep outside your room. I can't cover both entrances to the house but if anyone breaks in they've got to come up the stairs.'

'I feel safer already – I've always dreamed of having my own tame man laying across the threshold to my room. Though one could hardly describe you as being tame.'

He unrolled his sleeping bag and withdrew a heavy hunting knife with a matt black handle and carbon blade, viciously serrated, and a US Special Forces Smith & Wesson .357 Magnum revolver with a thick silenced barrel.

'And there I was thinking you could do all of it with only your bare hands. It's the telly that gives us these illusions, you know.'

'I'll be back,' he said, ignoring her. 'Lock the door behind me.'

'Do I wait, heart a-flutter for your knock?'

He pointed at a board fixed to the wall which had a series of electronic alarms screwed to it, all numbered. 'Two is the trip-wire out back – anyone who approaches the kitchen will hit it. I'll blip it three times.'

'What are all these others?'

'Perimeter, immediate area – the whole place.'

'So who were *you* trying to keep out?'

'Anyone.'

'Except me?'

'You come as part of the deal. Or people like you.'

'What deal?'

'The house.'

'So the house is a reward for past services?'

Wilder stepped outside but turned the light out first.

'What did you do for them?' she whispered in the dark, but he had already slipped away.

She felt her way to the door, pulled it shut and slammed the double bolts across then leaned against it, still in darkness wishing she was back at home. Except that home is even more dangerous, she thought, and wished instead she had never allowed herself to be seduced by greed into betraying her country and a way of life she wanted more than anything else to enjoy to the full. All she wanted now was to get out alive and not be exposed because that would mean a living death which she could never stand. The thought of death terrified her but at least she did not know what came after it. The possibility of prison or forced defection to her former masters in the Soviet Union chilled her to her soul. She doubted if she could face any of the possibilities with any courage at all.

'At heart, Rhoda James, you're a weak, greedy bitch,' she said aloud, then nearly fainted when a buzzer sounded three times.

She worked the bolts frantically.

'Why didn't you put the light back on?' asked Wilder.

'Because you turned it off.'

'Silhouette,' he explained. 'It's all right when I'm outside.'

'Next time tell me.'

He walked past her and flicked the light switch then saw the state she was in. 'You want to tell me about it?' he asked.

'You know damn well I can't.'

He hefted his sleeping bag. 'You'd better think about sleeping.'

'Do you really think I can sleep!'

'I think you should try.'

'I need a bath.'

'You go ahead, I'll be right outside.'

She went upstairs while he checked the windows and doors. 'I'm not locking the bathroom door,' she warned.

He stood at the bottom of the stairs seeing her clutching a cream towelling robe to herself. 'No one will come through the window, take a look at the locks. This is a Company facility.'

'I don't care.' She entered the bathroom and drew water, slipping off her robe. The mirror showed her all she did not want to see: bruised eyes much too bright and high cheekbones which instead of lifting her face seemed only to emphasize the hollows of her cheeks. She swore at her reflection. 'You'd better pull yourself together, love, or you'll turn into an old crone overnight.' The steam had put a fine sheen on her skin and the sight of her full breasts pleased her, their nipples proud. This did not surprise her, she had learned quite early in her life that fear acted upon her body like a strong aphrodisiac.

There was a musky scent to her skin as she ran a finger over its damp surface. Sweat, she thought, recalling her moment of fear in the darkness, breaking out all over me in a salty flood which had nothing at all to do with heat. That icy chill still touched her core but the steam and the heat given off by the pouring water thawed her – if only on the surface.

Outside the bathroom she could hear muffled sounds, then, after a few moments silence. A footfall sounded directly outside the door, a distinct creak on a floorboard.

Wilder opened the door, his eyes on her slick, naked body.

'I thought you'd never get around to it,' she said.

Simon Adeane sat in the lounge-bar of the inn he had booked into, drinking a pint of their real ale. He was playing the English gentleman and part of him enjoyed this charade while below the surface he was distinctly unhappy with his superior's secretiveness which indicated that Weidenstein did not entirely trust him. Still, he decided, perhaps it was better, in the long term, to be on the outside.

The bar had filled with both tourists and locals and Adeane allowed himself to be drawn into conversation with a group propping up the bar by his side, always fascinated by the way the British, who would cross a street to avoid getting into conversation with an acquaintance, would, contrarily, engage in conversation with total strangers once they entered a pub.

The talk, inevitably, zeroed in on politics and, of course, the forthcoming general election.

'What I want to know,' said one customer, 'is what alternative we have? This lot begun by telling us we married the bleeding Continent of Europe and got ourselves a nice fat dowry in trade – but all we've ended up with is some foreign parliament overturning our laws. As for more trade – well, I mean, just take a look at the figures.'

'And the dole queues,' put in another.

'Well at least they built some mountains out of each other's molehills!' suggested a wag.

'We should have gone in with the Yanks and bugger Europe – they've got it right. Always have,' argued the first.

'We're already one of their aircraft-carriers,' said an intense woman with a small CND badge on her jacket. 'They're absolutely paranoid about the Russians.'

A serious-looking man further down leaned inward. 'Both America and Russia will do anything to stop the Common Market from working effectively. It was Hitler's dream, wasn't it – and Napoleon's: the United States of Europe; a power-bloc which would have more clout than both the super-powers. Both of them will do anything to split the community – the Russians through subversion and the Americans by buying us up. They're halfway there already.'

'Well at least they're both tough,' said the first man, bringing his fist down on the bar. 'I mean look at the way they handle criminals. All we do is give them a paid holday. Even our kids aren't safe any more – another one got murdered yesterday.'

'Yes, but someone shot the bastard that did it,' the landlord cut in. 'Good luck to him. I reckon the coppers will let him get away with it. Should do anyway. That's my view for what it's worth.'

'Excuse me,' Adeane said, cutting in. 'Was that the case near Cheltenham?'

'That's the one, sir. Gloucester way.'

'The man who did it was shot? You mean shot dead?'

'While the coppers had him. In one of their cars. They're looking for the man who did it – I reckon it must be one of the kid's relatives. Got a name and a photo. Haven't you seen the news today? Big manhunt going on, they say. Here, Alice, switch on the nine o'clock. Gent here wants to see what happened to that evil bastard who strangled the kiddie. On in a couple of ticks, sir, same again?'

'I'll have a scotch instead,' said Adeane, considerably shaken.

The news came on, halting the conversation at the bar. The lead story was of Gerald Parminter's death which the newsreader described as being 'a brutal execution by a cool attacker which the police describe as possibly being a vengeance killing.' A nationwide hunt was in progress and the public were warned not to approach the killer who was extremely dangerours, she announced. The man's name was Alan Cade – known as Jack – and it was believed that he may have had connections with the SAS in his past.

This latter piece of information brought a ragged cheer from around the room.

Simon Adeane sat, glass in hand, looking at the cold prisoner's face staring out with bitter eyes from the television screen.

Yes, vengeance, he thought, but not for a child. He swallowed his drink and walked out to the Jaguar. Inside he used the in-car telephone, scrambling the call with equipment in a briefcase taken from the boot.

He spoke with Weidenstein briefly, suggesting he should watch the next news on television, then went back inside and ordered another drink.

He smiled to himself imagining Max Weidenstein's face when he heard that the conspiracy was being run from such a high level that they were using one – or possibly more – members of the crack Special Air Service Regiment to carry out their will.

Chapter Eleven

Cade was awoken by a hand clamped firmly over his mouth and a hiss from a face close to his own in the darkness. He could see the rotten teeth of the gypsy youth as blue light swept his face at rapid intervals.

Cade nodded and the youth released his grip, moving swiftly like a shadow as he drew back a rug on the caravan's floor. Underneath was a small panel, barely visible, which the gypsy prised up using the flat blade of his knife. Forcing himself through the tight aperture, Cade squeezed his body into the long, shallow false bottom.

His body touched both the floor of the false bottom and the supports of the caravan floor above, affording him barely enough room to expand his chest as he breathed. He silently blessed his SAS training, part of which had taught him to withstand the claustrophobic effects of confined spaces.

The floor-supports pressed down on his chest as footsteps sounded above him and in one mad moment he thought he might be crushed if any more men entered the caravan. Then air swept into the shallow space and he was dragged out.

John was sitting on the bunk with the youth who had woken Cade.

'Police,' the gypsy leader explained. 'They checked our vehicles. I listened to the calls on their radio. I think they hunt everywhere for you. There were only two men but even so they were very cautious.'

'They must have seen my van,' stated Cade.

'They looked at all the vehicles – but not inside. Yours was only one of many. I told them they all belonged to us. They

198

accepted this. Usually they ask for papers and make trouble. Sometimes they make us move on. These two only wanted to go, I sensed it. They carried their fear badly.'

'They had my number – must have done.'

'We can hide you.'

'Thank you – but they've spotted the van so you're already in enough trouble.' Cade rubbed his stinging eyes, then his cropped head, his mind almost numb with fatigue. 'I must finish what I started. It is my way.'

'It is a good way – unless it finishes you also.'

'I'll make it.' Cade looked at his watch. Past three o'clock. He had to move. 'I need some things from the van.' He touched John on the shoulder then leapt down to the grass and raced across to the camper.

Inside, he took camouflage clothing from a locker and put them on over the clothes he was wearing. This done he found a pair of combat boots and laced them up over the double thickness of trousers. He stopped for a moment and sat, his head in his hands, then forced himself up and took the four folders from where he had hidden them and replaced Rhoda James's photographs. From under the camper he removed the Browning and spare magazines from the box clamped to the chassis, adding extra rounds to the magazines, which he always stored two-thirds full to ease the spring tension.

John played his torch over Cade as he emerged from under the vehicle, the Browning under his camouflage jacket.

'You too are a soldier,' said John with a nod which might have been confirmation of his thoughts. 'Like the men who may be waiting for you.'

'I was.'

'In your heart you are still.'

Cade held out the four folders. 'Will you burn these – right now?'

'Yes.'

Cade tossed him the keys to the camper. 'You told the police it was yours – now it is. The log-book is inside. Tell them you bought it from me – make up some place where we met. You haven't got around to re-registering it yet. There's clothes and stuff in there, you'd better hide them or burn them.' He tapped the zipped pocket of the combat jacket. 'I have money . . .'

John clicked his tongue. 'You may need the vehicle?' he questioned.

'Not now. I couldn't use it anyway. I'm sure the police know about it.'

'We thank you for your gift, then.'

'You're welcome to it. Just point them away from me.'

John nodded, then said. 'Remember. The man – the strange one – you will give him responsibility for a child. I see this.'

'Do you see me dead?'

'I see you have a choice but only you know the path you will take.'

'I'll see you, then,' Cade said and made a gesture which the Romany returned.

The police came back minutes later, in force, with many vehicles and armed men some of whom had already circled the camp with stealth but Jack Cade slipped right through them.

Cade decided he was far enough away to risk the beam of his small pencil-torch. The detailed map which had been inside the envelope Harlow had given him confirmed that he should head due west. Around four miles, maybe less, he thought; so keep moving.

His legs felt leaden but as he moved onward the muscles warmed and the constant crouching, waiting, then rapid silent spurts between gaps in the densely packed trees became easier. He halted at intervals to check the tiny compass he always carried inside the combat jacket but it only served to confirm his own well-developed sense of direction.

He could hear, well behind him now, but still clear in the still night, the rasp of a police loud-hailer and even thought he heard his own name barked out. They were bloody quick, he thought. What led them to him? Old Sullivan? Had they traced the Triumph? He'd smudged the number-plate but the bike itself was a dead give-away. Had the old boy decided that what he had done was wrong? If he had, had he told Lettie? And had she fought him over it? He imagined she had – and cried a lot as well. Cade grinned warmly: great people – whatever they had decided to do.

The trees were a real problem, coming at him out of the dark when the moon slid behind clouds. Several times he found

himself on his back, cursing, yet, despite complete awareness
of his dire situation, fighting the urge to laugh at himself – out
loud. Get a grip on yourself, he scolded silently, or you'll be so
screwed up you'll get blown away without knowing it.

Morning seemed a century away. And the house as distant
as the stars which hung in spangled patches an eternity above
the tree tops.

He rested for a while, flat on his back, staring at the stars. He
thought of little Amy. Could she see him now? He wept and
curled himself into a ball, stifling his sobbing with the hood of
his combat jacket.

His grief subsided, as it always did, leaving the usual dead
numbness which in some ways was worse. Then the fire
burned in him and he took out her photograph – but not for
her beaming smile. He read the names on the reverse and
memorized every letter of the address where he would kill
next. This time for himself – not for Queen, not even for
Country. For Jack Cade and his daughter.

He wouldn't kill them. They would just give up from the
pain. He knew more ways of inflicting pain – in varying
degrees – than any man should know. He'd learned well from
the different races, the different countries, where he had
served. He thanked God, actually praying and saying it under
his hood: Thank you Lord for giving me this knowledge. It did
not seem blasphemous to him as he mumbled the words. God
had shown him these things, placed him where he would learn,
and now he would put the knowledge to use. Every soldier, he
told himself, fights for a cause – right or wrong – and as the
gypsy had said, he was still, in his heart, a soldier. Now, or very
soon, when this was over, he had his own cause to fight for.

He stood up and moved onward, always westward.

He sensed the clearing before he reached it – a shift in the air
– a widening of silence; the constricting sound-deadening trees
opening up like the bell of a horn, allowing passage for the
compressed note. He dropped, quite flat, snuggling himself
into the leaves and grass. Silence. All around him like feather
pillows, yet out in front it was wide and open, and dangerous.

The only way to go was forward but the moment that every
soldier fears the most spiked him to the forest floor. The
enemy, shielded by night and deadly beneath its cover. The

same inevitable questions rolled through his mind – useless as always because no one could give an answer to them, excepting the enemy himself: How many? Where? How armed? How well trained? And how scared?

Go on you bastard! *Forward*. There's no going back now.

He inched forward, slithering, never lifting his stomach from the ground, his progress marked with a muted swish of sound which might have been breeze sweeping low through leaves and bushes.

It would take for ever, he told himself. If he made it at all? Then it really would take for ever.

He had made it to the edge of the clearing, though he still did not quite know how.

By rights they should have nailed him already.

Perhaps I'm better than I thought, he grinned. Or perhaps they're not so good themselves.

Or perhaps they're so bloody good and so bloody well-equipped that they can afford to wait and pick me off where they'll know I'll go down and never get up again.

Ever.

'Let me make your position quite clear,' said the uniformed Hampshire police chief inspector. 'At the very least you can be charged with suspicion of stealing one Volkswagen Caravanette, colour dark green. On the other hand there is the very real possibility that you may be charged with harbouring a man who we have reason to believe is the murderer of a suspect being held in police custody. Also, being involved in conspiracy to murder.'

'I know nothing of these things,' said the gypsy leader.

'You do however know about the caravanette.'

They were sitting in John's large, comfortable caravan, facing each other across a rosewood veneered stow-away table.

'I bargained for the vehicle – the price was right so I purchased it.'

A burly uniformed sergeant put his foot on the caravan steps and leaned in. 'We've been right through the lot, sir. If he was here he must have heard us coming.'

'More likely he got moving right after the patrol-car reported sighting the suspect vehicle. Have the men extend the sweep of the woods – he may just have gone to ground.'

'It's black as pitch under those trees sir.'

'They'll just have to do their best. Thank you, sergeant.'

'You have destroyed our homes,' John complained.

'Disrupted, not destroyed. You can replace everything once my men have completed their search. Now, I want you seriously to consider your position. You have been arrested previously for receiving stolen goods so a conviction now would certainly mean prison. Surely you owe no loyalty to this man? He's not one of your people, we both know that. So he's spent time with another group in the past – does that give him the right to jeopardize your freedom?'

'A man sold us the vehicle last night – he needed money – we gave him food, then he left us.'

'He walked?'

'Yes, he walked.'

'And what time would this be?'

John shrugged. 'We do not watch time as you do. Perhaps it was nine o'clock. After we finished eating.'

'In which direction did he walk?'

John waved vaguely toward the main road.

'Towards Bournemouth?'

'Perhaps. I did not go with him. None of my people did.'

A man in civilian clothes rapped on the open door. 'Sir, you'd better come out and take a look at this.'

'Have a long think about your situation,' advised the chief inspector, rising.

He walked with the CID officer through the debris left by their intensive search of all the caravans and vehicles, arriving at the smouldering pit – now excavated. Scorched clothing was laid out under arc-lights and, at one end, the partially burned remains of four buff-coloured folders.

The detective bent down, indicating that the chief inspector should do the same. Without speaking he flicked open each one with a ball-point pen. The stiff material of the folders had saved much of the contents inside although the heat had caused the triple-posed photographs in each to contract.

'This little lot could cause an explosion somewhere, I'd say,' said the chief inspector quietly, reading the unburned passages.

'Like a nuclear blast,' the detective responded. 'Special Branch?'

'Oh, most definitely. You'd better see what Forensic can do with these. The clothes could be his – is that your conclusion?'

'Got to be.'

'I wonder if the dogs could get any scent from those? What with the fire and whatever they've been cooking in there.' He wrinkled his nose.

'Luckily they were close to the top. I'd say chummy hasn't been gone long.'

The chief inspector hauled himself upright with a groan. 'Bloody back! Always tweaks in the early hours. Very well, I'll have more men drafted in – and more dogs. In the meantime I'll see what Gypsy Joe in there has to say about burning official secrets.' He walked back to the caravan, clutching his lumbar region and climbed up painfully. 'Now,' he began, sitting down with relief. 'Let me review your position, but this time with additional facts. What can you tell me about possessing material which could be classed as official secrets belonging to Her Majesty's Government, which, it would appear, you have unsuccessfully attempted to destroy?'

John stared at him blankly.

'In the fire. Out there. Documents which could put you away for a very long time indeed. Your people originate from Eastern Europe I believe – or at least some of you do – and I shouldn't be surprised if you stay in contact with the old country. Perhaps you travel there now and then. Maybe even pass on the odd piece of information? Documents? Microfilms?' His voice hardened. 'I'm talking about espionage and that gets you thirty years' high security – no remission. We've got the evidence, so you're nicked – unless you want to point us in the right direction that is?'

John sighed. 'Sometimes life leave a man no choice.'

'Never a truer word spoken,' agreed the chief inspector.

The negro lay in his hide, completely covered by a thatch of damp branches and leaves. He munched a portion of his acquired United States Air Force air-crew survival pack, his heavy jaw working continuously, well after he had finished; a motion caused by the need to create saliva in his dry mouth brought on by the benzedrine tablets he had swallowed to ward off sleep. He knew the benzedrine was necessary and enjoyed the buzz it gave him but it also caused an intense craving for nicotine which he fought desperately to quell.

He had lain perfectly still for hours, clenching and relaxing his muscles to aid his blood-flow, regularly sweeping the killing-ground with the big, powered, night-vision device. Beside him, ready at hand, lay a Remington .223 rifle, chosen by the two contract gunmen for two reasons. The first being that it was a non-automatic weapon and could, convincingly, be passed off as small-calibre hunting rifle if found in their possession, and the second that the .223, when fitted with a heavy-duty silencer, produced a report no louder than a fierce expellation of breath. Despite the small calibre, a .223 hollow-nosed round could be devastating upon impact.

The negro's craving for nicotine had reached such a high pitch that he could no longer resist it. He considered the position of his hide and the effectiveness of the cover it provided.

One slow, deep draw, he tempted himself. Just one. He could use his special hunter's lighter, a battery-powered device which made no flame but instead heated an element like a motorcar cigar-lighter. He would light-up inside his camouflage jacket and any smoke would be dissipated by the thatch above him.

But his partner would kill him.

He chewed his cheeks, then silently slipped in a slab of gum which had nicotine content, but in his heightened state it tasted like a mouthful of dead cigarette-ends. He shifted position in agitation, determined to fight his craving, laying down his night-vision device for a moment.

Cade saw a ghostly glow appear for the briefest moment to his right and slithered in its direction, thanking God that the summer had been ruined by rains and that the leaves were sodden. If it were autumn I'd be dead, he thought.

The faint back-glow from the NVD had vanished and despite his eyes remaining on the spot where it had materialized he could not be certain where his enemy might be.

The moon had him now, sliding from behind clouds. He felt

as exposed as he might be had a parachute-flare hung above the clearing. His nostrils flared as he caught an acrid scent and he smiled. He was so close he could see wisps of smoke emerging from different points on a rising mound of leaves. He watched for where the smoke was most concentrated and tensed himself, raising his haunches carefully off the ground to give him impetus for the strike.

He sprang forward, landing flat and lengthways along the mound, his left hand feeling the hardness of bone where the skull lay, the knife in his right already through the cover of vegetation and across the throat. From beneath him came a deep gurgling noise and violent shuddering from head to feet. He forced down with all his weight to minimize the death-throes then a tiny bright circle alighted on his body like a stray firefly, followed by a thump as he rolled fast to his right, his left arm already wet and nerveless. Despite the pain and the urgent need to assess the damage, he lay perfectly still, eyes forward, judging the trajectory of the bullet which had struck him.

Just keep using that laser-sight, he told his unseen enemy. Don't be clever, don't unclip it, forget the moon, my son, let me see that little bright spot which tells me I'm dead. Then I'll blow your head off.

He inched his near-useless arm into the ready-made grave, watching the firefly flit nearer, then locked his numbed fingers around the weapon he knew had to be there, clenched his teeth against the pain and in one rapid movement, snatched the rifle out and rolled over and over, his eyes always forward the way he had been trained, ignoring the deadly whips which lashed at the leaves behind him, seeing only the tongues of fire far off in the night.

His return of fire was so quick that the rapid triple-snick of the Remington's bolt-action was a blur of sound, with little recoil from the totally silenced rifle. Somewhere, something fell heavily, snapping branches which seemed to cut off the cry of pain which began, then, as quickly, died.

Dead-eye Jack, thought Cade. Never anyone better. And cups to prove it – all in the bloody bitch's attic turning brown. Don't be stupid, she's already flogged them, hasn't she?

His shoulder was crucifying him with pain, and there were needles of fire in the left side of his chest.

206

Fucking hollow-points, he swore. Bastards!

Then he remembered how he had dum-dummed the round for Parminter.

In his combat jacket was a field-dressing pack, he removed it and peeled off his jacket gingerly. The sight, even by moon-light, was not pleasant – a worse wound than he'd imagined. He probed with his fingers, eyes squeezed shut in agony. The solid bone of his shoulder seemed intact, but definitely dam-aged. Chipped all to hell, he thought with the round opening up like a banana-skin after it hit. There were several exit wounds but that did not mean that half of it was not still in there scattered amongst the ripped muscle and tissue.

He bound it tightly after applying the field-dressing and a tourniquet then lay back deciding whether or not to inject himself with one of the morphine ampoules. He forced himself up and replaced his jacket.

Not yet, he decided. Morphine puts you to sleep – pain won't let you.

The house was completely dark, no light from any of the rooms at all.

That doesn't mean a thing, he warned himself. If there were two out here there'll be more inside. You hope there were only two out here! He moved, found a heavy stick and tossed it far to his right, but it was only a gesture. Any decent sniper would already be aware of his position and would be pinning him down with rapid fire while others closed in to finish him.

Just the two, he confirmed. And whatever's inside.

Cade began making his way around the clearing to the point where the trees were nearest to the house. He stopped at their edge, tears squeezed from his eyes by the pain. Give it a moment, old son. Take a few deep breaths, sit yourself down and check the Browning. Go for it when you're ready – there's all the time in the world to die – give yourself a bit more of life. He hefted the Browning one-handed, feeling its weight but unable now to work the slide with his left hand. Sod it, you know damn well there's one up the spout, you're just bloody procrastinating. Time to go, old son. Now or never.

He heard a rustling and turned to his left. To his astonish-ment, a section of the ground lifted very slowly. He was so close he could have slammed it shut with one unstretched boot. Then it flipped backward and a man, seemingly naked, crept out on his belly like a reptile emerging from a hole.

It took only one rapid movement by Cade to be above him, the Browning pressed hard against his spine and one boot rammed between the man's thighs, jammed against his testicles.

'Move and you're done,' said Cade.

'Okay, Charlie,' murmured Declan Wilder, his face in the dirt.

Cade kicked with his boot then, as Wilder curled up in agony, reached under his body and found the silenced magnum. The knife was in its sheath fixed to the belt on Wilder's jeans; this he threw into the bushes while the gun went into his combat jacket. Despite the agonizing kick, Wilder had made no cry.

'How many inside?'

No reply.

Again the boot struck.

'Try harder.'

Wilder was curled double, face contorted.

'It's not worth it, mate,' said Cade but he knew men and guessed that this one could be booted into oblivion and still not crack.

'All right, we cross over together – which means you get it first.'

Wilder was sucking in air with rapid breaths.

'Up,' ordered Cade, switching the Browning for the silenced magnum, jamming it into Wilder's spine as he stood, the filed-down hammer back. 'I'm going to stay right up against you – now you know the poundage on this trigger so if you think you can risk a trip or a throw you just go ahead.'

They traversed the clear ground quickly, approaching the back of the house. At the kitchen door Cade said. 'Open it.'

'I can't do that,' said Wilder.

Cade frowned at the unexpected American Southern accent but discounted it. The woman had been bought so the Yank was too.

'Don't fuck around!'

'Can't be done,' said Wilder.

Cade struck him hard with the revolver, about the temple.

Wilder attempted to parry the blow moving quickly with it, but there was still enough force to fell him.

A sound came from inside, very close to the door, followed by a harsh, terrified whisper.

Cade's mind refused to work and he knew he was losing too much blood. A roaring filled his ears and it took all his will to remain conscious. He tasted blood and wanted to vomit. Then the voice came to him again: 'Wilder? I heard the alarm. *For Christ's sake, Wilder!*'

The woman, Cade's rocking mind told him. She sounds alone and petrified. What the hell? Why was no one inside baby-sitting her? It had to be a set-up. Two snipers and this other one in the hole as back-up in case I managed to beat the rifles. There had to be another in the house!

Wilder was regaining consciousness, retching.

'Are you all right?' came the frantic voice from behind the door.

Cade moved to survey the windows. They were set very high and were narrow with metal frames. Even if he could reach up to them he would be silhouetted against the moonlight. And she could be armed.

'Don't open the door,' Wilder moaned softly, hunched over. 'Wilder?'

Cade held the gun on him and pressed himself against the door, his face close to the hinges. 'Open the door,' he whispered. 'Quickly.'

He heard the bolts being worked, then two locks. He stood back against the wall as Rhoda James came out, falling to her knees by Wilder. Cade lowered the revolver from beside his head and aimed at the back of her neck.

Wilder tossed her over his head with a judo throw, missing taking the silenced bullet himself by fractions, then launched himself at Cade's legs, overbalancing him. Cade slammed to the ground on his wounded shoulder and screamed in pain but still he gripped the magnum, swinging it toward Wilder.

Rhoda James shrieked and leapt at his arm but Cade kicked out, felling her.

'Stop it!' she shrieked hysterically. 'He's an American! For pity's sake, you've got it all wrong.'

Cade's wound was pouring blood: too much blood. He

knew the flow had to be stemmed or he would definitely pass out. He struggled to hold the magnum on them, dragging himself toward the wall and leaning his back against it. He .raised his knees and supported the revolver on them.

'I'm with them,' she said, almost a whisper. 'The Americans. He is too. *Please!*'

Cade dragged himself upright. 'Inside,' he gasped, looking down on them.

She became aware her robe was open and pulled it closed, standing. Wilder stood up, fingering the place where Cade had hit him with the magnum.

'Inside,' Cade repeated. 'Her first – and put on the light.'

Inside, with the light on, she gasped at the state of him. 'Who did that!'

'Fucking Americans!' Cade snapped. 'Out there! But you didn't know about them did you? 'Course you didn't. Like you didn't know this bastard was dug in waiting for me?'

'It's a tunnel,' said Wilder. 'You tripped the alarm out back, in the trees.' He turned to Rhoda James. 'You slept right through it.' He sucked in air as a spasm of pain pincered his groin.

'You left me alone!' she accused.

'I tripped the second one to warn you. If you'd stayed inside you'd have been okay. This place is secure. Nothing could get in as long as you stayed inside. The Company even fitted splinter-proof windows. You shouldn't have opened the door.'

'He means the CIA,' she said, her arms clutched tightly across her body. 'I told you I'm with the Americans.'

'You need to do something about that,' said Wilder, looking at the blood collecting on the floor. 'I can fix it up for you.'

'And fix me,' Cade retorted, lifting the magnum.

Wilder shook his head.

'Let him,' she pleaded, turning away from the sight. 'Then we can sort out this mess. Let me make a call?'

'You stay right where you are,' warned Cade. He felt for his field-dressing pack with his dripping red fingers and dropped it to the floor. 'Use that,' he told Wilder.

'I've got a para-medic pack,' said Wilder.

'You just use that.'

'Please put down that gun,' she pleaded. 'We won't hurt you.'

Cade looked at her disdainfully.

'Shut up,' Wilder ordered, casting a warning glance at her before turning back to Cade. 'You'll need a shot against infection or you'll lose the arm for sure.'

Cade struggled out of the blood-soaked sleeve of the combat jacket keeping the magnum on them. He searched Wilder's eyes and found something of himself staring back at him. 'Go ahead,' he said. 'You'd better be straight, mate.'

Wilder moved away and stood before his olive-green pack hanging behind the door leading to the hallway.

Cade nodded.

Wilder took out a US Army para-medic battle-pack, opening it for Cade's inspection before emptying the contents on the scrubbed pine table.

Cade sat down, placing his arm on the table, grinning weakly as Rhoda James quickly turned away as Wilder peeled off the now-useless field-dressing.

'You're still carrying metal,' Wilder warned, as he examined the wound before injecting Cade, his face grim. 'It could be anywhere.'

'I'll boil some water,' she said, lifting a kettle.

'Right Florence Nightingale,' muttered Cade, wincing with pain.

'Don't need it,' said Wilder.

'Suit yourself,' she said.

'You army?' Cade asked, very pale now.

'Was.'

Cade nodded.

'I need a drink,' she told Cade. 'What about you? You look as though you could do with one as well.'

Cade looked suspiciously at her.

'Lousy for shock,' Wilder said.

'Sod the shock. You got any scotch?' said Cade, grey-faced.

'We've got everything,' Wilder answered.

'A real little America,' said Rhoda James, acidly. 'They've got everything except the ability to stop one man getting close enough to nearly put a bullet through my head.'

'Don't feel too confident,' Cade warned her. 'They told me

211

you're a traitor – just like the rest – and they don't get things wrong.'

'*Who* told you?' she demanded.

'People who know,' said Cade.

'Let me make a 'phone call. You'll be told who I'm working for. They'll straighten all this out with your people.'

Wilder finished binding the wound and sat down opposite Cade, his eyes questioning, but very steady. 'She's a Soviet agent? You were told that?'

'You stay out of this, Wilder, it's not your business,' she snapped.

'One of four,' Cade answered

'They've killed three,' she said to Wilder. 'They don't know about my arrangement with your people.'

'Not *my* people,' Wilder corrected.

'Your country then.'

'Those guys outside – Americans?' asked Wilder of Cade. 'You're sure?'

'I didn't stop to ask. They tried to finish me, so as far as I'm concerned they're with her. And so are you.'

'I'm not working for the Russians!' Rhoda James almost shouted in frustration. 'I'm a double agent, damn you.'

Cade looked sharply at her.

'Which means she *is* working for the Russians,' Wilder said, quietly.

'Of course I am, that's how it works, any fool knows that. Look, whatever your name is, let me make contact with my controller and you'll get all the confirmation you need.'

'Don't let her near the telephone,' warned Wilder.

Cade looked from one to the other. 'You telling me she's lying?'

'I'm telling you that if she gets on that 'phone we've both got serious problems.'

'Shut up, Wilder!' she shouted.

'What's going on?' Cade demanded.

'She's just told us she's a double agent. If whoever sent you are official and they don't know that . . . it means they're not supposed to know.'

'You bastard!' she spat, starting forward.

Cade turned the magnum on her. 'You carry on, mate.

212

Convince me we're fighting the same war.'

Wilder smiled. '*No one's* fighting the same war. They're all fighting different wars for their own reasons, their own gains – which means they're all fighting each other. You and I are just stragglers in the middle of no-man's-land – and as of now we know too much to be allowed to roam free.'

'You're a lunatic,' she said, icily. 'They should have killed you in the jungle.'

'They probably did,' said Wilder.

A series of sharp buzzes from the trip-wire alarms announced that they were no longer alone and somewhere, not too far away, dogs barked, too many to be pets.

'Turn off the light,' Cade ordered. 'That's the coppers.'

The glow through the window was now a dull orange. The new day was beginning. Cade's drawn face turned to it, as if for guidance.

'Now you'll have no choice but to let me go,' said Rhoda James.

'Lady, for someone who plays both sides in the most dangerous game in the world you have lousy judgement,' observed Wilder.

'The police are here, there's no point in him killing me now. I'm going to walk right out of that door.'

Cade shook his head, the magnum steady on her. 'You go when I go. Whichever way that happens to be.'

Chapter Twelve

The Hampshire Police chief inspector who was in charge of the raid on the gypsy camp was named Dawkins. He sat, cat-napping, in the mobile incident room as the call came through. Opening his eyes, he leaned forward and listened to the voice of one of his officers coming through on the receiver.

'The dogs have turned up two bodies, sir. One black, throat cut, very nasty; the other, possibly Spanish or Italian, Latin anyway, shot. Both men were armed with sniper's rifles – silenced. The black was in some sort of hide – the other must have been up a tree. Shot while in it by the look of it – broke his neck in the fall. Looks like they were waiting for someone – possibly the suspect. If they were, he got them first. There's a cottage adjacent to where the bodies were found – doesn't seem to be any life inside. It's still early though, could be sleeping. No approach has been made. We had trouble holding the dogs back from the cottage.'

'Keep it that way,' Dawkins replied. 'How far away from the cottage are your men?'

'Well back, sir, what with the sniper's rifles and all, I didn't want to take any chances.'

'Very wise. You do not approach the cottage under any circumstances – not until we know a hell of a lot more about what's going on. Is that understood?'

'Understood, sir. I've already passed on the location.'

'Right, we're on the way.'

Dawkins turned to the communications officer. 'Get on to Headquarters Control Room. First I want to know who owns that cottage and who occupies it at this precise moment.

214

Second, inform them that I may well have a siege situation here – possibly involving hostages. Third, have them contact Thames Valley Police, the Reading Factory, and get hold of that chief super who knew this man Cade – name of Rand – and request him to make it down here by fastest possible means to aid in negotiations.'

'We can't be certain Cade's in that cottage, sir,' put in the CID officer who had found the partially burnt folders and Cade's clothes. 'We may be dragging him down here for nothing.'

'Always put your trust in a dog's nose,' Dawkins replied. 'Or if not, then in an old copper's, like mine. This business stinks higher than that curry old Gypsy Joe's people were cooking.'

'Anything else, sir?' queried the communications officer.

'Call Gloucester Headquarters, have the officer in charge of the case advised that we may have his suspect cornered.'

'I've had a message through from Gloucester, sir. A Detective Chief Inspector Murray is already on his way here. He left after we put out the call that the suspect was confirmed in this area.'

'Is he, by God? Left already? He's keen to grab this collar. I wonder how much of the story he hasn't told us? All right, fourth: I shall need to know if there is a telephone connection to that house. If there is, have the GPO alerted to be ready to block the number so that only we have direct communication.'

'British Telecom, sir.'

'Don't be clever, son, I'm too bloody weary. GPO it's been all my life and GPO it shall remain. Fifth: Ambulances and a doctor at the scene, right away – and no wailing sirens, please, nice and quiet if that is at all possible. Better alert the nearest hospital that they may have to receive casualties suffering from gunshot wounds.'

Dawkins hesitated.

'I'd guess this could be a long one – and it could turn bad. I'll need a second-in-command to relieve me, also a press liaison officer to deal with the vultures. And tell HQ that I appreciate we're dealing with a whole damn forest here but I'll need enough men to form a perimeter group, unarmed and uniformed, naturally – and armed officers of course for the Cover

215

Group. They'll just have to bring men in from other areas if necessary.'

'Is that it, sir?'

Again Dawkins hesitated. 'No. One final thing. This man Cade's formerly SAS, isn't he? Tell them I advise notifying London that we shall almost certainly need D11. Right, let's get at it.'

'Let me go,' pleaded Rhoda James. 'I'll make sure no action is taken against you. I daren't be involved in any publicity.' She turned from Cade to Wilder. 'Make him understand that. He doesn't understand what's at stake here. If this carries on, the wretched media will be crawling all over the place – they'll soon find out that an American lived here and Moscow will conclude only one thing from *that*!'

They were in the front room of the cottage, away from the windows. In the early morning light, the shapes of the police were shadowy as they moved cautiously among the trees and bushes. Only a plaintive howl from one of their dogs gave reality to their presence.

Cade felt desperately weak, lying slumped on the sofa, but the magnum was still held on them. He looked up at Wilder who was standing, very loose, against the wall by the door, his eyes fixed on the trees beyond the murky glass.

'So where do you stand?' Cade asked

'I told you. She should have kept her mouth shut.'

'I had to tell him!' she argued. 'It's me he was sent to kill.'

Cade raised the hand holding the gun and wiped the sweat from his forehead.

'Fever?' Wilder asked, studying him with concern.

'Never,' Cade retorted with a slight grin. 'I thought it was my bottle going.'

'He means his nerve,' said Rhoda James, translating the London slang.

'I've been there,' Wilder replied.

'What is this – an old soldiers' reunion?' she questioned with growing impatience. 'The police are all around us by now. They'll soon be armed, if they're not already. They've tracked you here and they'll shoot you down if they have to. For God's sake, one telephone call can stop this!'

216

'How much do they know?' Wilder asked Cade.

'Plenty, by the look of that lot out there.'

'Did you shoot any policemen?' she asked, afraid of his answer.

'I don't kill coppers.'

'Then they won't hurt you. Just give it up. Wilder, you go out there and tell them he's ready to negotiate. Tell them to bring someone from the Security Service – they'll have to back his story – they're the ones who sent him. Max told me.'

Wilder shook his head.

'Why not!'

'They're not going to admit anything now it's reached this stage. The British are no different from anyone else. Whoever sent him was mounting a clandestine operation – that seems obvious – and when they get news of this – and they will – they'll disappear into the woodwork.'

'Don't you want to get out of here alive? Have you got a death-wish or something?'

'I react badly when I see someone being screwed.'

'You *are* mad,' she snapped. 'Just take one look at him!' she told Cade.

Wilder said to Cade. 'Let's talk. What do they call you?'

'Jack, that'll do.'

'Okay, Jack. If you go out there, what happens? Prison?'

'For sure. But I'm not about to let that happen.'

'You've done time before?'

Cade nodded.

'What for?'

Cade's eyes hardened. 'For doing my bit for Queen and Country. Northern Ireland. I hit four of the Boyos. Later they told me that they were only kids out for a bit of fun. Fun – with a couple of Armalites, and sidearms to even-up the odds. 'Course those were gone by the time the army and the coppers arrived – and I hadn't stuck around because I was working undercover and had orders not to be blown whatever happened.'

'So they played politics.'

'They're good at that. Gave me eight years and blew my cover, which pointed the Boyos straight at me and what was mine. I did four years. Someone must have forgiven me.'

217

'So you got away with half your sentence,' said Rhoda James. 'Hardly a lifetime. You're lucky the IRA didn't kill you.'

'They did worse than kill me,' Cade snarled. 'They butchered my kid! All of six years old. You want to see her face?' He scrabbled with his wounded arm inside his clothes, his anger blotting out the pain, and threw a wallet at her. He raised the magnum. 'Pick it up and take a good look at the picture. She didn't look like that when they'd finished. Know what they did? *Everything!* Then they burned my initials into her cheeks with cigarette-ends. The stupid coppers thought they were hunting some religious nut. Jack Cade, JC. The Boyos were letting me know, weren't they. Well now *I* know. Turn it over. See the names? They're my price for finishing you. I told them I wouldn't do a woman – so they told me they'd give me those names. I'm not going inside. I'm going to get those animals and burn my name on their balls – every fucking letter.'

She placed the photograph back in the wallet and held it out to him. 'I'm so sorry. How could I possibly have known?'

'You know now,' Cade retorted, slumped and weakened by his outburst.

The telephone by the window rang.

'That's them,' said Cade, his face contorted with pain and clammy with sweat. 'You answer it,' he told her. 'Tell them there's no problem. They can't be sure I'm here. Get rid of them – and maybe I won't finish you.'

She lifted the receiver.

A steady, deep voice with a Hampshire burr said: 'Mrs James? This is the police. Will you please confirm that no one else is listening by touching your hair. We can see into the room with binoculars.'

She obeyed, slowly, then said: 'You must have the wrong house, everything is all right here.'

'There's nothing to worry about, Mrs James,' said Chief Inspector Dawkins. 'The house is totally surrounded. We just want to keep the gunman calm. If the man's name is Cade, C-A-D-E, pull your dressing-gown together at the neck. If you don't know, do nothing.'

She clasped the towelling material. 'How did you know my name?' she asked. 'I'm only a guest here?'

'Now is not the time to discuss that. Listen carefully. If the second man in the room is a friend and there are no others present in the house, transfer the telephone to your left hand.'

'Get off the line,' Cade ordered, in a harsh whisper.

She covered the mouthpiece. 'I'm trying to get rid of them.'

Dawkins spoke again as she switched hands. 'Now replace the 'phone.'

'Goodbye,' she said, replacing the receiver, her face deeply troubled.

'They knew your name,' said Wilder, watching her closely.

She nodded, very aware of the binoculars trained on the room.

'What's it matter?' muttered Cade.

'It matters. Only her controller and the guy who came with him should know she's here.'

'So they've tipped off the police.'

'Not a chance. The last thing they need is a link established between her and them.' Wilder frowned. 'Jack, you're sure you know who you're working for?'

'MI5. Saw the ID, didn't I. Said they couldn't use their own people for the job because of all the leaks you read about in the papers.'

Wilder shook his head. 'You're too straight, Jack. You're mixed up in the wrong world. If I were you I'd give up and tell the police all you know. I think you've been suckered by people who've uncovered four Soviet agents and decided that they didn't want them brought to trial. They'll have reasons – they always do – and usually the reasons are political. They've got themselves out of trouble by employing someone who is totally deniable – and expendable. You, Jack.'

'How come you've worked all this out?' Cade asked, warily.

'Because I've lived too much of my life in that world.' Wilder turned to Rhoda James. 'So who do you work for?'

'Go to hell,' she answered.

'GCHQ, Cheltenham,' Cade told him.

Revelation dawned on Wilder's face. 'She's run by NSA. United States National Security Agency. That makes it big league.'

'Is he right?' Cade asked Rhoda James.

'I work for GCHQ – which means I'm in contact with NSA.

219

So are most people employed at Cheltenham. It's part of the job. But I'm British and my loyalty is to Britain.' She glared, defiantly at Wilder.

Wilder moved closer to the window and looked out, his hands stuck in his jeans, shoulders slightly hunched. He sighed and relaxed then turned to face Cade. 'She either worked it out, or they've told her – the police – that there's a directional mike aimed at the windows. What she's forgotten is that this is a CIA facility and that means there's counter-measures against electronic eavesdropping built in. She doesn't want anyone out there to take what we've been saying seriously – which means that the Brits don't know she's on NSA's payroll. I'd bet the rest of my life that she's under orders to give Moscow classified material from inside GCHQ and pass on doc-tored NSA material at the same time. And the British have no idea that they're being screwed by their cousins across the water.'

Cade was lost. 'You're saying she's spying on *us* – for your lot? For the Yanks?'

'You'll get me killed, Wilder,' she warned.

Wilder ignored her. 'Not spying on you, Jack. Just giving away British secrets so that the disinformation she's also passing to the Russians is believed.'

'That's the same thing.'

'Not quite, but it's getting there.'

'What's your game?' Cade demanded, his bewilderment becoming suspicion.

'I don't have a game,' Wilder said, wearily. 'That's the point. I've had it with games. That's why I live this way. I've played their games for too long and I told them I wanted out. But no one ever really gets out from that world – on either side. I think you should go out there and tell the police all you know. Do that and maybe you'll bring down a few roofs. You'll never bring down their whole crazy world – no one can ever do that, they're too powerful.'

Rhoda James turned on Cade, her eyes wild. 'Don't listen to him. He's against everything we stand for – *you and I*! He's one of those loonies who want to destroy democracy but has no idea what to replace it with. Just *look* at him. What do you see? Nothing less than a degenerate with no standards at all.

Half an animal — except that animals at least have loyalty to their own kind.'

Wilder said: 'I know exactly what I want to replace it with. I want a world which doesn't manipulate people by making them believe they're doing their goddam duty. I want a world that doesn't buy people. I want to live my way without being coerced into believing that what I'm getting is freedom.'

'You're a dreamer, Wilder — and dreamers in the real world are dangerous. They get people killed, then walk away saying I told you so.'

Cade's pallor had turned grey, his skin pouring sweat. He blinked as it stung his red, feverish eyes. Then, the whites showed.

Rhoda James dived for the falling magnum but Wilder was too fast and too experienced for her.

'You son of a bitch!' she spat.

'They've even sold you the worst of our language,' he said. 'Now you just close those curtains, lady.'

Chief Superintendent James Rand viewed the police operation from the air, the police helicopter he had requisitioned sweeping over the scene at height as the pilot headed for the rendezvous point where the emergency services had already gathered. He could see that despite the road blocks where passing motorists were being diverted, crowds were already forming, held back by uniformed police.

Rand tapped the pilot's shoulder and pointed down to where a group of roughly dressed youths had somehow broken through the perimeter cordon and were already in the forest.

Rapidly, the police pilot passed on the information by radio.

'Stupid buggers!' he cursed when this was done, his voice reaching Rand through headphones.

'They'll run smack into the Cover Group!' Rand shouted, forgetting, as he had done all the way, about the microphone before his mouth.

The pilot winced, then banked the helicopter, indicating another group of figures below. 'TV camera crew,' he said and lost height, hovering over the equipment-laden group as he radioed their position in.

221

Rand watched the camera crew scrambling for shelter as the down-draft from the rotors blasted them in a storm of leaves and twigs.

'One day they'll catch a packet and blame us for being trigger-happy,' he said with feeling.

The pilot landed on a cleared area of the main road, Rand alighting quickly, head ducked low, despite the improbability of the blades touching him. He saw a senior uniformed officer running toward him, cap clutched to his head.

'Chief Superintendent Rand? Dawkins. I'm the one you've got to blame for bringing you all the way down here.'

'What's the state of play, chief inspector? You're sure it's Cade you've got in there?'

'Absolutely certain. Had the woman on the 'phone – she confirmed it.'

'Woman? The householder?'

The noise of the helicopter died with a long whine.

'That's better,' said Dawkins. 'Ah, the woman! Yes, well that's a development you won't know about. Come on, let's get a bit closer in.'

'So tell me about it,' Rand said, following the big lumbering figure.

Dawkins had acquired a walking stick which he beat the bushes with as they moved deeper into the forest. 'You know we found Cade's caravanette at a gypsy camp about four or five miles up the road – your direction not mine – all right? Well, during our search we turned up some documents the gypsies had tried to burn along with some of his clothes, which is how the dogs tracked him. Files, really – only partially burned, thank goodness. They gave details of four people employed at GCHQ Cheltenham.'

'What sort of details?' Rand enquired.

'Watch that dip,' warned Dawkins. 'Fell in it myself earlier. Lifestyle, work and leisure patterns, the whole bloomin' lot. Rum eh? Took one look and said to myself: This is for the Special Branch if anything is. Called them in straight away – and ended up with the Security boys. Turned up same manner as you – in one of those blasted things. Except they had the army do it. Locals hereabouts must have thought the Russians had landed, what?'

The big man trudged on, seemingly tireless, while Rand, who prided himself on his physical condition, found himself breathing raggedly.

Dawkins noticed. 'Ought to get yourself out more often. Oh, the woman, yes. Well, she was in the files, y'see. Along with the three others.'

'One named Parminter?'

Dawkins slowed and gave Rand an old-fashioned glance. 'That's the chappie. We know all about *him*, don't we? Mind you, not in this context, though obviously you do –?'

'He's not important.'

'Isn't he, by God?'

'Not as far as we're concerned. Go on.'

'The photographs, full-frontal and both profiles – like mugshots – were still recognizable. Didn't know that she was in the house of course but a check with GCHQ personnel told us that she was off sick and was staying here for a few days. Heart murmur or something similar. Strain. All that concentration, I suppose. Codes and stuff. Anyhow, we placed a couple of our lads up in the trees with binoculars and blow me down if they don't see her – name of Rhoda Anne James – in a dressing-gown, chatting with two men. One was Cade, for certain, even had a revolver, with silencer fitted. Looked badly shot up, left shoulder bound up – fairly professional-looking job – but still bleeding. Wearing combat clothes, heavily blood-stained, the jacket half off for the wound.'

'Who shot him – not one of ours? The other man?'

They were nearing the clearing and Dawkins turned off the path, directing with his stick.

Rand saw a large bundle on the forest floor, covered by a blanket and fenced off by tape and supports.

'My guess, he did,' said Dawkins. He lifted his stick to the tall tree above the body. 'Then took a couple himself, neither fatal, but bloody marvellous shooting anyway considering it must have been pitch black on my reckoning.'

'Cade's a marksman. A Bisley shot.'

'Ah! Well there's the proof. Neck snapped clean. Fall did that.' The stick pointed again, this time horizontally. 'Over there is another one,' he said, as Rand peeled back the blanket to examine the body, which still lay in the position it had fallen.

'Another one?' Rand queried.

'Coloured chap. Throat cut. Caught from behind as he lay in his hide. This way.'

'Any ID?'

'Nothing. Plenty of cash but no plastic.'

'Professionals by the sound of it.'

'More your world,' Dawkins remarked. 'I'm just a country copper.'

They were very close to the edge of the clearing now but behind sufficient cover to be out of sight from the cottage. An officer, lying prone with an Enfield Enforcer 7.62 rifle fitted with telescopic sights – a member of the Cover Group, there to keep armed criminals contained in a specific area – ignored them as they passed, saving his attention for the cottage.

'What do you know about the other man?' asked Rand.

'Odd one that. Long hair, looks like a rock and roll merchant. No shirt, Western belt – one of those snakeskin jobs with a big buckle – holding up tatty jeans. Strange thing, he was covered in mud.'

'Mud?'

'Could have been blood – hard to tell through the windows – but he didn't seem to be hurt in any way. Oh, except for a cut, here, on his head.'

'The cut couldn't have accounted for the stains on his body?'

'If it did he wouldn't be walking around. The lads say mud. Could have been one of those waiting for Cade I suppose but as a type he doesn't fit with the other two. What we do know is that he's down as the tenant.'

'So who's the owner?'

'Our enquiries led us to an estate agent, local bod, who sold the property some years ago to a company in London that turned out to be a holding company for another company – you know the way these things work. Anyway, to cut it short, the house is rented on long-term lease to one Declan Barret Wilder, American citizen, domiciled here for the past two years.'

'You've contacted the American Embassy?'

'Naturally. Fast movers those chaps,' Dawkin's observed, turning, a dry smile beneath his tawny moustache.

'You mean they've sent someone down here already?'

'Sent? By some amazing coincidence there's an accredited American diplomat staying not ten miles from here. You saw his Jag sports, back there.'

'So what did he have to say for himself?'

Dawkins negotiated a fallen tree trunk. 'As little as possible. Identified Wilder through the glasses, claims he's a minor military hero doing a bit of solitary out of choice. Shell-shocked or whatever the modern term is. Looked about as jumpy as a hibernating tortoise to me.'

'The James woman? Is she married or single?'

'Married. Yes I thought that too. A prolonged jump in the hay while hubby worries back home about her heart problem. The physical kind I mean.'

'What's the US Embassy chap's view?'

'Oh, he plays it as a domestic incident. Two men, one woman. Mind you, I don't believe for one minute that he believes that. He's a spook, stands out half a mile. Spends all his time on his car-phone – plugged through one of those briefcase scrambler jobs.'

'Where's his interest lie? Wilder or the woman? Or both?'

'As I said, he doesn't say much. Just keeps using that damn 'phone. But he's only asked about Wilder directly, which of course he would do. Interested in all that's going on though, in a quiet sort of way.'

'Has he spoken to the Security boys?'

'They've spoken to him. Long conflab. I get the feeling in my long-suffering back that we're only involved in part of whatever is going on.'

Rand nodded knowingly. 'I've had that feeling ever since I became involved in this whole Cade business. If I were you, chief inspector, I'd let the feeling stay right where it is.'

'Don't worry, I know when I'm walking on eggshells.'

Rand shook his head. 'Razor blades.'

'Like that is it?'

'I'd say, very much like that. All right, let's see if Mister Jack Cade is ready to talk.'

A constable scrambled from a tree, his uniform covered by a dark raincoat. 'He's on to us, sir. The woman's drawn the curtains.'

'Any problems inside?' Dawkins asked.

225

'Hard to say, sir. There was some fast movement – could have been a scuffle – but I couldn't swear that the situation has changed. There's no light inside and what with those filthy windows and full daylight now it's really murky in there. Sorry, sir.'

'Just do your best, son,' said Dawkins. 'Well, chief superintendent, you'd better try and have a word with your chap in case he's decided to do something he'll regret.'

Rand mused for a moment. 'I have a worrying feeling that Cade really doesn't care any more.'

'That bodes ill for my lads,' Dawkins replied, sombrely. 'That type usually like to take a few with them.'

'Yes,' said Rand. 'I know.'

Chapter Thirteen

The Prime Minister sat in the Cabinet Room opposite the Secretary of State for Defence. They were alone, both forgoing their regular cabinet chairs.

The Defence Secretary's mood was one of growing hostility, yet held firmly in check, with only the movement of his fingers on the table betraying his agitated state.

'There's no doubt whatsoever that she's in there?' questioned the Prime Minister for the second time since he had arrived after his call requesting – even demanding – a private meeting that Sunday morning.

He breathed impatiently. 'No doubt at all. The woman and two men – one definitely the killer of the other three traitors. The second man is an American. The police have also found two dead gunmen near the house. You know of course what all this means?'

'As I am unaware of the extent of your intrigue – not entirely, no.'

'It means that the Americans now know that you've passed on the location of their safe-house. The killer had only one way of finding out where they had hidden their agent. You, Prime Minister. Only you received that information.'

She studied him. 'And, of course, the fact that I passed it on to you makes no difference at all.'

'You could drag me down with you if that is your wish.'

'Which would mean the Party would be in serious danger of being caught up in the scandal. One rogue decision by the Prime Minister is bad enough but if the Defence Secretary could be shown to be involved also then the media would start playing dominoes with the entire Cabinet. You know very well that I would not involve you. You could be next in line for the Leadership.'

'That is immaterial, Prime Minister. What is pertinent right now is that this incident —'

'Scandal,' she corrected.

'As of now it is still only an incident. An incident which can be contained.'

'How?'

'Give the order that the house be stormed. I would suggest that you use an SAS Killer group. Since the man holding the woman and the American is SAS trained himself, he's likely to kill members of a police unit. Even D11 officers. No one need know we used the SAS — that's happened before.'

'He's wounded. Surely that raises the odds against him being completely effective?'

'An SAS man with a wounded arm could hardly be called ineffective. If anything he'd be more prepared to go down fighting. In this case I can guarantee it, I've seen this man's record. I believe you once met him yourself.'

'*I* did!'

'Some years ago. You expressed a wish to meet an officer, an NCO and a trooper from the Regiment. He was the NCO. They'd all acted courageously in some incident but naturally could not be publicly acclaimed.'

'This is on record?'

'It need not be.'

'But it could be construed that I had personal contact with him.'

The Defence Secretary shrugged. 'It need never get that far.'

She tilted her head, questioningly. 'Of course, we're not simply talking about the death of this ex-SAS NCO are we, Defence Secretary?'

'No, Prime Minister.'

'All three?'

'Yes.'

'The agent ORACLE especially.'

'Yes.'

'And the American bodyguard? I assume that's what he is?'

'If he survives, then the deaths of the other two mean

228

nothing. I'm afraid that your decision must encompass all three.'

'Do we then order the assassination of the woman's controller? And his deputy? Not forgetting those members of the conspiracy in Washington who began this treacherous exercise in deception.'

The Defence Secretary sighed. 'Prime Minister, with the woman dead, the Americans no longer have any hold over us. They can hardly complain if we kill two of our own citizens – and to be realistic, I cannot see them shouting from the roof-tops that we killed an American who was protecting one of their agents who was – with their connivance, indeed on their orders – passing British secrets to the Russians.'

She shifted her position, gravely disturbed by such calm discussion of murder by her minister, who, it seemed, could be as ruthless as she could be determined. It had all gone too far. She was no longer in control, and the realization hit her hard. From now on, she could well be in the hands of the man before her every time she had to make a decision. It really came down to a choice. Did she want to be controlled by the Americans, who at least would give her some leeway, some independence, for fear of their own position – though of course they certainly would lean on her when they chose – or to be under the whip-hand of the ruthless politician who confronted her now?

'No SAS,' she said firmly. 'No storming of the house. There is every chance that the police will be able to negotiate an end to the siege and that the matter will be decided by the courts. In camera, if necessary.'

'No,' stated the Defence Secretary.

'*Yes*. That is my decision – and I am still the Prime Minister of this government.'

He arose, his face livid. 'You cannot possibly understand the gravity of the mistake you are making.'

'Perhaps not. It is, however, my mistake to make.'

'I shall do all in my power to stop this.'

'Not while staying within the laws of the land. If you outlaw yourself then you must accept the consequences of your actions.'

'And you yours, Prime Minister.'

229

He stormed out, leaving her sitting at the long cabinet table, well aware that – if this incident could be overcome – she must move very swiftly to destroy him politically. She had learned · one lesson that day: his deceptive ice-cool charm could be turned into explosive, ill-considered action when the circumstances demanded total commitment from him.

God willing she would soon put that lesson to good use. And the Americans she would deal with in her own way.

Chapter Fourteen

Wilder dragged Rhoda James upstairs, ignoring her protests. Crouched low, using his own binoculars, he surveyed the scene outside.

Back with the slumped figure of Cade he told her to clean him up and to remove the outer layer of combat clothing he wore. With Cade lying dressed only in a tee-shirt, jeans and his combat boots, he took a hypodermic syringe from his paramedic's battle-pack and injected the measured dose of morphine into the unconscious man.

'You're mad,' she told him as he withdrew the needle and exchanged it for the silenced .357 Magnum in his belt.

'But straight, like him,' he replied.

'Real moralist, aren't you, Wilder? So how many children did you butcher in Vietnam? Is that what sent you scuttling away from the rest of us? Real fallen hero, are we?'

'Open the door under the stairs,' he ordered, aware of the fear behind her anger.

She obeyed, watching as he hefted Cade's body over his shoulder with astonishing ease.

'Now go on down,' he told her, 'Stand well away from the ladder at the bottom.'

Again she obeyed, mutely.

He followed her down the ladder, Cade moaning now as he laid him down on the rough concrete floor.

The underground room, too small to be called a cellar, had one wall filled by four loop-reeled tape-recorders rigged for voice-activation and set on steel racks. A second wall had more electronic equipment which was the CIA facility's

231

communication system with their London Station and other out-stations.

'Your people disconnected the recorders,' observed Wilder. 'That might have saved some embarrassing questions between the Company and NSA.'

'Might?' she questioned, watching him intently as he picked up what appeared to be a regular cordless telephone but which in fact had a range of more than five thousand kilometres with inbuilt circuits to defeat bugging or elecronic eavesdropping.

'The questions are going to be asked anyway. What's your emergency contact number in London?' he demanded, resetting the recorders.

'No.'

'I've shot children, remember? What difference is a woman going to make to my conscience?'

'The Agency will kill you.'

'They'll want to do that anyway. The Company might have other ideas.'

'I thought you were sick of playing games.'

'This is no game. It's survival. Whatever happens after this, if you're still alive, you'll tell NSA that I'm conscious of your role. Which brings in an insecurity factor they might find too high to risk. *Me*.'

'The police will arrest you anyway.'

Wilder flicked the heavy silenced barrel at Cade's prone form. 'They have their killer. They know you're targeted by him – that's why they're here.'

'He'll tell them.'

'He won't be here.'

'You'd kill him too?'

'I said, he won't be here.'

'You'd let him go? He won't get out alive!'

'Maybe he doesn't want to?'

'Don't be thick, Wilder. He wants the men who killed his daughter.'

Wilder nodded. 'That's why he'll take the risk. The number?'

She gave it to him.

He punched in the digits and waited. 'Your code-name?' he

asked and she gave him that too, looking defeated, her arms clutching her body while she stared lifelessly at Cade's grey face.

'*Oracle*,' said Wilder and heard breathing on the line. 'This is the Company 'phone. Don't hang up.'

'All right, Wilder,' said Max Weidenstein, his voice on foldback into the room.

'She's here – under my gun.'

Weidenstein was silent. 'So she's told you,' he said finally. 'Listen to me, I know the police are there. I know about this man Cade and who sent him. You're safe, I guarantee that – if you get her out of there without publicity. Cade's dead?'

'He's alive. Your guarantee is worth shit. I'll take this to the Company.'

'This is not Company business.'

'But it's all being recorded for them. Let them decide.'

'We'll break you, Wilder. Together, us *and* the Company. You don't know what you're into.'

'Sure I do.'

Weidenstein paused. 'So what do you want, Wilder?'

'Tell the British. Clear Cade.'

Weidenstein laughed. 'They already know. Right at the top they know. How do you think they got your location? I told them – right after Washington ordered me to. I told you you don't know what you're into. Washington will square the Company. You're finished Wilder.'

'If the British gave Cade this location then they want her dead. How are you going to keep her operating now?'

Weidenstein's amusement was clear in his voice. 'Because now we know who sent him after her.'

'And you'll destroy them.'

'We're talking about the future, Wilder. We've brought down governments for less.'

'And you'd do it now? Even to friends?'

'They were given a choice of enemies. The decision to choose was always in their hands.'

'It was never in their hands. Britain is too weak.'

'No,' said Weidenstein. 'America is too powerful. Look at the world as a football game, Wilder. There are only two teams strong enough to play. The rest watch the game from the

233

sidelines – or maybe they're allowed to be cheerleaders if they prove their loyalty.'

'Maybe some don't care for the tactics?'

'Then they don't get into the ball-park. Goodbye Wilder. Leave her alive or you'll end up as the ball.'

The line went dead.

Rhoda James smiled and Wilder shot her right through it.

Rising, he completed the coup de grâce. There was little sound from either bullet.

Upstairs the telephone rang and Wilder waited, then lifted the extension on the communications desk.

'I'd like to speak to Jack Cade,' said the caller. 'Tell him this is James Rand. He may remember me. I'm the police officer who escorted him to his daughter's funeral – I handled the case. Tell him I'm sure we can work this out without bloodshed.'

Wilder covered the mouthpiece and stood silently for a few moments, then said: 'He says he not ready to talk yet. He needs time. One hour.'

'Is everything all right in there?'

'No problem.'

'Is that Mister Wilder? Is Mrs James all right?'

'I said no problem,' Wilder answered and hung up.

Cade had regained consciousness and had dragged himself to the steel racks, leaning his back against them, his eyes glazed from the effects of the drug. He looked down at his clothes then at the splayed body before him.

Wilder pulled the undone robe together. 'This is how it is,' he said. 'She's dead – don't ask for reasons. They saw what you were wearing through the windows, they were watching her through glasses. I could tell. With different clothes you might make it. Use the tunnel.'

'You gave me a shot,' accused Cade, still disorientated.

'That's right.'

'It'll slow me down.'

'Without it you couldn't move at all. You're just about done. You sure you don't want to give it up?'

'I never give up on anything,' mumbled Cade, drifting.

Hanging behind the ladder was a bulky padded jacket – one the CIA had given Wilder when they had first flown him in to

234

England, because somewhere along the way he had lost any luggage he had. To that day he still could not remember where or how. He took it off the hook.

'Time to go,' said Wilder. 'I'll walk out front and draw them off you when you're out of the tunnel.'

'Why're you doing this?'

'That could be me on the floor.'

Cade struggled to his feet, rejecting Wilder's help, then stood shaking, one hand gripped firmly on the steel rack. He shuddered, then shook his close-cropped head. 'Jesus,' he muttered.

'You've still got the option,' Wilder said, watching him.

'Things to do,' Cade said, very weak but determined.

'Sure.'

'I could use a drink.'

'You couldn't handle it – right now.'

Cade grimaced. 'Yeah. A taste then – to lose the crap in my mouth.'

'That's the fever – and the morphine.'

'I could do with it,' said Cade.

Wilder nodded and disappeared up the ladder, returning quickly with a bottle.

Cade said: 'You first.'

'I don't –' Wilder began, then opened the bottle. 'Okay, me first, Jack.'

Cade accepted the bottle from him, swallowed, then gagged and leant back against the racks. 'Better give me both the small-arms. They'll never believe I left one behind,' he said, when he had recovered.

'No,' Wilder said. 'They'll blame you for her.'

'I've done three already – one more won't make any difference. Come on, hand 'em over.'

Wilder shrugged and complied.

'So where's the tunnel then?'

'Here.' Wilder dragged a large cardboard box containing blank tapes aside, revealing a jagged opening in the concrete with earth beyond in the darkness.

'You crawl through that? You a tunnel rat in Vietnam or something?'

'When it was necessary.'

Cade shook his head. 'Not me, mate. I'll do it now – but only because I have to.'

'There's no light in there – you don't need it. Goes straight out into the trees, no bends. At the end is a vertical shaft about twice your body width. The foot-holes take you straight up to the flap. From there you're on your own.'

Cade studied him, blinking to retain focus. 'Why the tunnel and the trip-wires?'

'Call it a way of life.'

'Some life.'

Wilder removed a plastic cover off one of the big recorders and stuffed the padded jacket into it. 'It's wet and the dirt comes off the sides in there. Wait until you're outside before you put this on.'

'Nothing else to say,' muttered Cade and held out his uninjured hand.

'Go easy,' Wilder replied, releasing his grasp and resuming his normal stance, shoulders raised and hands thrust into his jeans.

'You too, mate. Thanks. I'll see you.' Then Cade was gone.

Wilder went back upstairs and sat on the stairs in the hallway, head down staring at the floor in exactly the same way he had sat on the doorstep when Adeane and Weidenstein had first arrived at the safe-house.

He waited, his startling eyes blank as his mind saw a broken figure creeping painfully, bent double in pitch blackness, through gouged-out earth before coming to a solid stop, hard, as the tunnel ended. Then, lying winded, enveloped in the soft blanket of the drug which would only be containing the pain and not cancelling it out entirely.

Then, struggling to stand upright in the narrow vertical shaft while fighting fever and probably panic because it was not easy to retain control in that black hole even when your mind was clear.

Then fingers feeling for the footholds until at last they found them. Then relief, and the upward climb to the trapdoor of hard wood upon which, on the outside, grass and weeds grew in soil, perfectly matching the surrounding area. Completely undetectable, as others had been in the jungle.

Wilder acknowledged his former enemies. He had learned

236

well from the Viet Cong. He had also admired their courage and their unstoppable will directed against the super-power which should, by all logic, have crushed them underfoot like insects. Instead the huge foot had stomped madly at the earth, totally unable to accept that, to the insects, the earth was their defence and their rallying ground for ultimate victory.

He did not believe in their philosophy, but he believed, very firmly, in the unalienable right to choose the manner of one's life – and, if necessary, of one's death. And also, as now – even if they were his own people – the right to choose his enemies.

Wilder saw, in his mind, the trapdoor open and a man move in that special way that only an experienced, highly trained soldier can move: at one with the ground which could be his saviour or his grave.

Cade raised the flap and peered through the narrow gap, knowing all the while that all he could do was to get out fast and hope.

If you're lucky, you're behind them, he told himself. And if they're in front of you, you've still got a chance because they won't be expecting you and you're better than they are. But if your luck is all used up and you're right in the middle of them, then that's it over. Good night Irene. Just don't shoot a copper, that's all.

He was out fast and into the undergrowth, ignoring his injured arm which, when he had caught it on the flap, felt as if it had been ripped from his body. He wished that it had.

He began moving steadily forward, trying with every part of him to discipline his wandering mind. He stopped because the pain had him crippled for a moment and any movement seemed to hurt him more than all the wounds he had ever suffered.

I'm coming home, Amy, he thought – or perhaps he actually spoke the words aloud. Come down here, God. Sit beside me like you did before. But this time *do* something!

He crawled forward, the pain moving with him. The fiery needles in his chest flared like small incendiaries and the blood in his mouth tasted sour.

Give it up, he told himself but then he remembered Wilder,

waiting, prepared to walk out into the sunshine, and the guns, to draw them away from him.

Sod the women, he decided. Give me a man any day. Like him. No questions, no arguments and no axe to grind. Straight. The best.

He dug deep into his reserves of strength and will, prepared now to squander them, because if he did not get off his belly and go forward upright, he would never rise again.

He dragged himself to a tree and pressed his face to the cool bark. Hello, God, some part of his mind said. You're a hard bastard, aren't you? And rough on those who need you when it really matters.

He used the tree to pull himself upright, clawing with his fingers wherever they found purchase in the gnarled wood.

Above him, through the branches, the sun was bright, casting dappled patches around and on him but the chill in him defeated the warmth. Yet the sweat ran from him in rivers. I'll sodding melt, he thought, but kept the padded coat on because Wilder had given it to him, though now he could not remember why.

He began walking, stumbling whenever his dragging feet contacted a rise or missed a dip in the earth, no longer with any sense of direction – and even his purpose lost to him.

He sensed figures around him, but hidden, and his mind cast him backwards so that he was with them, in the safety of the wood and the leaves, with the smell of oil from the weapon nestled against his cheek. He was a trooper again, in some other lifetime, with his comrades around him and only the terse, hushed command of his officer, in the silence. *Let the buggers come on.* Yes, boss. I love it, he thought. Take me back, God.

He heard the rifle bolts and the sound thrilled him.

'Cade!' a voice cried. 'Jack! Stop there.'

The voice was real and he did not want its intrusion.

Men stepped from the trees. Two of them, moving forward cautiously, but still some way off. Time and distance seemed to have no measure for him any more.

One of the men came ahead and Cade swayed, looking at him. He tried to recall the face. Someone he knew from somewhere. Someone who knew little Amy. Someone who cared.

He remembered the voice which fitted the face, remembered it speaking, tight with anger – as his own had been, except his own words were locked inside. The words were far away, from some other place where grief was a small box being lowered into the ground, except when the soil covered it it escaped, because not all the soil in the world was heavy enough to press it down.

What were the words? Good words, from a fair man.

'The bastard killed her for three weeks. If I get him I'll take a lifetime,' Cade heard in his mind. A moment of pure clarity. He remembered the man too and knew that if he showed him the names he would get the bastards.

He reached inside the padded jacket for his wallet.

Declan Wilder stood up and put on Cade's combat jacket, then stepped outside into the morning sunlight, his arms raised as he walked forward.

All around him, at the edges of the clearing, sunlight pierced the trees, like lances embedded in the forest floor.

There was more silence than he could remember, even in that peaceful place, then realized that the presence of man, armed and poised to kill, had driven away the game.

He continued forward, still naked to the waist under Cade's bloodstained jacket, his bare toes sinking into the good earth he had made his own.

The gunshots were flat and distant; a barrage in miniature. A dry rattle which seemed too brittle and too impotent to kill.

Wilder closed his eyes and stood dead still, only opening them when the rushing figures were upon him.

He stood motionless, as they searched him then stood back staring at him quizzically, still unsure of him but unable to act further.

He put his hands into the pockets of Cade's combat jacket against the chill which spread through him only half-hearing loud voices explaining to whoever was listening, that Cade had reached for his gun. His fingers curled around a square of leather and he smiled. Inside, he knew, he would find a smile far brighter than his own.

Brighter in fact than any he had ever seen.

Epilogue

The house was on its own, well chosen, set at the furthest end of the cul-de-sac in an area of London which was neither deprived nor privileged. Those other houses which were near to it were easily identifiable as homes, whereas this one had a transient aspect, a place where change was normal, though by its inhabitants and not its structure.

Yet it was neither lodging house nor hotel.

The young woman who opened the door to the confident double ring of the bell saw the man and his suitcase against the sickly glow of the tall, spaced street-lights. He was immediately different from those she welcomed on other occasions. Well dressed, with a smart, very new raincoat and polished shoes which seemed to have had little wear. Overall, everything he wore appeared new, yet in some strange way she could not quite pin down, he wore them badly. They seemed almost to be placed over his body rather than worn.

'NORAID,' said the man, as she closed the door behind him, fast.

The young woman's manner changed perceptibly, becoming at once deferential and much less confident or even, as was her nature, aggressive. Also, studying his chiselled face and obviously recently cut and dressed hair, she fancied him wildly. She felt she had a good chance too, because he was committed to the cause and had come all the way from America – oh, that Land of Dreams – to aid it in its hour of need.

'I called this evening,' he said in a calm Southern drawl. 'From the airport. I rented a car – is it okay to leave it outside?'

240

'You know your way around then?' she asked, flirting, her Belfast accent harsh, destroying any charm she had.

He fixed his startling amber eyes on her in a manner that rebuked her curiosity.

'Sorry, shouldn't've asked, should I? They're upstairs, I'll go get 'em.'

'Just take me to them,' he said.

There was another door at the top of the stairs, very strong, with mortice locks matching those on the main entrance. He stopped her before she mounted the stairs.

'I hope my instructions were followed? Just the two I named. I don't want my face known by any of your people who operate in the Province.'

'There's none of them here. The house is empty right now – apart from the ones you want. You were lucky to find them here at all – paymasters get to move all over the country.'

'I knew they were here,' he stated. 'We don't move without knowing everything.'

' 'Course,' she said, feeling stupid. 'You Americans get it right. Not like some of those we have to deal with.'

There was a bell on the door which she operated with signalled rings.

A fat man opened it immediately, obviously waiting. He nodded, his eyes dropping greedily to the suitcase in the man's hand.

'She goes out,' said the man, coldly. 'I said only the two of you.'

'She had to cook our dinner,' the fat man argued.

'For one hundred thousand dollars you should have starved.'

The fat man licked his lips and again his eyes fell to the suitcase.

'You get yourself out, Moira,' he ordered the girl, who sulked and made a protracted exit, tossing her top-coat angrily over her shoulders.

'Sorry about that,' said the fat man. 'What do we call you?'

'Call me Declan,' answered Wilder.

'A good name. Call me Pat; he inside is Sean.'

The fat man moved aside to let Wilder pass.

'After you,' Wilder urged.

'Polite, you Americans, aren't you?' said the one called Sean who was sprawled on a settee, legs outstretched. He pulled himself up, a beer-can in his hand, and switched off the television set.

Wilder eased the fat man aside and took his hand out of his raincoat pocket. He shot Sean accurately through the upper thigh then raised the small .22 automatic to the fat man's temple.

'It's very small and it doesn't make much noise, but it'll blow your brains out same as a Colt .45, so take it easy.'

'You fucker!' Sean cried, down on the carpet, squirming as he pressed both hands to the small wound.

'What's this all about?' the fat man gasped, already trembling uncontrollably.

'Go and kneel down, hands on your fat head next to Sean,' ordered Wilder.

With the two men positioned as he wanted them, Wilder flicked open the locks on his suitcase and drew out a length of rope and two metal one-gallon containers. These he set down on a table littered with the remains of a meal but kept hold of the rope.

'What're you up to, you fucker!' snapped Sean, his eyes squeezed tight with pain.

'Some might call it justice,' said Wilder and shot him precisely in both upper arms. .

Sean howled and the fat man ducked over, cowering, hands over his head, blabbering: 'Mother of God! Mother of God!'

Wilder also shot him in each bicep, moving in close for each shot. His victim shrieked and his arms flopped to the floor as though they, like his shuddering body, were composed of fat.

'You can make as much noise as you like,' said Wilder. 'I know about safe-houses.'

He returned to the table for the two containers and emptied the jellified substance inside over each squirming man, ensuring that they were well covered.

'What's that!' blubbered the fat man, his tears mixing with the slopping chemical, his terror negating his sense of smell.

'It's called napalm,' said Wilder. 'Now normally it's dropped by aircraft and the effect over a large area is something you boys should see. There's nothing in this world like it. Beyond this world, though, I'd say hell might come a close second.'

The fat man screamed.

'Shoot us, you fucker!' Sean shouted, his mouth filling with the jellied petroleum.

'Then you'd miss the pain. That's why I used the Two-Two. A heavier calibre might have made you pass out.'

'You're the fuckin' Devil himself,' Sean spat through the lethal jelly.

'I want you to think of me as an avenging angel. Here, this is for both of you.'

Sean blinked as Wilder held up two copies of Amy Cade's photograph – but the fat man lay whimpering doubled over so he had to be pulled up and forced back onto his knees. 'You probably don't even remember, so I'll just pin these reminders to both of you so that you'll never, ever, forget the face.' The rope was already knotted like a western lariat and this he looped over both men's heads, pulling sharply so that their skulls cracked together. Keeping the tension on he took two heavy-duty drawing pins from his raincoat pocket and impaled one photograph to each forehead, the face of the child inward to their horrified eyes.

This done, he walked to the door and reached in his raincoat pocket for a metal Zippo lighter which flared into life as he spun the wheel with his thumb.

Both men screamed as Wilder called: 'Jack Cade and his daughter say they'll be seeing you.'

He tossed the lighter and was out of the door before the napalm ignited in a monstrous flame.

Outside the house he walked to his rented car, started the engine and drove away.

The house, as always, kept the screams secret, even as the fire burnt out its heart.

It was autumn, and the avenue of trees leading down almost to the banks of the Mississippi had shed part of their leaves and glorified the earth with countless shades of gold.

Declan Wilder sat on the porch of the white ante-bellum mansion, his family's home for centuries, watching the timeless river. He sat on one of the many steps not as he might have done in the past, head down, his amber eyes on the ground

243

between his feet, but instead, relaxed on an ancient rocking chair, which, like the mansion – and himself – had survived harsher days.

He thought of England, whose government was now going through turbulent times – despite being returned with a massive majority after a general election, a few years before. The cost of power, he mused, was sometimes greater than the achievement of it.

Upon his knees he dandled a young child, whose golden hair and large, astonishingly bright amber eyes shamed even the glories of nature which faced them both.

He looked at the trees and the shaded tunnel which they kept secret from the unknown power of the heavens, high above their tallest branches.

He remembered an honourable man, and a soldier, in another place and time; then recalled words which, to his mind, suited all.

There in a silent shade of laurel brown
Apart the Chamian Oracle divine
Shelter'd his unapproached mysteries:
High things were spoken there, unhanded down;
Only they saw thee from the secret shrine
Returning with hot cheek and kindled eyes.

A woman's voice called out, raised, but loving. Declan Wilder pushed himself up from the rocking chair, lifting the child high and gaining the reward of her beaming smile, then laughter.

'Time to get on with living, Amy,' he told her, and, kissing her, carried her inside.